FIRST NOVEL

Nicholas Royle is the author of six previous novels, including *The Director's Cut* and *Antwerp*, as well as two novellas and a short story collection, *Mortality*. Born in Manchester in 1963, he runs Nightjar Press, reviews fiction for the *Independent*, and is a senior lecturer in creative writing at Manchester Metropolitan University. He divides his time between Manchester and London.

ALSO BY NICHOLAS ROYLE

Novels

Counterparts

Saxophone Dreams

The Matter of the Heart

The Director's Cut

Antwerp

Regicide

Novellas

The Appetite

The Enigma of Departure

Short Stories

Mortality

Anthologies (As Editor)

Darklands

Darklands 2

A Book of Two Halves

The Tiger Garden: A Book of
Writers' Dreams

The Time Out Book of New
York Short Stories

The Agony and the Ecstasy:
New Writing for the
World Cup

The Ex Files: New Stories
About Old Flames

Neonlit: Time Out Book of
New Writing

The Time Out Book of Paris
Short Stories

Neonlit: Time Out Book of
New Writing Volume 2

The Time Out Book of London
Short Stories Volume 2

Dreams Never End: New Noir
Short Stories

'68: New Stories from Children
of the Revolution

The Best British Short Stories
2011

Murmurations: An Anthology
of Uncanny Stories
About Birds

The Best British Short Stories
2012

NICHOLAS ROYLE

First Novel

A Mystery

VINTAGE BOOKS
London

Published by Vintage 2014

2 4 6 8 10 9 7 5 3 1

Copyright © Nicholas Royle 2013

Nicholas Royle has asserted his right under the Copyright, Designs
and Patents Act 1988 to be identified as the author of this work

First published in Great Britain in 2013 by
Jonathan Cape

Vintage
Random House, 20 Vauxhall Bridge Road,
London SW1V 2SA

www.vintage-books.co.uk

Addresses for companies within The Random House Group Limited
can be found at: www.randomhouse.co.uk/offices.htm

The Random House Group Limited Reg. No. 954009

A CIP catalogue record for this book
is available from the British Library

ISBN 9780099575245

The Random House Group Limited supports the Forest Stewardship
Council® (FSC®), the leading international forest-certification
organisation. Our books carrying the FSC label are printed on FSC®
certified paper. FSC is the only forest-certification scheme supported
by the leading environmental organisations, including Greenpeace.
Our paper procurement policy can be found at:
www.randomhouse.co.uk/environment

Printed and bound in Great Britain by Clays Ltd, St Ives plc

for John Saddler

I

Very Low-flying Aircraft

'The greatest hazard of all, losing oneself, can occur very quietly in the world, almost as if it were nothing at all.'

Kierkegaard

I am sitting, alone, in my shared office at the university. On the walls are flyers for readings and a large poster advertising a local literature festival. The bookcase behind me is filled with books – books that I have brought in from home and others that I have acquired from the second-hand bookstalls across the road and the Paramount Book Centre in Shude Hill. In addition to these are bound volumes of literary magazines – *Antaeus*, *Transatlantic Review* – and books that I have claimed out of unwanted stock from the university library. My eye runs along a shelf two-thirds of the way down the bookcase. *Nineteen Seventy-Four* by David Peace, *Robinson* by Christopher Petit, *Berg* by Ann Quin, Gwendoline Riley's *Cold Water*. I skip along. *Friction* by Joe Stretch; *Dreams of Green Base*, Terry Wilson. First novels.

I take down a book from the shelf above: James Lasdun's *The Horned Man*. I hold it to my nose and flick through the pages using the soft pad of my thumb. It has a woody smell. Trampled grass, funfairs. A hint of caramel? I put it back on the shelf.

I turn back to the desk. On it are a PC, switched off, and a pile of books. Between them, right in the middle lying flat on the desk, is a Kindle. My colleagues and I in the writing school have each been given a Kindle. I look at it. The screen is blank. My finger hovers above it, as if reluctant to touch it. The screen is cool, slippery. I press a random selection of buttons on the keyboard. Nothing happens. I have not plugged the device into a power source and charged it. I pick it up. Its weight is difficult to judge. The back is more tactile. It has a sort of rubberised feel to it. If I were to drag my fingernail across it, it would leave a mark.

I drag my fingernail across it. It leaves a mark.

I put the Kindle back down and study it. It looks impenetrable. There are no screws, or feet, no catch, just a seam that runs around the edge on the back of the Kindle. It's too narrow to get a fingernail into.

To the right of my desk is a unit comprising three drawers. I open the top one and take out a small box made of transparent plastic containing six precision screwdrivers. I place the case on the desk and open it. I take out the smallest of the four flathead screwdrivers and insert its head into the seam on the back of the Kindle. There's a little bit of give. I push the screwdriver outwards at the edge and manage to release one of a series of little plastic clips that hold the rear piece in place. Once one is free, it is easier to release the others. After a few moments I manage to pop off the back piece, which I put to one side. I place the device down on the desktop and take a good look at it. A large flat battery takes up a third of the space. Most of the rest is occupied by the motherboard, which is comprised of a green background and numerous tiny parts. There are four little protective shields with a finish like stainless steel. Using one of the bigger screwdrivers I undo two screws that hold the battery in place. I remove the battery, which has writing in English on one side and Chinese characters on the other. Revealed beneath where the battery had been is a portion of the back of the e-ink screen.

I lift the Kindle up off the desk and hold it to my nose. It doesn't smell of anything.

I start removing tiny black screws from the motherboard. When I think I have removed all of them, I try to prise the motherboard free, but it won't come and when I inspect more closely I see another little screw hidden towards the bottom. Once I have taken that out and disconnected the little red speaker cable, I pop out the L-shaped motherboard, which bristles with minuscule parts. Using the screwdriver, I lever off the stainless steel protective shields to find a number of computer chips whose various functions I would only be able to guess at. Putting the motherboard down next to the rear casing piece, I turn my attention to the last set of tiny screws that hold in place a final board made up of two interlocking sections, one shiny, the other matt. Beneath this I find the back of the screen. I can neither see nor figure out how the e-ink interfaces with the inside of the screen.

I place all the separate pieces next to each other on my desk, the screws and widgets that had held it all together sorted into piles according to size and type. I pick up the screwdriver and replace it in the transparent plastic box.

Either I would be able to put the Kindle back together, or I would not.

Pushing back my swivel chair I get up and walk around to the front of the desk. I pick up the waste-paper bin and return to my side of the desk. I hold the bin under the edge of the desk and use my other hand to sweep all the various parts and pieces of the Kindle into it. I take the bin and put it back where I got it from, then I come back around to my side of the desk and sit down.

My hand reaches out and takes a book from the top of the pile on the right-hand side of my desk. Jane Solomon's

Hotel 167. It is a Picador, a paperback original, dating from 1993, when Picador still gave all of their books a clean white spine with plain black lettering. I open the book and feel the slightly rough fabric-like texture of the yellowed pages under my fingertips. I lift the book to my nose and breathe in.

I turn up the volume as the front wheels make contact with the tarmac and the rear of the car leaves the driveway. The road is lit at regular intervals, neighbours' houses standing in darkness. Speed bumps force me to stay in low gear until I reach the main road where I signal to go right. A bus drives past the stop on the other side of the road, empty but for a single passenger on the top deck. His silhouetted head narrows as he turns to look at the car nosing out of the side road.

I follow the bus, making no attempt to overtake. At the lights it goes straight on while I turn sharply to the left, sensing the pull of the car towards the front offside. The road surface is made up of flat blocks of orange broken up with lines of reflective white. The street lights are topped with misty coronas like dandelion clocks. The next set of lights changes to red as I approach and I knock the gearstick into neutral, allowing the car to coast. Another car sits at the adjacent stop line waiting to go, the driver's face ghostly in the glow of the dash. The traffic lights change in his favour and he moves forward.

I go on through one more set of lights and turn left into Burton Road. The restaurants and bars that earn this district its reputation are all closed. I slow down as I approach Somerfield, indicate left and pull into the car park behind the shuttered supermarket.

There's one car parked behind the store itself, another two at the other end by the recycling bins. I roll down towards them and back up into a space a few yards short, switching off the engine. The CD, *Full on Night* by Rachel's, stops as I do so.

I peer into the darkness – the car park is unlit – and turn the key halfway in the ignition, then pull down the stalk to activate my right indicator. Its rhythmic clicking is the only sound to be heard apart from the hum of traffic on the Parkway, even at this hour. After a couple of minutes I start the engine and a dissonant guitar riff accompanies my rolling the car back out on to Burton Road, then turning right into Nell Lane and heading for the Parkway.

Traffic on the motorway is light. I take the exit for Cheadle Royal and the patient piano work of Rachel Grimes ticks off the lighting poles on the wide loop around the back of the former Barnes Hospital and nearby disused Cheadle Bleach Works. The frantically bowed viola towards the end of 'Full on Night' is a suitable accompaniment to the scratching of the treetops at the purply-orange sky.

I take the third exit off the roundabout at Cheadle Royal, skirting the miniature lake and heading deeper into the business park behind the sports and leisure centre. Behind an anonymous building of blond brick and green smoked glass I reverse into a parking space and sit and wait. The car park is divided by a line of low shrubs, beyond which two cars wait in darkness. In an hour or so, the bright lights of the day's first flights will appear in the sky 1,500 feet above the Stockport Pyramid. Shortly after, they will rumble over Cheadle Royal, travelling at a speed of 150 knots just 700 feet above the roof of the car. For now, though, all is quiet.

I turn the interior light on and let it burn for less than half a minute before switching it off again.

Nothing happens. No lights are lit in the other parked vehicles. No one approaches the car on foot.

Either I stay a bit longer or I leave.

I twist the key in the ignition and turn the wheel to drive down the other avenue on the far side of the island on the way out of the car park. The two cars, expensive saloons parked three spaces apart, appear empty, but the shallow angle of the windscreens makes it impossible to be sure.

I negotiate the roundabouts and head south on the Wilmslow Road, turning right at the lights in the direction of Heald Green. A man in high-visibility clothing waits at a bus stop. A delivery van sits outside a convenience store, its rear doors folded back. I turn left into Styal Road and right into Ringway Road. The Moss Nook restaurant approaches on the right. I can either turn into the little car park or keep going. I allow the car park and restaurant to retreat in the wing mirror. Moments later, again on the right, there is a sudden break in the line of small, modest houses. On the other side of the road a bank of yellow-white approach lights marks the beginning of runway 24. I take the next road on the right and shortly afterwards another right turn into the Ringway Trading Estate. A light shines brightly on to the apron outside a depot on the left. I turn to the right and then go left in front of Air Freight Services. In the car park at the end, I turn around and back up to the chain-link fence.

I switch off the CD but keep the engine running and the lights on. Further down on the other side is a parked car. A dark shape is lodged in the driver's seat.

I reach down to kill the engine and extinguish the headlamps, then raise my hand to switch on the interior light and turn towards the passenger seat.

◆

I say something as they come towards me. I can't remember what I say but they take exception to it. I ask them for money and they start to taunt me. One of them, maybe she feels bad for me, I don't know, sticks her hand in her pocket and pulls out a fiver. As I go to take it, she pulls it away, so I snatch it and the others start pushing me and pulling me, trying to get the fiver back, but I'm not going to let go of it. I bury it deep in a pocket and back away from these idiots. I feel a push and suddenly I'm falling, falling, falling.

Thursday morning. I am running a workshop at the university. Just over half of the two dozen students who should be present have actually turned up. My eyes flick from face to face as I see who is there and try to work out who is not and whether they are persistent absentees who need to be sent a formal letter. Grace is there. I wonder if she has remembered what she wanted to ask me.

'I'd like you to write a short scene,' I say. 'No more than a page. Pick something memorable that has happened to you in the past week involving at least two people and write about it from a point of view other than your own. It can be that of someone else present, but it doesn't have to be. Be as imaginative as you like.'

'What if,' asks a boy called Iain with fixed braces and a glossy black fringe, 'nothing memorable has happened to us in the past week?'

There is a ripple of laughter.

'Then write about the most interesting dream you have had in the past week, and the rule remains the same. Switch the POV.'

Another student starts to ask a question, but I cut him off. 'If nothing memorable has happened to you and you can't remember any of your dreams or they weren't interesting, just make something up. And change the POV from yours to that of someone – or something – else. You've got fifteen minutes. And please,' I add, 'don't write your name on it.'

Amid much sucking of pens and scratching of heads, the students slowly settle into their own thinking space. At the end of fifteen minutes I ask them to finish the sentence they're writing and I walk around and collect up the sheets. I shuffle them and redistribute them. If anyone ends up with their own piece back again, they don't say so. I ask Iain to read out the piece he has in front of him. It's about a confrontation in a nightclub in town. It's not particularly interesting, but there's nothing actually wrong with it. I ask Grace to read out what she has been dealt. She reads a piece about an argument with a ticket inspector on a train that turns into a river running between high, snow-capped mountains guarded by two-headed lions. Someone has taken me at my word.

I ask a boy whose name I can't remember if he will read out what he's got. He reads out an account of an attack on a tramp, from the tramp's point of view.

I realise I am going to have to check out the path down to the dismantled railway line, after all, and have a look for Overcoat Man.

Late afternoon. Wednesday. I am standing in my study at the top of the house looking out at the back gardens of my neighbours and the rear elevations of the houses in the next street. Behind me, my study, with its square hip or pyramid roof, the vaulted ceiling rising in four converging triangular planes to a single point. Built-in bookshelves cover two walls, floor to ceiling. Fiction, film, biography – each has a different section. Short-story anthologies, literary journals in magazine files. Books are ordered alphabetically, little magazines chronologically. Perched on the four-drawer filing cabinet looking down at my desk is a head-and-shoulders mannequin, female; standing in the corner close to the anthologies and magazines, a full-size tailor's dummy. Curled up asleep on the armchair in the opposite corner, my black cat, Cleo. Above her, hanging on a nail on the wall, a stuffed fox's head.

My desk is as tidy as that in my office at the university. Laptop, empty mug (on coaster), pile of scripts for marking, A4 wallet-style folder marked 'Writers' Rooms'. On the wall over the desk, a number of pictures of aeroplanes – some cut out of newspapers and magazines, others printed at home on photographic paper – pinned to a small corkboard. Against the fourth wall under the window is a long free-standing bookcase. On top of this at the left-hand end is a pile of books, first novels – *Fermentation* by Angelica Jacob, *Pharricide* by Vincent de Swarte, *Glass People* by Tom Darling. John Banville's *Nightspawn*, Philip N. Pullman's *The Haunted Storm*. Among others. At the right-hand end, a pile of six identical trade paperbacks. Orange spine, black type.

To the left of the rear gardens that I can see from the window, the main road climbs gently towards a humpback bridge over the trackbed of a dismantled railway line. I can see Overcoat Man making his way slowly up the incline. Overcoat Man is one of numerous instantly recognisable characters that I see around the village, such as Laundry Bag Man, Umbrella Lady, Polling Station Man and Dog Man. Overcoat Man wears several overcoats one on top of the other. All of them are filthy, his trousers likewise. His shoes are coming apart, which perhaps accounts for his shuffling gait and extremely slow progress. His features mostly hidden behind unkempt grey hair and a long reddish beard, he is inscrutable.

Often he can be heard muttering to himself and occasionally he will ask passers-by for money or utter an offensive remark.

As he reaches the point towards the top of the humpback bridge where a path leads down to the trackbed of the former railway line, he turns to confront an approaching crowd of rowdy young people. Maybe he asks them for money or growls unintelligibly at them, but something prompts them to gather around him. I am unable for a few moments to see clearly what is happening, but soon I realise that he is being jostled. He seems to try to edge away from the group down the path to the old railway line and either loses his footing or is pushed and falls over. He rolls once or twice and then I can no longer see him.

In what resembles the protective gesture of a threatened organism, the group of young people closes in. They form a huddle, from which one and then two members abruptly break out, leaving the group. Others depart and soon there's only one person standing at the head of the path, peering down into the undergrowth. After a moment, this person also leaves.

During the incident, which is over in less than a minute, no one else has crossed the bridge. A dog trots by off its lead, its owner nowhere to be seen.

I continue to watch the road and the humpback bridge, but there is no sign of Overcoat Man emerging from the bushes that border the path.

I look at the backs of the houses in the next street. A light has come on in one of the flats. A man fills a kettle at a sink in a first-floor kitchen.

I continue to stand at the window as the sky above the houses turns a deeper blue and the lights in the windows glow more brightly and the gardens below fall into deeper and deeper shadow.

*   *   *

Tuesday morning, just after eleven o'clock. I am sitting in my office at the university. None of my three colleagues is in. This is deliberate. We choose our office hours so that they do not overlap. It is not good to be talking to a student about his or her creative writing while a colleague sits listening – trying not to perhaps, but listening all the same – just the other side of the room-divider. It is not good from the student's point of view, as writing can be a personal thing, and nor is it good from your own, since your colleagues might find it impossible not to judge your performance as a teacher.

On the desk in front of me is a PC, switched off. When I need a machine, I bring in my own. The PC is cumbersome, clunky, slow. I have moved the keyboard out of the way next to the printer, which is also redundant. These items of hardware occupy the left side of the desk. On the right-hand side are two books – Jane Solomon's *Hotel 167* and Sylvia Plath's *The Bell Jar*, both first novels, which I am intending to read in the next few days, the latter for the first time – and a small, neat pile of newspaper cuttings.

There is nothing else on the desk, no clutter.

The newspaper cuttings are all single pages from the review section of a national broadsheet. They are part of a series called Writers' Rooms in which a half-page photograph of an author's office, study or workroom is accompanied by a sidebar of copy written by the featured writer. I take the top one off the pile.

It is the turn of Scottish novelist Andrew O'Hagan. In the foreground is a comfortable-looking armchair, a newspaper draped over one arm. The position of the armchair traps an open door against the wall. Hanging on the door, on the side of the door that would be outside the room if the door were closed, is a blackboard. Both these details suggest the door is, in fact, never closed. Maybe any other members of the O'Hagan household are on instructions not to enter, since a comment – 'The laptop is there for work but it's not online because I hate the idea of some boring email popping up while I'm trying to fix a paragraph' – suggests he does not like to be interrupted. On the blackboard is a chalked reminder: 'Tuesday: Burns essays.'

I picture O'Hagan bent over a pile of manuscripts in a back garden somewhere in north London, striking a match.

There is a knock on the door – my door, the office door, not O'Hagan's. I get up and walk around the desk, slip between two of the room-dividers and cross the office to open the door, which cannot be opened from the outside unless you know the code.

'Hello,' I say to the student who is standing there.

Her name is Grace, I think. I see a lot of students, hear a lot of names.

'Hiya.' Her voice is slightly uncertain and her eyes look everywhere but at mine. With her dyed black hair and pale skin, she has the androgynous look of an emo kid or a goth. 'It's Grace. I'm in your First Novels class.'

'I know,' I say. 'I remember. Come in.'

We sit with my desk between us, and she still doesn't look at me, until I briefly turn away and then I am peripherally aware of her gaze momentarily settling on me.

'What did you want to see me about, Grace?' I ask.

'The . . . er . . . First Novels class.'

'Yes?'

'I'm having trouble finding copies of some of the books on the list.'

'Maybe you weren't at the introductory session,' I say. 'I explained then that a number of these titles are out of print but that in most cases second-hand copies are easily available from online booksellers or second-hand bookshops, where they still exist.'

'Right,' she says, looking at the two books on my desk. 'I managed to find this actually,' she adds, pointing to *The Bell Jar*. 'But it looks different.'

'This is an old copy,' I tell her. 'Second-hand. But *The Bell Jar* is in print. The Jane Solomon is not in print, but you can pick up copies online very cheaply.'

She nods, looking at the floor.

'Was there anything else?'

'I can't remember,' she says. 'I mean, yes, there was, but I can't remember what it was.'

'Email me when you remember.'

'My Internet connection is down. Can I call you?'

'OK.' I look at my Spartan desk. 'I don't have anything to write my number on.'

She rummages in her pockets and comes up empty-handed. From her bag she produces a dog-eared five-pound note and a pen. I dictate the number and she writes it on the banknote.

I see her to the door. The cutting I had been looking at is still sitting in the middle of my desk. I pick it up again.

O'Hagan's desk is old, square, solid, four drawers either side, two in the middle. He claims it came from a Victorian lawyers' office in Doughty Street, next door to Dickens' house, and it may well have done but it looks identical to that of Antonia Fraser, previously featured in the same slot. Behind the desk is a bookcase with glazed doors full of volumes the uniformity of which suggests they are copies of O'Hagan's own titles. Between the armchair and the desk is a small three-shelf book-case of the type that tips books at an angle, but the spines are too far away to be legible. Closer to the camera, an urn sits on the floor next to the armchair. Three books sit on top of it in a neat little pile, clearly the books O'Hagan was last looking at as he sat relaxing, but they cannot quite be made out. All I can say with any certainty is that none is a trade paperback with an orange spine and black lettering.

After the workshop I head straight for home. I stand at the window of my study and look down across the back gardens of the houses in the next street towards the humpback bridge over the dismantled railway line. I think about the incident involving Overcoat Man and the crowd of young people. Is there any doubt in my mind that the piece read out in the workshop was a description of that actual event? Could it not have been an account of a similar incident, perhaps even an imagined one? Was it not simply a generic event easily called to mind or one that could have happened anywhere in the city in the last week? The local papers are full of accounts of happy-slapping incidents.

In the cupboard under the kitchen sink I find a box of lightweight rubber gloves that I bought off an unemployed teenager from Middlesbrough who came to the door with a bag of dusters, microfibre cloths, clothes brushes, tea towels and other poor-quality household items. You can close the door on them, but then how do you know they will not target your house when you are out? The simplest and safest way to make them go away is to buy something off them.

I leave the house. Didsbury is an affluent area of south Manchester, a village in the way that Highgate in north London is a village or Greenwich Village in New York. I walk around to the humpback bridge. I take the path that leads down to the dismantled railway line, which is overgrown, a haven for goldfinches, foxes and occasional junkies and alcoholics. I peer into the tangled vegetation on either side of the little path that runs down the slope. Nothing. At the bottom, the main path – the trackbed of the dismantled railway line – leads south past Didsbury Park, past the Tesco where TV presenter Richard Madeley once walked out with two bottles of wine for which he had forgotten to pay, and eventually to Parrs Wood, an area of East Didsbury bordered by the River Mersey and the A34 and known for its eponymous high school and extensive entertainment complex. The other way, a dead end, leads north towards the humpback bridge, but is blocked off before reaching it. There's a thicket of trees and bushes and brambles, all of which will have to be cleared if they do ever extend the tram system out here. I pick my way through razor-sharp coils of raspberry and blackberry, taking care to minimise my trail. In the shadows at the heart of the thickest vegetation, lighter patches turn out to be sweet wrappers, fast-food cartons, a copy of the *South Manchester Reporter*. I am about to head back up to the road when I notice what looks like a discarded pile of light-coloured textiles towards the back of an extensive nettle bed by the fence that separates the path from the new block of flats on the south side of School Lane. I realise I can get around the back of the nettle bed by creeping along the narrow ridge between the fence and the nettles, using the chain-link fence for support. This means I do not disturb the nettles. I have to make a single footfall between the fence and the light-coloured material, which I can now see is the outermost of Overcoat Man's many coats.

He is lying on his front with his face turned away from me. He is unmoving and makes no sound. There is a strong smell rising from his body, but then there always was. I take the gloves from my pocket and put them on.

The pockets of his outermost overcoat – a filthy mac – are

empty. He has two further coats and a suit jacket underneath, but all I find in the pockets of these are a dry-cleaner's ticket stub, a button, part of a page torn from a religious tract bearing a subhead in bold type, 'The Way Forward', and a playing card – the seven of diamonds. I have to move Overcoat Man's body – a deadweight – to get at his trouser pockets, which contain two scrunched-up paper napkins, a few coppers and a door key on a split ring with a cheap plastic fob and the words 'Side door' written on the label in a spidery hand.

I leave everything where I found it and am about to retrace my single step to the chain-link fence when I realise I didn't check to see if the suit jacket had a top pocket. I bend down again, joints creaking, and feel my way through the outer layers to the suit jacket – cut from once-fine wool-rich cloth, 'hand-tailored by Howard Lever', according to the label – and in the top pocket I find a crumpled five-pound note.

I uncrumple it and study it closely on both sides. Nothing has been written on it. No phone number, nothing.

I return the note to the jacket pocket and roll Overcoat Man's body back into its original position before retreating to the chain-link fence and extricating myself carefully from the scene.

I climb back up the path to School Lane. As I reach the pavement by the side of the Scout hut, Umbrella Lady is making her way slowly past. She wears dark glasses, pink ankle socks and carries a plastic carrier bag in one hand and a small grey umbrella in the other. I wait for her to pass and then I cross the road.

It is half past eleven in the morning. I am sitting at the kitchen table with a cup of green tea and my laptop, answering emails. There's one from AJ and Carol inviting me to a barbecue at their house. Either I will accept or I won't.

There's an email from the editor of a food and drink website asking me if I want to do another restaurant review.

And there's an email from the latest editor to turn down my proposed article about Vincent de Swarte's *Pharricide*.

Pharricide, Vincent de Swarte's first novel, is the story of a young man, Geoffroy Lefayen, who becomes the lighthouse keeper at Cordouan, a tiny island in the Atlantic close to the mouth of the Gironde. To mark his appointment, Geoffroy catches and stuffs a conger eel. For Geoffroy, taxidermy is an art form, as well as a way of conferring immortality. 'If you stuff a living creature, death is not the end, whether it's a conger eel, a lion, even you or me,' writes Geoffroy.

De Swarte died in 2006 at the age of forty-one. Shortly after, I started writing to literary editors, but few are interested in articles about untranslated foreign-language novels that are not set to become the latest publishing sensation, fewer still if the book in question is about a psychopathic loner with an interest in taxidermy.

I hear the snap of the cat flap in the cellar, which will be Cleo coming in from the garden. She will stop at her food bowls before coming upstairs. I wait a moment, listening, and then I hear her running up the wooden steps from the cellar. I wonder if she has brought anything. Lately she has started bringing birds into the house. Dead birds. Birds I've never seen alive. Goldcrests. A blackcap. I don't know where she finds them, where in the garden they are hiding.

Cleo enters the kitchen and jumps up on to the table, sitting on her haunches next to my laptop. She is not an affectionate cat, but she is at least sociable. She has not brought any birds this time.

I look again at the email from AJ and Carol. Either or.

* * *

AJ and Carol's house is a short walk from mine.

On the way, I take a detour down the path at the side of the humpback bridge. At the bottom, I turn right on to the path of the dismantled railway and pick my way carefully towards the nettle bed. I stop and peer through the overhanging foliage. I approach a little closer but I can already see that Overcoat Man's body is no longer there. A telltale patch of damaged nettles shows where he lay, but I can see no clear evidence of which route he might have used to drag himself out of the nettle bed – or by which route his body was removed.

I search the rest of the area, but there is no sign of him.

At AJ and Carol's I encounter Lewis. He has a shaved head, which he may think disguises his male-pattern baldness, and the few extra pounds he carries are noticeable despite the untucked stencilled shirt and baggy linen trousers. His moon-like face is given a certain definition by strategically trimmed facial hair. He's standing a little apart from everyone else eating a greasy chicken leg.

'Lewis,' he says, licking grease off his fingers before holding out his hand. He laughs: '*Ksssh-huh-huh.*'

'Hello,' I say as I take Lewis' hand, which turns out to be dry but has a soft grip as if made of rubber.

'I'm helping AJ with the barbecue,' Lewis says. 'By eating it. *Ksssh-huh-huh.*'

'Hey stranger,' says AJ as he notices me for the first time. 'Let me get you a drink.'

'You carry on, AJ,' I reply. 'I'll go and say hello to Carol.'

I see Carol some mornings, if neither of us is working, as she walks their children to school past my house.

'Paul, darling,' she greets me with mock affection, a hand on my shoulder and a kiss on each cheek. 'What can I get you to drink?'

'You're not on duty now,' I say, bending down to get myself a beer from the cooler.

Carol is a flight attendant, cabin crew. She has a wavy curtain of thick auburn hair that I'm more used to seeing tied back and she's wearing a white linen dress cut daringly low. Although my eyes don't leave hers, I am peripherally aware of the meringue-like swell of her breasts.

I sense she wants to introduce me to the Asian woman she had been talking to when I arrived.

'Paul, this is AJ's mother, Nina,' she says. 'Nina, this is Paul. He's only recently moved to the area.'

'How are you settling in?' asks the older woman, who is wearing a bright turquoise sari.

I know what to say. 'Your son and daughter-in-law have been very kind.'

As everyone sits down to eat, a shadow falls over the garden accompanied by a thunderous roar of an intensity that some of those present appear to find uncomfortable.

'That was low,' complains a thin, orange-skinned woman called Juliet, whose only contributions to the conversation so far have been sharp and vituperative. Her bad mood seems to stem from the fact that her husband, who is delayed due to the overrunning of a Sunday league football match, has still not turned up. She seems embarrassed, as if AJ and Carol might regard it as bad manners.

'That wasn't low,' says Lewis with a distinct sneering tone to his voice. He has a chicken bone in one hand and a trickle of grease at the corner of his mouth. 'That was, what, 1,500 feet? *Ksssh-huh-huh*. Low-flying is classified as 250 feet.'

He looks around, as if expecting most of those present to agree with him.

'It depends,' I say, looking at Carol, who flicks her hair behind

21

her ear before raising her wine glass to her lips. The tiny pink tip of her tongue emerges to meet it. I cross my legs and dust away an imaginary mark, like a batsman prodding his wicket.

'Paul's a writer,' AJ says, reaching for his own glass. AJ is one of those people, increasingly few in number, who think that because you are a writer you know something about the world. 'Like Elizabeth,' he says, as a petite woman with long silver-blonde hair enters the garden from the house. 'Paul, this is Elizabeth Baines. Elizabeth, this is Paul Kinder.'

'All these bloody writers!' Lewis exclaims. 'At least you're not a pilot. *Ksssh-huh-huh*. I've never come across so many fucking pilots as I have since moving here. Excuse my French,' he adds with a glance in Nina's direction. 'What is it with this place and pilots?'

'What do you write?' Nina enquires, ignoring Lewis.

'I write for the papers,' I say, smiling thinly and noticing the look that Juliet seems to be giving Lewis.

'On what subject?' asks Nina.

'Food. Books. Art. I'm a bit of a jack of all trades.'

'And master of none. *Ksssh-huh-huh*,' splutters Lewis, emitting a fine spray of saliva as he falls into the trap I had decided to lay for him.

'Actually, Paul's a novelist,' AJ adds.

'I'm a journalist and I teach creative writing,' I say hurriedly, mainly to head Lewis off, since I suddenly know with absolute certainty what his stock question would be on meeting any novelist: *Would I have read anything you've written?*

Instead, he asks the other question that people always ask: 'Do you write under your own name?'

It occurs to me to answer *No, I write under the name D. H. Lawrence*, but I force my lips into a smile and change the subject: 'You're new to the area, then, Lewis?'

'You are, too, I gather,' he counters.

'I lived in the south for twenty years,' I say, 'but I was brought up round here.'

He reclines expansively, extending his arm along the back of the wooden bench towards Carol who is sitting at the other end.

'I lived in Chorlton,' he says, 'then spent some time in the Far East. Been back a couple of years now. Of course,' he adds with a smile in Carol's direction, 'the upside of living around here is I've never met so many trolley dollies either.'

'Trolley dollies,' I say, also looking at Carol. 'That's a term you don't hear so much these days.'

Carol gives a half-smile and looks away at AJ.

'Surely, trolley dollies was a derogatory term for *male* cabin crew?' Juliet remarks.

'I wouldn't know. I don't do boys. *Ksssh-huh-huh*,' he laughs, looking round for support and not finding any.

'My husband is a pilot,' Juliet says. 'We can ask him when he gets here. *If* he ever gets here.'

'Fucking hell. *Ksssh-huh-huh*. Here's to trolley dollies anyway. Girls *and* boys,' Lewis says, jerking his bottle of Beck's and splashing beer on his shirt.

Lewis' laugh is like the laugh of someone who has had to learn how to laugh as an adult.

AJ turns to Elizabeth Baines, and Nina adjusts her sari.

In the ensuing silence the doorbell can be heard.

'Saved by the bell,' I say, before Lewis can, as AJ leaves the garden.

'*Ksssh-huh-huh*,' Lewis responds on cue.

'What have you got against pilots?' I ask.

'Unreliable. Untrustworthy.' He screws his face up, tight little lines fanning out at the corners of his eyes.

'One would hope not,' I say. 'Maybe the answer to your question—'

'I wasn't aware I'd asked a question,' he interrupts, his eyes suddenly cold.

'—is because the airport is only ten minutes away,' I continue, 'and this is the kind of neighbourhood pilots like to live in.'

'And can afford to live in,' he adds, the chill lifting.

'What pilots get paid is an interesting subject,' I say. 'They don't get paid as well as one might imagine,' I say and immediately I see Juliet's head snap around towards me.

'Anything at all is too much,' says Lewis.

'I would have thought the better paid they are the safer we feel,' I say, but it's obvious from Juliet's expression that it's going to take more than that, despite the challenge I might represent to Lewis.

'Oh look,' says Nina, 'what's that?'

There's a scurrying beneath the hedge.

'Just a squirrel,' I say.

'Pests,' snaps Juliet.

'Like pilots,' says Lewis.

'Elizabeth and I are reading a very good novel in our book club at the moment,' Carol cuts in, placing her hand momentarily on my arm. She names the latest must-read title and asks me if I have read it.

'No,' I say.

'A bit mainstream for you, I suppose,' she says.

I try to smile. 'I'm a bit weary of this type of novel. The Something of Somewhere. The something is usually a humble occupation like a librarian or a cobbler, and the somewhere will be somewhere either tropical or topical. Sometimes both. Afghanistan, China, Iraq. I'm sure it's my loss, Carol, but there are so many books and so little time. If only we had eternity to read them all in.'

'What are you reading at the moment, then?' Carol asks.

'You mean apart from students' work?' I say, lightly grimacing. 'I'm reading something called *The Garden of Earthly Delights* by Lawson Davies.'

'I've not heard of that,' says Carol brightly.

'It came out a long time ago,' I say. 'I found it in Hay-on-Wye some years back. They had a whole shelf of them. First edition, too. In fact, I'm quite sure it was the only edition.'

'What made you buy it? What made you want to read it?'

I think for a moment. 'I met the author years ago at a party in London,' I say, 'and he told me he'd written a novel that was due to be published. I remember being impressed and promising myself not only that I would read it, but that one day I too would meet someone at a party and they would ask me what I did and I would say that I was a novelist.'

'You should read Elizabeth's book,' Carol advises.

'I intend to,' I say.

AJ lopes into the garden followed by a short, dark man in sports gear.

'Sorry I'm late, everyone,' says the newcomer, looking straight at Juliet.

'Don't you think you should go and get changed?' Juliet suggests.

'*Ksssh*—'

The rest of Lewis' laugh is drowned out by the roar of another 747 looming over the apex of the roof and dragging its shadow across the garden.

From a distance of thirty yards, Ray saw immediately what was happening. There was Flynn, in his new full uniform, which the two older men, in engineer's overalls, would have insisted he wear. Ray stepped back behind the trunk of a palm tree, observing.

Several ginger-cream chickens pecked in the sand, looking for seed that the two engineers, whom Ray recognised as Henshaw and Royal, would have scattered there. Ray could see Henshaw talking to Flynn, explaining what he needed to do, Flynn looking unsure in spite of the new recruit's desire to please. Henshaw was a big man with red hair cut severely short at the back and sides of his skull. Royal – the shorter of the two engineers, with a greased quiff – who had been bending down watching the chickens, stood up and took something from the pocket of his overalls, which he handed to Flynn.

Ray caught the flash of sunlight on the blade.

Henshaw mimed the action Flynn would need to copy.

Ray considered stepping in, stopping the ritual, for it was a ritual. He hadn't had to suffer it on his arrival on the island, but only because he had been a little older than Flynn on joining up. Henshaw and Royal were younger than Ray, which would have been enough to discourage them.

But for the time being, he remained where he was.

Flynn, his golden hair falling over his forehead, took the knife in his left hand. With his right, he loosened his collar. He would have been very warm in his blue airman's uniform and he clearly wasn't looking forward to using the knife. His shoulders drooping, he made a last, half-hearted appeal to the two engineers. Henshaw made a dismissive gesture with his hands as if to say it wasn't such a big deal. It was just something that had to be done. The squadron had to eat.

Flynn tried to catch one of the wary chickens, but found

it difficult to do so and hang on to the knife at the same time. Henshaw swooped down, surprisingly quickly for such a big man, and grabbed a chicken. Flynn bent over beside him and switched the knife to his right hand, looking set to do the job while the bird was held still, but Henshaw indicated that Flynn needed to hold the chicken himself. He passed it over and swiftly withdrew. Royal took several steps back as well.

Flynn secured the chicken between his legs and encircled its neck with his left hand, then glanced over his shoulder for encouragement. Royal gave a vigorous nod and as Flynn turned back to the chicken the two older men exchanged broad smiles.

Ray knew this was the moment at which he ought to step in, but still he made no move from behind the tree.

To his credit, Flynn got through the neck of the struggling chicken with a single slice and then leapt back as a jet of blood spurted out. Liberated, the chicken's body spun, spraying the airman with arterial blood until his uniform was soaked. The recruit dropped the severed head as if it were an obscene object.

The butchered bird ran around in ever decreasing circles still pumping out blood. At a safe distance the two engineers laughed. Ray glared at them as he approached. He put a protective arm around the shoulders of Flynn and muttered comforting words, but the young airman, not yet out of his teens, seemed traumatised.

'Come on,' said Ray. 'They were just having a bit of fun.' Though he didn't know why he should excuse their behaviour.

Flynn wouldn't move. The chicken's body had given up and had slumped to the sand. But it was the bird's head that transfixed Flynn. It twitched. The eye moved in its socket. A translucent film closed over the eyeball and then retracted again.

'It can still see,' Flynn whispered.

'It's just a nervous spasm,' Ray said.

'No, it's still conscious,' said the teenager. 'Look.'

As they watched, the bird blinked one more time, then the eye glazed over and it finally took on the appearance of death.

Ray looked over his shoulder and saw that Henshaw and Royal were now a long way down the beach, their dark overalls shimmering in the heat haze, which caused their bodies to elongate and become thinner, while their heads became distended, like rugby balls hovering above their shoulders.

◈

Three days after AJ's barbecue I'm working in my own back garden, removing ivy from the crown of a hawthorn tree and stripping it off the remains of a fence that separates my garden from the one beyond. The hawthorn is a big tree and there may be a danger the ivy is going to make it unstable if I don't deal with it. My approach is not very scientific. I begin by pulling bits of ivy off the fence, aware all the time of several thick stems sunk into the rockery. Clearly they are what feeds the profusion of shiny green leaves among the hawthorn branches. If I don't attack the stems I won't make any actual progress. But the fence part is easy to do and it's quick to see an improvement. All I'm actually revealing, however, is the extent of the damage to the fence itself, which is rotting and giving way where it isn't being penetrated and pulled apart by the ivy.

I'm thinking about the barbecue and remembering the tension that was in the air while Juliet's husband, Kelvin, was off getting changed.

I had been wondering if Lewis was going to keep going

with his pilots routine. An attempt was made to steer the conversation into safer areas, but the moment Kelvin reappeared, in a pale-blue polo shirt and chinos, another aircraft passed directly over the garden.

'What's with all these planes, Kelvin?' AJ asked him. 'I thought the flight path was down over Cheadle Royal.'

Kelvin had just lifted a bottle of Beck's to his lips and I saw Lewis take in a deep breath and prepare to hold forth.

'I see you need a beer, Lewis,' I said to him, pointing to his empty bottle. 'Let me get you another one. What would you like? Same again?'

He raised his eyebrows. 'Sure. OK.'

As I returned from the coolbox I heard Kelvin beginning to answer AJ's question. I handed Lewis his beer and sat down on his other side, encouraging him to turn his back on the others.

'I imagine you've got your own answer to AJ's question,' I said to him.

'The "extended runway centre line" . . . OK?' He paused for acknowledgement of his having used an impressive piece of technical language, which he'd signalled by curling two sets of fingers in the air. I merely shrugged.

'The extended runway centre line,' Lewis repeated, dispensing with the air quotes, 'runs back from the airport out towards the Peak District. It passes over the David Lloyd gym at Cheadle Royal and the Stockport Pyramid. In non-busy periods, pilots coming from the north are sometimes asked if they would like a "six-mile final", allowing them to loop in over Didsbury and join the "extended runway centre line" at Stockport instead of the usual ten miles out. *Ksssh-huh-huh.*'

It sounded rehearsed, as if it was a speech he had given before. While he was giving it, in the gaps between the words, I was able to pick up bits of Kelvin's explanation, enough to understand that all that was happening was that while planes normally landed and took off at Manchester towards the west, today, due to the wind having changed overnight, they were taking off (and landing) towards the east. These planes, which Lewis thought were coming in to land, had in fact just taken off and were turning left to head for destinations in the north and west.

'I'm going to stretch me legs,' Lewis said, getting to his feet and wandering off to the end of the garden where the children had established their own territory under the leadership of a nurturing eighteen-year-old, Samantha, and her excitable thirteen-year-old brother, Thomas – Carol's children from an earlier marriage.

Kelvin, meanwhile, was talking to Elizabeth Baines, asking her if she lived locally and she said she lived a couple of minutes' walk away on Victoria Avenue.

'Where they filmed *Cold Feet*,' AJ said.

'Just a few doors down from there,' she added.

From time to time, I could hear Lewis' laugh over the cries and shrieks of the children.

When the doorbell intrudes on my thoughts, I decide not to answer it. I need to continue working on the ivy.

It goes again. And then a third time.

I leave my muddy boots at the back door and walk through the kitchen in my socks. I see the figure of a man through the stained glass. I open the front door. Cleo chooses that moment to run in from the front garden, flowing around our legs like a river of molten tar.

'*Ksssh-huh-huh.*'

I don't say anything for a moment. I don't know what to say.

'Lewis,' I manage finally.

'That gave me a fright,' he says, pointing up at the manne-quin positioned in the bedroom window. '*Ksssh-huh-huh.*'

When I don't say anything, he digs his hands into his jeans pockets and looks at my front garden. I don't intend to help him out. Instead I just wait.

'Looks like you're pretty busy,' he says eventually, eyeing my gardening clothes.

'Yes. I'm trying to get rid of some ivy.'

'As long as it's not Himalayan balsam,' he says. 'Still, it can be very persistent, ivy. *Ksssh-huh-huh.*' He shakes his head. 'Do you want an 'and?'

'I've got it, thanks. I'm OK.'

He nods, pushes his hands deeper in his pockets.

I have no intention of giving in.

'I could murder a brew,' he says, plaintively.

I breathe in – and out.

'Of course,' I say.

I step back into the hallway and he clumps on to my carpet in dirty shoes.

'You've also been gardening?' I say, looking deliberately at his shoes.

'Just tidying,' he says, failing to pick up the hint.

I lead Lewis through the house into the back garden, because the prospect of standing with him in the kitchen for the length of time it will take the kettle to boil is not a good one.

He looks at the ivy and the fence and the rockery in turn.

'Are you going to cut it off at ground level?'

'Either that or try and get the roots out.'

'*Ksssh-huh-huh.* That's a big job. You'd be looking at taking the rockery out and you've got a skip's worth of rockery there.'

'Yes,' I say, unconcerned whether my tone conveys irritation.

'You'd need a wheelbarrow and everything.'

'Mmm.'

'You're welcome to borrow me wheelbarrow.'

'Thanks.'

'Just let me know.'

He steps closer to the fence.

'It's made a right mess of your fence,' he observes.

'Yes, I'm going to have to replace it.'

He takes hold of a weak section and pulls at it. With a creak it bends and snaps off in his hand.

'*Ksssh-huh-huh.* Yeah, you are.' He peers through the jagged hole into the garden of the house beyond. 'There's your problem. They've let it go. Completely overgrown.'

'The ivy's mine, though. The roots are on this side of the fence.'

'Yeah, but it's grown up into their tree and all over the fence from their side.'

'It's a rented house. Flats,' I say. 'Apparently, the guy who used to own the house committed suicide. In one of the back bedrooms.'

I thought Lewis would relish the detail, but he doesn't react, just places his eye closer to the large hole he's torn in my fence.

'Who told you that?' he says finally, with, it seems, a trace of scorn.

'My neighbour,' I say.

Lewis stares through the hole in the fence again and remains silent for a while.

'So,' he says, stepping back from the fence, 'you're a writer?'

'Yes.' I feel my head beginning to hurt.

'What name do you write under?'

'My own.'

He nods.

'It must pay well,' he says, taking in the garden and the house with a sweep of his hand.

'No,' I say, 'it doesn't pay well. I wouldn't recommend it as a career.'

'Have you written anything I might have heard of?'

My head throbs.

'I doubt it. I wrote one novel several years ago. No one's heard of it. I'll just go and see to that brew.'

I leave the garden and while I'm in the kitchen, watching through the window as Lewis conducts a further examination of the ruined fence, I swallow 400 mg of ibuprofen and two co-codamol. Behind me on the table is a cutting from the weekend's paper featuring another one in the series of writers' rooms. This one is Adam Thirlwell's. Thirlwell got on to the 2003 *Granta* Best of Young British Novelists list on the strength of his first novel, *Politics*. Although there's an open laptop just off-centre, Thirlwell's desk is dominated by a red Olivetti typewriter (he's learning to touch-type); there's also a pewter hip flask standing on a floral mouse mat. The hip flask is empty, according to Thirlwell. Under the desk, which looks like the kind of ash-and-chrome affair you might pick up for a few hundred pounds from one of the smarter furniture shops on Deansgate, but could just as easily be a self-assembly job from Ikea, is a line of books standing snug up against the skirting board. None of the titles or authors' names can be clearly read, but one at least is the right colour and approximate thickness. It's impossible to be certain either way, but on balance I'd have to say it's unlikely.

When I go back outside with two mugs of tea, Lewis seems to have got the message: he asks no more questions about my writing. The conversation, such as it is, flags until Lewis ends up raising the subject of football, about which I have nothing to say, and as soon as he's drained his mug, Lewis leaves.

I carry on with the ivy removal, but the further I get, the clearer it becomes that I am going to have to attack the root cause. Lewis would laugh his strange little laugh at that, perhaps. I am going to have to hire a skip and borrow the man's wheelbarrow. He had written his address and phone number down on my kitchen calendar before leaving. That in itself seemed to me like a further trespass on my property, but what's the point of keeping a blank calendar?

◆

Insulated from the pain that had cut him off from England for ever, Raymond Cross prospered in the Royal Air Force, which had a small presence on Zanzibar. Prospered insofar as he seemed to find satisfying the narrow range of tasks assigned to him. He ticked boxes on checklists, got his hands dirty in the engines of the few planes that were maintained daily. They were taken up only once or twice a week, to overfly the island and to hop across to Mombasa to pick up supplies. Ray was allowed to accompany the tiny flight crew if he wasn't busy: he could be made useful loading and unloading.

In his spare time in the barracks, Ray listened to jazz records on an old gramophone the base commander had picked up on a trip to the mainland. Milt Jackson and Thelonious Monk riffed until the needle was practically worn away. No one could say where the records had come from. Some nights he got out of his head on Kulmbacher lager they had flown over from Germany. It was dropped at night, illegally, in wooden crates that burst open on the beach, scattering the ghost crabs that rattled about on the foreshore. He drank steadily – sometimes with the other men, usually on his own – and spoke to none of his comrades about his reasons for joining the RAF.

When the conditions were right – and they usually were between June and March, outside the rainy season – and Squadron Leader William Dunstan was piloting the mission, they would take a small detour before heading for the airstrip. On returning from Mombasa or a tour of the island, Billy Dunstan would take the Hercules north to Uroa where he would swoop down over the beach and buzz the aircraftmen and flight lieutenants stationed there. Ray was soon organising his time around Dunstan's schedule, so that when the flamboyant squadron leader was in charge, Ray was invariably waiting at the airstrip to go up with the crew. Dunstan ran a pretty relaxed ship.

The men at Uroa station would hear the Hercules' grumbling approach rise above the constant susurration of the wind in the palms and run out on to the beach waving their arms. Dunstan would take the plane down as low as possible; on occasion he even lowered the landing gear and brushed the surface of the beach a few hundred yards before or after the line of men, raising huge ballooning clouds of fine white sand.

After his pass, the line of men on the beach applauding as they turned to watch, Dunstan would tilt to starboard over the ocean and climb to a few hundred feet before doubling back and flying down the coast to the base at Bwejuu. Every time, Ray would be standing hunched up in the cockpit behind Dunstan for the best view. The squadron leader enjoyed showing off; Ray's pleasure lay in watching Dunstan's reaction as he risked going lower and lower each time, but there was more to it than that. There was another element to it for which Ray had yet to find expression.

* * *

The next day, during a break from duties, Ray saw a lone figure standing by the shoreline. He wandered over, clearing his throat once he was within earshot, and came to a halt only when he had drawn alongside. The two men looked out at the horizon. Some 300 yards out, the reef attracted a flurry of seabirds. They hung in the air as if on elastic, a short distance above the water.

'I'm sorry I didn't get there sooner,' Ray said. 'In time to stop them, I mean.'

Flynn shrugged. 'They'd have got me another time,' he said. 'Probably. No harm done, eh?'

'I was scrubbing away at my uniform for at least an hour this morning,' the younger man said.

Ray felt the breeze loosen his clothes and dry the sweat on his body.

'I've heard stories,' Flynn continued, 'about beheadings in the Mau Mau Uprising. They used machetes. They'd cut someone's head off and the eyes would still be blinking, still watching them. What must that be like? Still being able to see.'

They watched the horizon without speaking for a few moments. Ray broke the silence.

'I'm not sure you should be left alone with your thoughts.'

They watched the rise and fall of the seabirds, at this distance like a cloud of midges.

'Do you leave the base much?' Ray asked.

'I go to Stone Town . . .'

Ray turned to look at the young airman. He was wearing fatigues and a white vest. His eyes, which didn't deviate from the view in front of him, were a startling blue. He didn't seem to want to elaborate on what he got up to in Stone Town. Ray bent down and picked up a shell. He turned it over and ran his thumb over the ridges and grooves.

'There you go,' he said, handing it to Flynn. 'Don't say I never give you anything.'

'Here. Pull in here,' I said, pointing to the opening on the left.

Susan Ashton swung the wheel of her Golf GTI and we pulled into the car park by Hatton Cross Tube station.

'I can give you a lift all the way back into London, you know,' she said, leaning back in the driver's seat, the upholstery sighing beneath her weight.

I smiled at her and shook my head. 'It's OK,' I said. 'It's out of your way.' I looked out of the window. It was early evening, late autumn, getting dark. Enough artificial light to see her eyes glimmering. 'I like this place. That's why I asked you to drop me here. And it's close to where you live. You're not far from here, are you?'

Susan Ashton's thick chestnut hair rocked forward whenever she moved, two acute angles sweeping towards her cheekbones. I looked at her right hand on the steering wheel. Her left on the edge of her seat, nearest to me. No rings. She and Tony didn't even live together. She lived in Feltham; he was down the road in East Bedfont. Or the other way around. They were thinking about moving in together. Considering buying a place.

She wasn't sure.

She wasn't sure about *it*, she wasn't sure about *him*.

I knew this because we had sat up in the hotel bar until four while she told me all about it. We'd been the only delegates on the staff development course who hadn't gone up to bed when the bartender had told us he had a home to go to.

I couldn't figure out if I'd ever looked at her twice before the course. Working in the same office for three years, I'd always found her pleasant, but maybe she was taken, and I definitely was, so it was never an issue.

Veronica and I had been together four years, both living in London but both from the north. The twins had been born two years after we got together – that's two years before Susan Ashton steered her car, with me sitting in the passenger seat, into Hatton Cross Tube station car park – and Veronica and I had found it difficult adjusting to life as parents. There's no point denying it. But still it was never an issue – me and Susan Ashton. Sometimes it just isn't. And then you get thrown together on a staff development weekend, even though you have no interest in staff development. No real interest in the company you work for. The event was compulsory, a residential course in a Thames Valley hotel. I had watched her in the group sessions. Delighting in others' company. Outgoing, fun, mildly flirtatious, yet clearly holding something back.

'It's just a couple of miles over there . . . Tony's more . . .' Susan Ashton waved vaguely to the south.

'I know.' I shifted around in my seat so I was looking directly at her. As I did so, the sky suddenly closed in around the car with a deafening roar, jet engines powering down. Flaps up, gear down, close enough to touch. Or so it seemed. We both swivelled in our seats to watch the aircraft descend further. The runway was only a few hundred yards away beyond the wire-mesh netting.

'That was a big one,' I said. 'Jumbo. 747.'

She nodded. Her body still angled backwards, she rested her head on her arm and looked at me. She was wearing a white cotton blouse with three, maybe four buttons undone. No necklace or pendant. I gave up trying not to look.

'It'll be all right, Tony and that,' I said, as if I cared. I imagined touching her face with my hand, stroking the backs of my fingers against her cheek.

Another plane overflew the car. It was smaller, a 737, but still the nearness of it was overwhelming. I was becoming an increasingly nervous flyer as the years went by, yet here I was, happy to sit underneath the flight path. I had recently read that statistically London was overdue for a major air disaster. That would be one for them to chew on, those poor bastards who took refuge in the comfort of statistics: it's safer than crossing the road; you're more likely to die in a car crash; hit by lightning. Those were the people who didn't mind who hit the ground at ninety degrees and 500 miles an hour still strapped into their seat, as long as it wasn't them.

And yet there I was sitting a few hundred feet beneath 250 tons of decelerating metal and flesh and I wasn't bothered. Far from it.

'Did you know,' I said to Susan Ashton, 'the engines on a 747 are designed to fall off in the event of excessive vibration? *Designed to fall off.* What kind of idea was that? Can you imagine coming out with that one on a Monday morning? You know, the design team sits down around the table to bash out a schedule for the week and you say, Hey, why don't we design the engines so they fall off if it gets a bit rough? Save the whole wing coming off. Why do they put engines on a 747 in the first place? Because it's a bit heavier than a fucking glider. That's why.'

Susan Ashton was smiling. She hadn't heard it all before. Unlike Veronica.

As a break from working in the garden, I walk into the village. On School Lane I pass Dog Man. Dog Man has a leaning-forwards gait so pronounced he would fall over if he stood still.

He has a red face and five o'clock shadow even first thing in the morning. His dog, a chocolate-brown Labrador cross with stumpy legs, struggles to keep up at his side. I must have seen him fifty times and never once without his dog.

I end up in Oxfam, but the selection of books has not altered much since my last visit a week ago. There's an extensive fiction section, but the only white-spined Picadors are the ubiquitous Kathy Lettes and a couple of Julian Barnes novels that I already have (and almost certainly will never read), and Carlos Fuentes' *The Old Gringo*, which I picked up recently elsewhere. In terms of A-format orange Penguins there's a volume of Dirk Bogarde's autobiography, but it's a later edition than the ones I like to collect. It's also Dirk Bogarde's autobiography, and while I collect almost indiscriminately within my chosen parameters, there are limits. There are three John Wyndham novels, but I have them all. Under classics there's *Middlemarch* and Gilbert White's *The Natural History of Selborne*, both of which I already have.

They have started playing middle-of-the-road pop music in Oxfam. A Whitney Houston track finishes and is followed by Sting, the equivalent of adding insult to injury. The manageress smiles at me as I walk past the till on my way out. I draw my lips across my teeth in response.

I cut around the back of Marks & Spencer to Barlow Moor Road and the Art of Tea. I pass through the café to reach the second-hand bookseller – the Didsbury Bookshop – where I can easily lose an hour in the narrow aisles between the tightly packed stacks.

'Hello, m'laddie,' calls Bob, the proprietor. 'Just having a look? Let me know if there's anything I can help you find.'

I make a non-committal reply, knowing from experience that a conversation with Bob will inevitably come around to the subject of Europe, and Britain's place in it. Bob holds strong views on this, but he keeps a good stock, which is all that is important to me.

There are no other customers. I can hear faint music coming from the picture framer's workshop at the far end of the premises. On the right as you enter Bob's domain is a section devoted to Penguins. My eyes move across the spines, looking for any new additions, checking first by author, then title. I slide out a copy of Isaac Bashevis Singer's *The Slave*. The front cover is coming away and there is a stain in the bottom left corner, but I have a number of these white-spined editions and I am fairly certain that this is one I don't have. I hold on to it while I check out the remaining shelves. I am never sure which Edna O'Briens I have and which I don't, and I can't remember whether I have started collecting the slim translated novels of Françoise Sagan or if I'm still saving her for another day. Bob has three, in uniform covers. I leave them for now and walk to the other end of the shop where he keeps the rest of the paperback fiction.

I am looking for the classic white spines of Picador, but for some weeks now I have been thinking that soon I will start collecting other white-spined books. Sceptre, Abacus, King Penguin. I spot a white-spined *First Love, Last Rites*, Ian McEwan's first collection of short stories. My copy has a photographic cover that bleeds on to the spine. I have been keeping an eye out for a white-spined edition for years. I reach up for it and as I'm taking it down from the shelf I am aware out of the corner of my eye of someone entering the bookshop. Indistinct, dressed in black, the newcomer walks past Bob's little table and is obscured by the stacks in the middle of the room. I hear Bob call out a greeting and make his usual offers of help, which are met with nothing more than a grunt.

I move to the left-hand wall, where there's a small selection of crime and mystery fiction. Numerous grass-green Penguins, including several Simenons, but I can never remember which Simenons I have, so many of the titles being so similar. Maigret this, Maigret that. I crouch down to look at them, as I have looked at them on previous visits, to read the titles and try to remember whether I have seen them here, or in another shop, or on my shelf at home. I can't be certain and so I decide that the two books I have found will do for today and when I stand up and turn I bump into the black-clad newcomer. I mutter an automatic apology and when she looks up I see that it is Grace, from the Year 1 workshop and First Novels course. There's recognition in her eyes, but no obvious surprise.

'I was just about to pay for these,' I say.

She asks me what I have chosen and I show her. Her hair needs a wash, I see, as she flicks through *First Love, Last Rites*. It's greasy and lank and there are some tiny flecks of dandruff on her scalp.

'I've never read McEwan,' she says. 'Is he good?'

'Very. The early stuff especially.'

'You like early stuff, don't you?' she says. 'First novels.'

'*The Cement Garden* is very good. Nice and short, too.'

'I was going to get a cup of tea,' she says suddenly. 'Do you want to get a cup of tea?'

I don't answer.

'I could do with a bit of help on the whole First Novels thing,' she says. 'If you don't want to, that's fine.'

'No, no. Sure.'

It can be like a tutorial, only over a cup of tea. In a café. It's not a problem.

I pay Bob for my books and we move back into the Art of

Tea. Grace picks a little table on the lower level and we order herbal teas. She asks what cake they have and orders a piece of lemon drizzle cake.

'For you?' the boy asks.

'I'll have the same,' I say.

There's a moment's silence. Grace picks up the Isaac Bashevis Singer and pretends to read the blurb on the back.

'So, what were you looking for?' I ask her. 'In the bookshop.'

'I'm still looking for most of those first novels,' she says. 'From your list.'

'I don't think you'll find many of them here. Maybe the Jane Solomon, although I'd have noticed it if they'd had it. *The Bell Jar*, but you've already got that, I think.'

She casually pushes up the sleeves of her hooded top and my eyes are instantly drawn to the angry red marks on the insides of her forearms. I look away at the framed artworks on the wall.

'Good stuff,' I say.

She gives them a cursory glance.

'So what is it about first novels you like so much?' she asks. Is there a hint of a challenge in her question or is it just her manner? She has a slightly abrasive way of speaking that I imagine is the product of shyness, of low self-confidence. The marks on her arms back this up. She is rather plain-looking, square-jawed; her skin is dry and pale, her eyes an indeterminate colour. I wonder, as I often do with students, how she found her way on to the course. I did not interview her and know nothing about her, where she lives, where she's from. It is possible she is local. I remember the piece that was read out in the workshop, which I assumed she had written, but the five-pound note could have been a coincidence. She might not have been among the group of young people on the humpback bridge that evening.

But someone in the workshop almost definitely was.

It could have been her.

The five-pound note I found on him might not have been the only one in his possession when he hit the ground.

'It's not just first novels,' I say. 'I'm interested in first novels that have been lost or suppressed or never followed up.'

I wonder if I have said too much. It is not usual for a lecturer to be forced to justify his choice of texts to an undergraduate.

The tea arrives, the slices of cake.

'What do you mean?' she asks.

I have a sip of tea.

'Well, like John Banville's *Nightspawn*. Every so often, when Banville brings out a new novel, his backlist gets reissued with new covers and so on. But you'll never find his first novel, *Nightspawn*, included in these reissues.'

She nods.

'Jane Solomon and Angelica Jacob both wrote brilliant, or at least very promising, first novels and then never wrote anything else. Or nothing else ever appeared.'

'Why not?'

I shake my head. 'Solomon became a tango instructor. Jacob – I don't know. She wrote art criticism. One or two short stories. But as far as I know she didn't write another novel. I find this very interesting.'

Grace raises her eyebrows, seemingly encouraging me to go on.

'It wouldn't be interesting if the novels were no good,' I say. 'You'd think they got it out of their system and let's just be thankful they don't feel the need to foist another worthless novel on the world. It's not like we're short of books. But *Hotel 167* and *Fermentation* were both good novels, so why no more? Why do we hear no more from these very talented writers while others, far less talented, continue to write book after book after book?'

With her fork, Grace divides her slice of cake into quarters. She places one of these into her mouth and chews it slowly, without any expression. She drinks some tea.

'What about your first novel?' she says.

'What about it?' I ask before I can stop myself.

'Why don't you put that on the list?' Her mouth is twisted into an approximation of a smile. 'I mean, is it any good? Why is it impossible to track down? Why haven't *you* written a second novel?'

Now I smile, and take another sip of tea.

'So many questions, Grace,' I say.

She gives a little laugh to acknowledge my having avoided them.

'I am writing a novel at the moment,' I say.

'Is it your first?' she asks, a sly smile playing around the corners of her mouth.

'It will be the first to appear under the name Paul Kinder.'

'So, what, your first appeared under a pseudonym?'

'This cake is very good,' I say.

'Hmm.'

'What about you?' I ask. 'Are you writing a novel?'

'Should I be?'

'As an undergraduate, you are not expected to.'

'But what's to stop me?'

'Nothing.'

We watch each other for a moment like two chess players between moves.

'If I were writing a novel,' she says, 'even though there's no expectation of me to do so for the course, would I be within my rights to ask one of the tutors to offer supervision?'

'There would be no harm in asking,' I say, choosing my words with the same level of care.

'Maybe,' she says, polishing off her last forkful of cake, 'I should make an appointment to see you in your office.'

'You've got my number.'

The following morning, I stand in the bay window of the bedroom, next to the mannequins, and watch as parents drop their children off at the school. I see Carol walk past on the opposite side of the road with her youngest – the two children she has with AJ. Her two older children, Samantha and Thomas, whom she must have had when very young, spend most of their time with their father – by amicable agreement, she once assured me – and attend school in Altrincham. Carol's hair is tied back in a ponytail and she is dressed in a smart blue jacket and skirt and white blouse, clearly about to drive to the airport once she has dropped the children off.

Just when I think she has gone too far, she turns and looks at the house, her eyes scanning the downstairs windows before looking up. She lets go of a small hand to wave. I raise a hand in response. The children look up and point and laugh; they think the dummies are funny.

The dummies are not funny. Sylvia Plath did not find dummies funny. There's a line in *The Bell Jar*: 'The figures around me weren't people, but shop dummies, painted to resemble people and propped up in attitudes counterfeiting life.'

Once Carol and the children have crossed the main road to gain entrance to the school, I turn away from the window. I am wearing my gardening clothes, but I am in no hurry to get started. On the landing outside the bedroom is a white bookcase. In it I keep Picador paperbacks from the 1970s, 80s and 90s. At some point in the 90s Picador abandoned the classic design of white spine and black lettering with uniform typography. They still occasionally publish some interesting books – Bret Easton Ellis' *Lunar Park*, John Banville's recent novels – but they don't look the same and so I don't collect them.

The way things look is important.

Dummies are all about look.

The first four shelves contain my collection, from Aragon's *Paris Peasant* to B. Wongar's *The Track to Bralgu*, and the last shelf and a half is where my wife Veronica's Picadors reside. She didn't collect them seriously, not like I did, but when we got together, I combined my Picador collection with those that she happened to have among her books, for she was a reader. Where her Picadors finish, halfway along the bottom shelf, eggshell-green Penguin Modern Classics fill up the rest of the space. As I buy more Picadors, from charity shops and the few second-hand booksellers that remain in business, the Penguins are edged out and shelved elsewhere.

I have read one or two of these books more than once. Perhaps half of them I have read once. The other half comprises books I intend to read one day and books I doubt I will ever read, either because I will run out of time or because I am not sufficiently interested, but they have the right look, so I buy them and keep them on the shelf.

The house sits silently on its foundations as I slide out my old copy of *First Love, Last Rites* and replace it with the one from the Didsbury Bookshop. I place the old one on top of the bookcase; I will take it up to my study when I am next going.

I run my finger across the spines of the Ss. Saki's short stories, a novel by Nicholas Shakespeare, Iain Sinclair's poetry anthology. And on to the Ts. Emma Tennant's *Hotel de Dream*: there are two copies of this novel. One on my shelves, one on Veronica's. I take them both out and lay them side by side on the carpet.

I can't work out what is more interesting, either their being virtually identical or that there are minor differences of appearance. One is creased at the top corner, the other slightly foxed along the bottom edge. I flick through both copies, one after the other. They smell exactly the same. They smell of second-hand bookshops, cardboard boxes, spilt tea. The faintest hint of cigarettes. Futility. Time.

I take out the five other books by Emma Tennant on Veronica's shelf. *The Bad Sister*, *Wild Nights*, *Alice Fell*, *Queen of Stones*, *Woman Beware Woman*. I place them next to each other. I compare them in terms of smell, cover design, number of pages.

Cleo comes and brushes against my leg.

'Hello, Cleo,' I say. 'What do you think? Either I mix Veronica's books in with mine or move them elsewhere.'

I stroke her back, tickle her under the chin. She lifts her head up to encourage me.

'You're not much help,' I say. 'Are you? She's been gone a long time.'

I collect the books up and put them back on Veronica's shelf. I'm tempted to integrate them into my collection, but I'm not sure it would be the right thing to do. At what point will it be, I wonder? Will it ever?

I look again at the Ss on my shelves. Sinclair, Stevens. Something is missing. I picture my copy of Jane Solomon's *Hotel 167* on the corner of my desk at the university.

I follow Cleo down to the half-landing, where the Penguin shelves – wide and shallow, designed precisely to fit A-format paperbacks – are a mixture of orange and grass-green. I look at the Simenons, trying to commit to memory the titles that are there, but I know that as soon as I'm back in the bookshop, or any other bookshop, I'll have forgotten.

There are occasional breaks among the orange and green for white-spined Penguins – Derek Marlowe, Isaac Bashevis Singer, D. M. Thomas' *The White Hotel* – which I am increasingly finding an unwarranted distraction, at least in this context. On these shelves. Nevertheless, I slip the copy of *The Slave* between *The Estate* and *A Friend of Kafka*.

I walk to the bottom of the stairs and sit on the last step to pull on my gardening boots.

A few streets away, a 1930s semi bristles with scaffolding. Sheets of heavy-duty plastic shift listlessly in the light breeze. The bell is one of those that cannot be heard from the outside, perhaps even from the inside, so I knock on the door. After a few moments, heavy footsteps come bounding down the stairs and the door swings open.

'*Ksssh-huh-huh,*' he laughs. 'That was quick.'

'My skip was delivered first thing. You mentioned a wheelbarrow . . .'

'Come in, come in.'

'I'll just take my shoes off,' I say, pointedly, then follow him down the narrow hall.

'It's in the garage,' he says over his shoulder. 'We could have opened it from the outside – it's not like I ever lock it – but there's stuff in the way that needs moving.' As he passes through the kitchen, he flicks the switch on the kettle. 'Make yourself at home. I don't tend to lock this either,' he says as he opens a door that appears to connect the kitchen directly to the garage. 'There's no need.'

While he rummages in the garage and I hear the scrape of a wooden door on the gritty tarmac of his drive, the kettle continues to boil and I look around his kitchen. There's a calendar from a local business with scribbled notes and ringed dates. Between it and the fridge is a large, cheaply framed collage of old snapshots featuring a vivacious-looking redhead and two little blonde girls at various ages. The woman's hair is longer in some shots, shorter in others. One shows her and Lewis in evening wear, about to set off for a party. They have their arms around each other: she looks proud and happy. He's smiling, but looks slightly tense or awkward, as if he knows something she doesn't. He had more hair then.

Lewis re-enters the kitchen and I step back from studying the picture.

'Being nosy,' I say.

Lewis edges past me and fiddles with the kettle. He drops the lid of the teapot, which clatters on the floor, masking the splutter of his characteristic laugh.

'Me family,' he says. 'Me ex-family.'

'You split up?'

Lewis pours the water. He shakes his head.

'There was an accident.' His voice threatens to break on 'accident'. He spills the milk. 'Oops. No use crying. *Ksssh-huh-huh.*'

I don't say anything, but watch Lewis' shoulders as he stands hunched over the sink, perfectly still.

'So, anyway,' he asks finally, 'how you settling in?'

'Fine.'

'You should come down the pub. Everyone's there. Thursday, nine o'clock. It would be good for you to meet some more people. Come down tonight.'

I imagine a load of blokes desultorily disagreeing with refer-
eeing decisions.

'Who goes?'

'Everyone. All the lads. It's not a piss-up. Very civilised.'

I drink my tea and make my excuses.

Ray had joined the RAF as a way of getting out of Britain
in the early 1960s. His wife had died giving birth to their
only child and it would have broken him if he hadn't got out.
Some say it did break him anyway. Others that it just changed
him. The pinched-faced moralisers among his family said it
had no effect on him: he'd always only ever been in it for
himself. These are the people you might have expected to
have got their heads together to decide who was best placed
to offer the infant a home, until such time as his father tired
of the tropics. But they didn't exactly fight among themselves
for that right.

Ray himself had been born into a community so tightly
knit it cut off the circulation. His own domineering mother
and subjugated father, all his uncles and aunts, were regular
churchgoers. Some gritty, northern, unforgiving denomination,
it would have been, where prayer cushions would have been
considered a luxury.

It wouldn't have mattered who Ray brought back to the
house in Hyde as his intended, they weren't going to like her.
They'd have looked down on her whatever she was, princess
or pauper. Not that they had any money of their own to speak
of, they didn't. But pride they had.

Perhaps Ray bore all of this in mind when he took the
Levenshulme bingo caller to the Kardomah in St Anne's Square.

Victoria. Vic, Ray called her – his queen. She may have been only a bingo caller to the family, but Ray worshipped her. She turned up in the Cross household one blustery night in a new miniskirt. 'Legs eleven,' he blurted out, ill-advisedly. 'Your father and I will be in here,' his mother said, frowning in disapproval and pointing to the front room; Ray's father shuffled obediently. 'You can sit in t' morning room,' she said to Ray.

The morning room, an antechamber to the kitchen, was dim and soulless in the morning and didn't get any lighter or warmer as the day wore on. Somehow it failed to benefit from its proximity to the kitchen. No one used it, not even his mother, despite her being temperamentally suited to its ambience.

Ray and Victoria's options were few, if they had any at all, and sticking around wasn't one of them. Ray got a job with the Post Office in Glossop, so they packed what little they had and moved out along the A57. He worked hard and earned more than enough for two, so that when the first signs of pregnancy appeared, they didn't think twice. It didn't matter that the baby hadn't been planned; it was welcome.

After the birth, Ray held the tiny baby once, for no more than a few seconds. Victoria lost so much blood, the hospital ran out of supplies. She suffered terribly for the next twelve hours, during which time Ray stayed by her side. Twice the nurses asked him if they'd thought of a name for the baby. Each time he waved them away.

When the RAF asked Ray his reasons for wanting to join up, he said he liked the uniform and had no objection to travelling, the latter being an understatement. They sent him to the island of Zanzibar, thirty miles or so off the coast of Tanganyika in East Africa. A greater contrast with east

Manchester must have been hard to imagine. The family declared him heartless and cruel, swanning off to a tropical island when he should have been mourning his wife and looking after his kid. Their hypocrisy galvanised him and he brought his departure date forward. He needed to put some distance between himself and his family in order to mourn. Five thousand miles wasn't bad going.

Ray wasn't surprised when Billy Dunstan invited the two girls to join them on a flight around the island. Joan and Frankie were English nurses working in a clinic in Zanzibar Town. Dunstan and one of his fellow officers, Flight Lieutenant Campbell, had met the pair one evening on the terrace of the Africa House Hotel where all the island's expats went to enjoy a drink and to watch the sun go down in the Indian Ocean.

On the agreed afternoon, the nurses were brought to the base at Bwejuu by an RAF auxiliary. Ray looked up from polishing his boots and saw all the men stop what they were doing as the women entered the compound. Henshaw stepped forward with a confident smirk, wiping his hands on an oily rag. The other men watched, with the exception of Flynn, whose uniform still bore one or two of the more obstinate traces of the engineers' ritual humiliation of him on the beach. The airman coloured up and looked away.

Dunstan appeared and made a swift assessment of the situation.

'Henshaw,' he said, 'shouldn't you be driving the supply truck up to Uroa? You'll have it dark, lad. Take Flynn with you.'

Flight Lieutenant Campbell had been called away to deal with a discipline problem on Pemba Island, Dunstan explained to the two women. Because of the nurses' schedule, there wouldn't be another opportunity for a fortnight and Dunstan didn't want them to go away disappointed. Ray watched him stride out across the landing strip to the Hercules, his white silk scarf, an affectation only he had the dashing glamour to carry off, and then possibly only in Ray's opinion, flapping in the constant onshore breeze. Joan trotted behind him. Frankie stopped to fiddle with her heel and while doing so looked back at the men watching from the paved area outside the low huts. Ray, who was among those men, was struck for the first time by her resemblance to Victoria. When she smiled, it seemed directed straight at him. A nudge in the ribs from Henshaw confirmed this.

'Didn't you receive an order?' muttered Ray.

'Yes, Corporal,' Henshaw replied sarcastically.

Ray looked away from Henshaw towards Flynn, who had also been watching the exchange of looks between Ray and Frankie with, it seemed to Ray, a look of hurt in his blue eyes.

'Corporal Cross,' came a cry from the airstrip. 'Get your flying jacket.'

'Now it's your turn to be ordered about,' said Henshaw. 'Lucky bastard.'

As Ray left to join Dunstan and the two girls, he passed close to Flynn.

'You'll get your chance, son,' he said quietly.

As they taxied to the beginning of the landing strip, Ray looked out of the cockpit to see the fair head of Flynn bobbing into the supply truck alongside Henshaw.

'Hold tight, ladies,' shouted Dunstan over the noise of the four engines as the plane started to rumble down the runway.

It takes a while to set up a protected route through the house for the wheelbarrow, but once I have, I make a start on removing the rockery. I soon realise it's a bigger job than I had thought it would be. The rockery is about fifteen feet wide and climbs to three feet above the level of the lawn. There are rocks, obviously, and a lot of impacted soil, but that doesn't go very deep, because a few inches below the surface the landfill starts: roof tiles, half-bricks, lengths of flex, old light fittings, bits of hard moulded red plastic and some unidentified cottony material that for some reason I find slightly sinister. The penny-pinching approach to upkeep of the former owners of the house has left me a wide range of problems to deal with, of which this is only the latest to emerge.

I kick down on the spade and receive a bone-jarring shock to hip and shoulder. Further, more careful shovelling reveals the ghostly white outline of an old Belfast sink. Inside the bowl is a collection of ash and burnt matter. I turn this over with the spade, but it's impossible to tell what it once was. I wonder if I should have bought a decorator's mask.

I work on, filling the wheelbarrow, pushing it through the house, emptying it into the skip. I keep promising myself a break – after the next barrowful, once I've emptied five barrowloads – but don't take one. Every time I unearth another section of the ivy's extensive root system, I down tools and try to tug it out. The results are mixed and I keep falling over on my backside. Every time this happens I get straight up and carry on, aware of pain radiating out from a small angry red knot of muscle, as I picture it, in the small of my back. Then one time I don't get up, but allow myself to rest for a moment, sitting in the mud. The root I've been trying to free has snapped, leaving me holding a six-inch stub. In the hole I've dug to gain access to the root is a white name tag from some plant bought at a garden centre. I feel a sense of futility settle on the scene, born partly of my insignificant progress and partly of an odd, almost malevolent stillness in the early afternoon air. There's a strange compressed quality to the light with a wall of slate-grey cloud building steadily in the west. The sun disappears behind the cloud. The sound of children's laughter, of which I have hardly been aware, fades out and ceases altogether as the light changes. The colours become muted. Lewis' face briefly enters my mind as I reach for the white tag in the hole. I see his face screw up as he laughs his spluttering laugh and turns away, then turns back, the laugh dissipating, to meet your gaze, almost challenging you to look away. At which moment, I suddenly realise, there's always a strange look in his eyes. Either sadness, or an emptiness of some kind. An odd ambivalence, as if his emotions could suddenly swing dramatically in any direction. The laugh itself carries a suggestion of hysteria.

I pick up the tag. It names a plant that presumably once grew in the rockery: *Crocosmia* 'Lucifer'. I allow myself a brief smirk at that. 'Hardy perennial' it says. It would have to be very hardy indeed to survive any length of time in this toxic dump. In the rockery since I've been living here, there's been no sign of what the tag describes as the 'flame-red flowers and sword-like foliage' of the *Crocosmia* 'Lucifer'. There's been very little, in fact, apart from rosebay willow herb and various other weeds. I wonder how far back in time the name tag goes. I presume the previous owners put the rockery in. The previous owners – who increased the price of the house substantially after a figure had been agreed – I do not feel well disposed towards. The overgrown ivy, and the landfill rockery, don't help.

The quality of the silence starts to alter. The sky – and

somehow the silence itself – becomes darker, even more ominous and unsettling, until it becomes clear that what I can hear isn't silence at all but the drone of an approaching plane. As I look up, it lurches over the roof of the house dragging an overwhelming downdraught of noise, in the same way that a thick black cloud might trail skirts of heavy rain. Despite the subdued light, I can see the aircraft's lower parts, its undercarriage and the curved plates of its tubular fuselage, in the sort of shimmering, hallucinatory detail you see in certain surrealist paintings. I see individual rivets glowing like white-hot pinheads. As the bass roar of the engines causes my breastbone to vibrate, I think of the neckline of the dress Carol wore at the barbecue, which in turn prompts a memory of the dashboard of a car. Numbers, needles and dials picked out in glowing jazz-club blues and traffic-light reds.

My right hand was resting on the edge of my seat, my body turned so that I was facing Susan Ashton. Her left hand was placed over my right, her fingers very gently closing over mine. She leaned back in her seat. Her white blouse billowed forward in sympathy with the upholstery either side of her shoulders. Because I was sitting slightly forward and she had slumped down somewhat in her seat, I could see down the front of her blouse.

As I looked, she tightened her grip on my hand a fraction.

Just enough.

I could see the fine down on the tops of her breasts. The dark cleft between them. They rose and fell as her breathing grew louder. I didn't want her to do anything more, neither to speak nor to unbutton the blouse further. She seemed to sense this.

When the next jet cast its enormous shadow over the car she watched our reflection in the windscreen as I unbuttoned her blouse, slipped her bra strap off her shoulder, peeled the cup away, caught her breast in my palm. I squeezed it gently, then more firmly, catching her nipple between my forefinger and thumb. I detected a slight wheeze in her increasingly loud breathing. I squeezed harder, heard her catch her breath, a slender moan beginning in her throat that matched precisely the whine of decelerating engines from the next airliner to pass over. With my right hand now I released the other bra strap. Still she sat facing forward as a procession of screaming jets came down low over the car. I made her lean forward far enough to allow me to unclip the bra, which I threw on to the back seat. She reclined again, shivering as my hands moved over her upper body. Cradling her breasts, stroking the back of her neck. Then, with her right hand, Susan Ashton leaned down to release the recline lever and kicked the seat back with her bare feet. The slightest opening of her legs and consequent upwards drift of her skirt constituted no more invitation than I needed. As I shifted across, she unbuckled my trouser belt and a moment later my knees were pressing into the forward edge of her seat. By now we were both breathing heavily and the Golf's windows were misted over, but every time a plane overflew the car we felt its passage stirring the marrow in our bones. Roughly one plane in every six was a jumbo or equivalent, the noise from which would drown out any sound coming from inside the car. I couldn't imagine that Susan Ashton was paying the same kind of attention to the air traffic as I was, but she timed her orgasm perfectly, climaxing with a great cry of release as the car shuddered under the sonic onslaught of a 747.

◆

They flew across the island to Zanzibar Town. Dunstan pointed out the Arab Fort and the Anglican cathedral. Frankie spotted the clinic where she and Joan worked on the edge of Stone Town. Dunstan turned the plane gently over the harbour and flew back over the so-called New City in a south-easterly direction so that he was soon flying parallel with the irregular south-west coastline.

'Uzi Island,' shouted Dunstan as he pointed to the right. The two girls leaned over the back of his seat to get the best view. Ray watched the way their hips and bellies pressed into Dunstan's shoulders. The squadron leader seemed to sit up straighter, flexing the muscles at the top of his back, as if maximising the contact between them, his hands maintaining a firm grip on the controls.

'Where's that?' asked Joan, pointing to a tiny settlement in the distance.

'Kizimkazi. Not much there. Hang on.' So saying, he banked sharply to the left, unbalancing both girls, who toppled over then picked themselves up, giggling. Ray watched a twitch of pleasure in Dunstan's cheek. Frankie smiled hopefully in Ray's direction. He smiled back instinctively, but then looked away.

They crossed the southern end of the island, then kept going out to sea before turning left again and describing an arc that would eventually bring the plane back over land north of Chwaka Bay. The horizon – an indistinct line between two blocks of blue – had become a tensile bow, twisted this way and that in the hands of a skilled archer; the plane itself was Dunstan's arrow. Ray watched the squadron leader's hands on the controls, a shaft of sunlight edging through the left-side window and setting the furze of reddish hairs on his forearm ablaze.

The RAF station at Uroa came into view: a couple

59

of low-lying buildings in a small compound, a handful of motorbikes, a Jeep and one truck that Ray surmised would be the supply vehicle driven there by Henshaw and Flynn. As the Hercules overflew the station, several men appeared from inside one of the huts, running out on to the beach waving their arms. Ray looked back as Dunstan took the plane into a steep left-hander and headed away from the island once more.

'They're moving the truck,' Ray said. 'They're driving it on to the beach.'

'They must want to play,' said Dunstan with a grin as he maintained the angle of turn.

The nurses grabbed on to the back of the pilot's seat.

'This is like going round that roundabout,' said Frankie to Joan, 'on the back of your Arthur's motorbike.'

Dunstan looked around.

'My ex,' Joan elucidated.

'What we're about to do,' Dunstan yelled, 'you can't do on a motorbike, no matter who's driving it. Hold on tight and don't look away.'

Dunstan took the plane lower and lower. The beach was a mile away, the altitude dropping rapidly.

'Five hundred feet,' Dunstan shouted. 'At five hundred feet you can make out cows' legs.'

'There aren't any cows,' Frankie shouted back.

'That's why I'm using this,' said Dunstan, tapping the altimeter with his fingernail.

Ray watched the needle drop to 400, 350, 300.

'Two hundred and fifty!' Dunstan roared. 'Sheep's legs at two hundred and fifty. Not that there's any sheep either. We are now officially low flying, and below two hundred and fifty,' he shouted as he took the rattling hull down even lower, 'is classified as very low flying.'

The ground looked a lot closer than 250 feet to Ray, who knew that the palm trees on this side of the island grew to a height of more than thirty feet. He watched their fronds shudder in the plane's wake, then turned to face forward as the station appeared beneath them once more. The truck had been parked in the middle of the beach, the men standing in a ragged line either side of it, raising their hands, waving at the plane. From this distance – by now, free of the palm trees, no more than fifty feet – it was easy to recognise Henshaw, and Flynn, who was jumping up and down in boyish enthusiasm. The girls whooped as the Hercules buzzed the truck, leaving clearance of no more than thirty feet. Ray turned to watch the men raise their hands to cover their faces in the resulting sandstorm.

'Fifty feet, ladies,' Dunstan boasted, enjoying showing off. 'We're allowed to fly this low to make free drops.'

'What are free drops when they're at home?' asked Joan.

'When we want to drop stuff without parachutes. Boxes of supplies. Equipment. Whatever.'

Frankie had fallen silent and was looking back at the line of men.

'What is it?' Joan asked her.

'That young one, the blond one, I'm sure I've seen him before.'

'He's been in the clinic, Frankie. I saw him in the waiting room. He must have been your patient, because he wasn't mine. I'd have remembered him, if you know what I mean.'

Frankie put her hand up to her mouth as she did remember.

'Oh God, yes,' she said. 'Such a nice boy. He was so embarrassed. I felt terribly sorry for him.'

Dunstan had already started to go around again. The blue out of the left-hand side of the plane was now exclusively that of the ocean, the sky having disappeared. Ray waited to see if Frankie would say more about Flynn. She saw him watching her and fell silent.

She was similar to Victoria, but when Ray looked at her he felt nothing. Victoria was gone and the feelings he had had for her were gone also. It didn't mean they hadn't existed. But they could not be reawakened. Something in Ray had changed, even if he didn't understand the full nature of the change. He didn't doubt that he was still grieving for Victoria, but living on the island, in the company of Dunstan and the other men, was altering him. He couldn't have said what he did feel, only what he didn't.

'Can you take it any lower this time?' Joan was asking Dunstan as she leaned over the back of his seat and the line of men grew bigger in the pilot's windshield.

'What's that boy doing?' Ray muttered, as Flynn clambered on top of the cab of the supply truck that was still parked on the beach.

'Sometimes we fly as low as fifteen feet,' Dunstan shouted, sweat standing out on his forehead as he clung to the controls and fought to keep the plane steady. He knew that one mistake would be fatal. If the right-hand wing tip caught the trunk of a palm tree, if the wake of the aircraft created an updraught that interfered with the rudder, control would be wrested from him in an instant, setting in motion a chain of events that would be as swift as it would be inevitable. Ray knew this and he knew that Dunstan knew it. He could sense that the two girls were beginning to realise it, as they watched, wide-eyed and white-knuckled.

The line of men was no more than a hundred yards away, the plane travelling at 140 knots.

'Be careful, sir,' Ray murmured. 'Watch Flynn.'

The youngster was standing on the roof of the cab, stretching his arms in the air, his face ecstatic, hair swept back.

As the plane passed over him, they felt a bump. It would have felt harmless to the nurses, but Ray knew nothing is harmless in a plane of that size flying at that kind of altitude. He twisted around and looked back through the side window. He saw a figure in a blue uniform falling from the roof of the truck and something the size of a football rolling down the beach towards the sea.

'Christ!' said Ray.

One of the girls started screaming.

The golden sand, the turquoise sea. Rolling and rolling. A line of palm trees, the outermost buildings of the station. Henshaw, eyes wide, mouth hanging open. Another engineer bent double. Over and over. The golden sand, darker now, black, the sea, fringe of white foam, the vast blue sky. The black cross of the Hercules climbing steeply, banking sharply, heading out to sea. The golden sand. A body, damaged, somehow not right, lying on the sand by the supply truck. A quickly spreading pool of blood. The golden sand, line of trees, the vast empty sky, the distant plane, a line of men, men running, a body on the sand. The golden sand. Ghost crabs. A shell. Shells. The vast blue sky, line of trees. The supply truck. The golden sand. Palm trees swaying, blown by the wind. Henshaw. The golden sand again, darker, wetter. White foam, tinged pink. The blue of the sky. The body by the truck. Line of men, line of trees. The golden sand.

Horror Story

He's a nice guy and everything. Well, he's OK. But you can't help but look at his track record and wonder. One published novel, I don't know how many hidden away in the bottom drawer. And the one that <u>did</u> make it didn't <u>really</u> make it, if you know what I mean. Yes, it was published, but it didn't set the world alight and it's been out of print for donkey's years. No one on the course has read it or even seen a copy – except me. How can we take instruction from someone who doesn't seem to know how to do it himself?

Am I being harsh? After all, he's a published novelist. He didn't self-publish either; a proper publisher bought it and put it out because they thought it was good enough (or because they thought they could make money out of it, but having read it, I kind of doubt it). That's precisely what all of us on the course dream of, to have a novel published. It's weird how books are meant to be under threat from all other forms of entertainment and kids don't read any more and bookshops and publishers find it increasingly hard to make ends

64

meet, yet everyone, from A-list actors to stand-up comedians to top poets to the woman down the street, everyone wants to write a bloody novel. And Dave, our course instructor, has done it and me and the other girls and our two token boys, who are really honorary girls since Vince is gay and Justin's so sweet it's like he's a girl, are all thinking big deal, so what, where's his second?

So, yeah, maybe I'm a bit hard on the guy. But you know what they say. Those who can, do; those who can't, teach. And that's a bugger of a sentence to punctuate. Not at all convinced I've got it right; Dave would know how to do it. One thing he does know about is punctuation. Use a semicolon correctly and suddenly Dave's your best friend, until you confuse it's and its, or there and their. Whatever. Still, the argument goes, if he were any good, he wouldn't need to teach. Right? Wrong. Look at Martin Amis. The moment the fifty-something enfant terrible of British letters announced his professorship at Manchester, hundreds of washed-up novelists in universities up and down the country received an ego boost the equivalent of Mariella Frostrup suddenly saying, in her gravelly voice, 'What we really need are more novels by X.' They felt valid-ated. They were able to take that resignation letter out of the print queue. They even started thinking about getting stuck into another novel – or resurrecting the last failed attempt.

Dave's got all of that going on, I reckon. Anyway, I'm waiting outside his office for a quick meeting, not really a tutorial, I haven't got time for that, but, amaz-ingly for me, I'm five minutes early, so I don't knock.

Suddenly his door opens and one of the three people he shares his office with comes out and Dave sees me and gets up and suggests, since it's so busy in there, that we go to the canteen, which I'm cool with. So we head downstairs and he's moaning about not having his own office. Something to talk about, I guess. I nod and make appropriate noises, but I'm wondering if he knows I've read his book. How could he? I've not told him. I've been careful not to let it slip. I haven't even told any of the others I've got a copy, let alone lent it out. <u>Salt</u>, it was called, about a guy whose wife dies from eating too much salt. That may be an over-simplification, but that's basically it. He does go on about it, does labour a point, but when you factor in the research that's been done, a lot of it since he wrote his novel, about the dangers of consuming too much salt, it kind of makes it OK, I guess.

Dave gets a duck-breast wrap with hoisin sauce or something equally Daveish, while I get a plate of chips. I'm sprinkling them with salt when Dave says, 'Go easy. It'll kill you,' and that gives me a jolt, but when I look up, he's got this weird half-smile on his face. I think it's Dave's attempt at a full smile, but he doesn't really do smiling. There's too much seriousness and tragedy in that big balding head. Stretching a smile across it must seem a bit like sticking a smiley badge on the door to the mortuary.

'I was thinking,' I say to him, 'you know you told us all to write a horror story for Halloween?'

He nods.

'I'm struggling with it. I'm trying to experiment with point of view and perspective, like you said, and frankly the further I get into it, the less I feel I know about how it's all done, and I really need a tutorial, but I can't get away for long enough during working hours because of my job. Anyway, you once offered to make yourself available out of hours and I'm wondering if I can make an appointment, and probably not here, either, cos it's a right bastard to get to. Oh, excuse my French,' I add because I just looked up and he had this, like, bizarre look on his face and I'm thinking do I really want to book to see this guy out of hours? But I tell myself he's been checked and double-checked or else they wouldn't let him work here and I really must stop being so paranoid.

'No problem at all,' he says and I'm like, 'Cool, thanks.'

So, a few days later, I'm walking down his street in a leafy part of town. Leafy, perhaps, but not particularly well lit. The houses are all big semi-detached jobs with drives and front gardens and loads of brilliant hiding places for muggers and rapists, and I know what you're thinking. Why did he suggest we have the tutorial at his house, and more to the point, why did I agree? Look at the alternatives. Coffee shop? There's only Starbucks and obviously I'm not going there. We could hardly meet in a pub, because (a) it's a Friday night and we wouldn't get a seat and we'd be shouting at each other to make ourselves heard, and (b) it could easily, and weirdly, start to feel like a date, and from Dave's point of view especially, that has to be avoided. From mine too, of course, but I'm not the one who'd face awkward questions at work on Monday morning. Although, from what I've heard, it's not like Dave's colleagues – or perhaps I should say former colleagues – have been models of propriety where relations with students are concerned. But still. As far as I understand it, Dave's got family. That's what his biographical note says, anyway. Dave lives in Manchester with his family and teaches creative writing at blah blah blah. This is his first novel. It's a bit like saying, 'This is my first wife.'

The appointment was set for six o'clock. It's the best time of day, at this time of year, for having a nose in people's windows. Too early to close the curtains but dark enough to have the lights on, so all these comfortable reception rooms with their framed pictures and their well-stocked bookshelves, their dining tables and upright pianos, they're like little stage sets each one, shining under the lights. Most are empty, but now and again you see someone drift in and wander out again. Maybe they glance out into the darkness and see me, my ghostly white face hovering at the end of their drive like something painted by Edvard Munch.

Dave's house is near the end of the street. It's the one with the group of mannequins in the bedroom window. I'll admit they gave me a fright as I looked up. Nice one, Dave. One dummy in a window, OK, but three, and two of them children? Each to his own, Dave. I squeeze past the knackered old car in the drive and ring the bell.

Dave opens the door and we get through the pleasantries and small talk and I can hear myself overcompensating for my shyness and generally being a bit of an idiot, and Dave's trying to make me feel at ease, but he's not a terribly relaxed person himself and so he's not that good at it. We shuffle down his hall to the kitchen at the end and he says he was having a beer and would I like something and I say I'll just have a glass of water if he's got one. If he's got one? Like his taps might not be working. He pours me a glass from the fridge and we sit down at his kitchen table at a slight diagonal, as if that might be less weird than facing each other directly, but of course it's weirder, because when would you ever sit diagonally across from someone if there are just two of you?

'It's quiet round here,' I go, meaning the area generally, but I can see he thinks I mean his house.

'They're upstairs,' he says.

I look away because I can't meet his eyes and on the shelf alongside is this weird-looking lizardy thing.

'What's that?' I ask before I can stop myself.

'It's a mummified lizard,' he says. 'My sister brought it back from Egypt years ago. I like it.'

'You're into mummies, aren't you?' I go. 'I guess it's the salt.'

Too late, I've said it. I want that nice wooden kitchen floor to open up and let me fall into the cellar that is no doubt underneath. He's looking puzzled.

'They use salt, don't they, as a drying agent?' I say.

'And why . . .' he begins.

I'm cross at myself, but I'm also starting to feel a bit cross with him, too. Why should it have to be a secret that I've read his novel? It was published. Why wouldn't his students – or one of his students, at least – be interested enough to get a copy and read the damn thing?

'You read us that short-short story by Christopher

Burns,' I said. '"The Mummification of Princess Anne". As an example, you said at the time, of a short-short that was actually worth writing, unlike all those Dave Eggers stories in the <u>Guardian Weekend</u>. Remember?'

'Of course, I'm just pleased <u>you</u> do.'

'It was great,' I say, overcompensating again. 'I'd love to reread it. What was it in again?'

'It was in an anthology called <u>New Stories 1</u>.'

'<u>New Stories 1</u>. I like that. It's confident. It's like saying, "This is my first wife."'

He looks at me, but I can't meet his eyes. I just want to die.

'I'll go and get it,' he says. 'You're welcome to borrow it. You strike me as someone who looks after books.'

He leaves the kitchen and while I listen to his footsteps going upstairs I find myself looking around, checking the table, the work surfaces, the island. I spot a pepper mill, but there's no sign of a salt cellar. I hear a muffled voice upstairs, but only one. I drain my glass and then he's back, with the book, which he puts on the table.

'Where's the nearest loo?' I ask. 'Weak bladder.'

'Downstairs. Just go out of the kitchen and turn right. The stairs are in front of you.'

I find the loo in the cellar. The seat is up. Hmm. I'm thinking this was a pretty terrible idea, coming to Dave's house, and I'm wondering how much worse it can get. Maybe there's another way out of the house from the cellar and I could escape and quit the course and give up writing and never have to see Dave ever again. Half with this in mind, although not seriously of course, and mainly because I'm a nosy cow, I check out the rest of the cellar. There's enough room down there for a student flatshare. I push open one door – it's already open really, I just have to open it a little bit wider – and see a couple of huge bags slumped against the wall. I see my hand reaching out to pull open the top of one of them to check out what's inside and I'm slightly weirded out to see that it's full of salt. Not table salt and you wouldn't want to cook with it, but salt all the same. Like the kind of salt they used to put on icy roads when you were a kid. Why's he got two great big bags of salt in his cellar? And why are his wife and kids so implausibly quiet? And then I hear his voice floating down the stairs from the hall.

'Are you all right down there?'

No, I'm thinking. Not really.

2

Campus

'The theory of flight is simple. Drag and weight try to stop an aircraft: lift and thrust have to overcome them.'

Brian Moynahan

I am interested in straight lines.

I was born in Manchester, but left at the age of seventeen to go to London. London doesn't really do straight lines. There are straight roads, of course; they stand out. The A5. The A1, for a bit. The A30 as it approaches Hatton Cross Tube station and the perimeter of Heathrow Airport. No one can miss those. On the ground, on the map.

When I moved back to Manchester I became aware of a number of less obvious straight lines. If I stand in the bay window of my bedroom and look into the bay window of my neighbour's bedroom, I can actually see through that bay into the bay of the next house and so on down the street.

If, on a dark night, you come off the M60 at junction 25 and head north up Ashton Road towards Denton, you see the road surface shining ahead of you in a straight line. Only at the last minute do you see that your road – Ashton Road – bends sharply to the right. The road that appears to continue in a straight line, Castle Hill, is actually a left turn off the main carriageway. To take it at speed would lead you quickly into difficulties.

Drive south down Holme Road in Didsbury, alongside Marie Louise Gardens, and turn right at the bottom into Dene Road West. Ahead of you the road is invitingly straight.

Certain features conspire to conceal the much bigger and busier cross street, Palatine Road: an overgrown bush hides the stop sign, a speed bump obscures the white markings of the junction itself. I always want to drive straight across Palatine Road and into Mersey Road without stopping. It looks as if you should be able to. There's a risk involved, perhaps, but a risk worth taking. A risk you should take, even.

The Modern Jazz Quartet's 'Pyramid' is playing on the car stereo as I turn left into Longley Lane. 'Pyramid' was written in 1957 by Ray Brown after hearing the gospel singer Mahalia Jackson in concert in Lenox, Massachusetts. The title came from the group's attempt to impose a 'tempo pyramid' on the song's arrangement. Very little remains of that experimental version of the song, but John Lewis' quick little runs up and down the keyboard have the power to suggest the ascent and descent of a pyramid.

Pyramids are another thing.

Pyramids and straight lines.

Longley Lane takes us over the M56 and eventually into Styal Road, which heads away from Sharston and Gatley. Styal Road is not straight, but it is my preferred route to Moss Nook and the airport because as you meander south down Styal Road, sooner or later you will hear a plane passing directly overhead. If it is big enough you will become aware of the vibrations too, in your chest cavity, in your breastbone. You may even become aroused.

Erica, my passenger, lives in Kenworthy Lane, Northenden. I hadn't known that when I had entered the Cooperative Bank two days earlier. I hadn't known her – Erica – at all. The Corporation Street branch in town is large enough that you can hang around without attracting suspicion. I watched the various tellers at their windows and eventually settled on the third from the end. Then all I needed to do was wait until the queue had gone down so that I could go straight to her window.

She looked up and smiled at me. Pleased that she didn't ask 'Are you all right there?' as everyone behind a counter seems to do these days, I did my best to smile back. I could see from the tiny lines around her almond-shaped eyes that she was a little older than I had thought. But that could work in my favour. The absence of a wedding ring – indeed, any rings at all – was promising. There was a good chance that a bank teller in her late twenties, if not married, was not seeing anyone either, or not with any degree of seriousness. She was wearing a pale-blue wrap top, without any necklace or pendant. She would have known that with the wrap top none was necessary.

I told her I was considering opening an account and wanted to know what the bank had to offer to prospective customers. She started telling me and I pretended to listen while I watched her lips move and I pictured her dressing for work. I saw her kneeling on the floor in front of a full-length mirror, inspecting the tired skin under her eyes while waiting for her hair-straighteners to warm up. I imagined her getting out the wrap top and a plain blue round-neck T-shirt and putting them side by side on the bed as she tried to decide between them.

I waited for a gap and when it came I asked her if she would like to go out for dinner. She recoiled slightly and a little colour appeared in her cheeks. I apologised and explained that I was a writer and I had just been asked to review a restaurant at short notice and I had no one particular in mind to go with. I had acted on impulse, I said, with a little smile, and hoped she would forgive me.

'Are you actually interested in opening an account?' she asked.

'Absolutely,' I said and let her go on outlining the benefits I would enjoy as a customer of the bank. When there was another pause, I said, 'It is meant to be a very good restaurant.'

If a half-smile hadn't appeared on her lips at that point I would have walked away.

'There is a dress code, by the way,' I added. 'You have to wear that top.' I smiled again so that she would think I was making a joke.

As I jump a red light at the junction of Styal Road with Simonsway and Finney Lane, I hear the deep bass rumble of a large aircraft. It flies over the roof of the car no more than 250 feet above us. I imagine pulling over and having sex with Erica right there in the car at the side of the road. Instead I watch the plane as it follows a straight line – no evident sideslip this close to landing – on a diagonal trajectory towards the start of runway 24 less than a quarter of a mile away.

'Look at that,' I say. '747.'

'You like planes?' she asks, amused.

'I like it when they go over. I like to think of all those people in there travelling at 150 miles an hour right above our heads. Some of them relaxed – reading, doing a Sudoku. Others terrified as the ground approaches ever faster. Toy cars revert to normal scale and ants become humans.'

I turn to look at her. She is wearing the pale-blue wrap top exactly as I wanted her to, but she has combined it with a simple amber pendant possibly as an act of mild defiance, or, more likely, self-protection. She smiles nervously.

I turn right into Ringway Road and then right again into

the restaurant's own small car park, which I notice has a lock-able gate currently standing open.

Almost the moment we enter the restaurant, I realise I have made a mistake. It's not the sense of stepping back into the 1970s: the patterned carpets, old-lady lighting, and tasselled swag curtains. I don't mind all that. It's not even the slightly uneasy combination of excessive formality with unconvincing overfriendliness, to which I am impervious. It's more that as we are shown to a table by the window, I see a plane passing 200 feet above Ringway Road and I can't hear a thing over the tinkle of cutlery and the rustle of conversation. I had anticipated it being the other way around. I knew the restaurant was a few hundred yards from the flight path rather than directly underneath it, but I had imagined diners straining to hear each other above the roar of jet engines. I had thought the mullioned windows would be rattling in their panes. Instead, the restaurant could be anywhere, double-glazed into oblivion. The place trades on its proximity to the airport, yet it goes as far as it can to eradicate any trace of aircraft.

I notice Erica looking out of the window.

'Do you ever get to go to the Pyramid?' I ask her.

'What pyramid?'

I sense her bristling slightly.

'The Stockport Pyramid. The blue one. It's got your bank's logo all over it.'

'No. If you don't work there, there's no need to go there. I work in town. You know that.'

'Right.' I take a sip of wine. 'Well, I do need to go there. I need to get inside. I wondered if you could help?'

'Is that what we're doing here? You think I can get you into the Pyramid?'

I try to assess how close she is to walking out.

'Of course not,' I say.

She lifts her glass and appears to be debating what to do with it. She opts to drink its contents and I refill it from the bottle, which brings the waitress scurrying to our table. It's that kind of place. The kind where they insist on filling your glass for you.

'Is everything all right?' asks the waitress.

I look at her. I can feel Erica looking at me. The waitress is of mixed race with light-brown skin and long, dark wavy hair pulled back into a ponytail accentuating high cheekbones. She's a tall, attractive woman but she looks worn out and it's only the start of the evening.

'I can't hear the planes,' I say.

'You want to try living here,' she says.

I raise my eyebrows. 'Do you live locally?' I can still feel Erica's eyes on me.

'Just down the road.'

'This side of the runway?'

'Just.'

'I like the planes,' I say, leaning back in my seat.

She directs her tired gaze at Erica, whose cheeks, I notice, are tinged pink.

'He does,' she goes on, for Erica's benefit, 'he wants to try living here.'

'Yes,' I say, so that she looks at me again. 'I do. I do want to try living here.'

'It's no fun when you're tossing and turning and a great big bloody jumbo jet goes over,' she says, her hands planted assertively on her hips.

'Well, I beg to differ,' I say, just about able to remember Susan Ashton. Her Golf GTI. Hatton Cross Tube station car park.

The waitress shrugs as a way of bringing the subject to a close and asks if we have finished with our starters.

Erica is looking around the room. Anywhere but at me, I suspect. I follow her gaze. We are the youngest people in, by some way. Most of the other diners are couples. Golfers and their wives. Golfers and their husbands. The acoustics are such that you can hear conversations from other tables quite clearly even though no one is speaking especially loudly. You try to distinguish one table's chat from another, as if angling a boom mic from one group of diners to the next, but find you can't. You watch one white-haired man's lips move and realise the voice you can hear is that of a retired headmistress on the other side of the room.

The waitresses, meanwhile, are wheeling a trolley towards the table in the far corner. On it are two plates, each covered with a domed silver lid with a small knob on top for a handle. They deposit the plates on the table in front of an elderly couple, and then, with practised ease, lift the lids in perfect synchrony with a flourish that comprises a girlish swing of the hips with the slightest genuflection like a half-curtsey. The elderly couple do not react; they've seen it all before. They've been coming here for years and now barely have the energy to lift their cutlery. For the waitresses the reveal is clearly a tiresome routine, one they yearn to leave behind, but it goes with the territory. If they had a contract, it would be written in.

The trolley is wheeled back into the kitchen and I swivel to look at Erica. She turns at the same time and our eyes meet for an awkward moment. I look down and my gaze snags on her amber pendant. She has large breasts. The clingy material of her pale-blue top wraps itself around one of them like a promise. I have to tear my eyes away.

'Are you married?' she asks suddenly.

'Kind of.'

'What does that mean?'

'She died,' I say. 'She's dead. Or she's enjoying eternal life, depending on what you believe.'

At that moment the two waitresses arrive at our table with their trolley. On it are two plates covered with the same silver domed lids. The girl with the ponytail and cheekbones places mine in front of me while the other waitress, a middle-aged woman with short, dyed blonde hair, serves Erica. Then they each delicately grasp the nipple-like handles and their eyes meet. On a signal invisible to us they swing, bend and lift in one fluid movement. All it lacks is someone to say 'Ta-da!' in an ironic tone of voice.

'I'm sorry,' says Erica as the waitresses withdraw, and she sits forward to communicate sincerity.

I look back at her and don't know what to say.

'Who does work there?' I ask eventually.

'Where?' she says, taking my non sequitur as a sign that she may start to eat.

'In the Pyramid.'

'Mortgage people. Business and personal banking. Smile.co.uk. Computer banking, training. All sorts. Why are you so interested? Are you a bank robber?' she asks before closing her lips around a piece of salmon caught on the end of her fork.

'No, more of a grave robber. You know, like Howard Carter.'

'Howard who?'

'Never mind. The Pyramid offers the promise of eternal life. I'm interested in that.'

'Who isn't?' she says, tipping wine into her mouth.

'I have a particular interest in it,' I say.

There's a pause before she apologises again and then there's a further pause while we both eat.

I see that she has finished.

'Shall we get out of here?' I say.

'I thought you had to write a review.'

'I've seen enough.'

We cause a bit of a stir by paying on the way out. The staff handle our sudden desire to leave with tact and aplomb; it's among the remaining diners that we detect the lightest of tuts and softest of glares.

'A short walk?' I suggest, heading away from the car park down Ringway Road. I watch the little houses on our right. The waitress with the ponytail will return to one of them later. She will down a glass of vodka, neat, then strip to her underwear and crash out.

On the left is a small layby where before 9/11 you could park to watch and listen to the planes thundering overhead. The landing lights loom over the fence on our left, burning in the darkness, casting a gauze of yellowish sparkles into the night sky above the road. I take hold of Erica's arms and pull her towards me. I place my lips on hers. At first she neither yields nor resists, then she softens, but I feel nothing. I move my head to one side, while still holding her close to me. In the sky above the Moss Nook Industrial Area on the north side of the road, twin white lights can be seen growing steadily larger and brighter. At that distance they will have passed over the Pyramid and be approaching Cheadle Royal. Erica tries to say something, but her mouth is pressed against my shoulder, her voice muffled. I can hear the plane now. It's a medium-sized passenger aircraft, a 737 or an Airbus 320. I can feel Erica squirming beneath me, trying to get free. The plane flies overhead, its deafening roar filling my ears. I turn my head to watch it overfly the landing lights and I release my hold on Erica.

From the layby you can't quite see touchdown, but you can hear it. The sudden exhilarating explosion of reverse thrust. The application of speedbrakes. The squeal of rubber on tarmac.

I look down. Erica is straightening her clothes. She seems upset.

'I'll take you home,' I say and turn and lead the way back towards the restaurant.

Several cars remain in the car park as we leave it, turning left to go back the way we came. The streets are quiet, splashed with pools of orange light. In the car neither of us speaks. When I look to the left to check for traffic, I see her face reflecting the glow of the city in the night.

As we approach Northenden I think about taking a short detour to Marie Louise Gardens and driving from Dene Road West into Mersey Road by going straight across Palatine Road without stopping. At this time of night there would be very few cars on Palatine Road. We would be unlucky to be hit. I stop at the lights at the end of Church Road. Right for Deane Road West, straight on for Kenworthy Lane. Either or.

The light changes to green. I sit there undecided. Erica's eyes are on me; she's wondering why I don't move forward. Eventually, as the lights are changing back, I do.

On Kenworthy Lane I stop outside the little house where I had picked her up at the start of the evening. She gets out without a word, then bends down to look back in before closing the door. I turn towards her, but her eyes are hard to make out, the wrap top and its contents lost in shadow.

'Goodnight,' I offer, my eye drawn by the amber pendant, which swings clear.

84

'Goodnight,' she says non-committally and then she is gone.

I drive on to the end of the road, which runs straight for a couple of hundred yards before meeting a confluence of cycle paths and pedestrian routes that extend under the interchange of the M60 and Princess Parkway. After a bend to the right, the road continues in a straight line beyond a row of four concrete bollards. I think about the electronically controlled bollards in town that rise and fall allowing buses to pass over them. At least once a week a car is written off in a collision with one of these. It seems there is an unending supply of motorists who think that if they follow the bus and put their foot down, they will get through in time, and on every occasion they are disabused of this notion by the swift and inexorable rise of the bollards, which strike the bumper or enter the engine compartment and jack the car up off the ground.

With my engine still running, I consider flooring the accelerator and driving at the concrete bollards in the hope that they might sink into the earth.

I remember Moss Nook and the sparkly glimmer of the landing lights. I think that if I return there now and drive slowly along Ringway Road I will see a tall, ponytailed figure walking slowly, tiredly, along the pavement between the restaurant and the runway.

I look again at the line of bollards.

Either I go for it or I don't.

I depress the clutch and select first gear.

I have tried to get an office of my own, since one was as good as promised to me when I joined, but other promises that were made at that time have not been kept and I don't suppose this one will be either. Actually, that is not true. What is true is that I was not discouraged from thinking that I might one day get an office to myself. As the months passed, it became clear that there was less and less chance of this happening until I finally accepted, within myself if not outwardly, that it would never happen. When I think about it, there were no promises made at all, but there were certain things that were not said.

I was told I would have contact with undergraduates as well as MA students, but it was not explained that this contact would take the form of teaching on a unit devised and run by another lecturer whose vision of creative-writing teaching was somewhat at odds with my own.

Nor was I told that there would be endless meetings about administrative matters that I would be expected to attend, in spite of my having nothing useful to contribute.

Nor that some of the students would barely be able to construct a sentence using correct grammar and punctuation. Fortunately they are outnumbered by the good ones.

As I walk towards the end of the corridor I note that no light is visible from within the office. This means that none of my colleagues is in. In truth it's rare that we are in at the same time. My own advertised 'office hours' are on a Tuesday morning. I unlock the door and walk past Will's desk. Will is a big man with big hair that he greases and combs back from his forehead. He wears bootlace ties and a leather belt with a big silver buckle in the shape of a steer's horns. When he is in, he listens to a wide variety of music on his computer, using headphones, from knockabout rockabilly to the most avant garde industrial noise, which he buys second-hand from Vinyl Exchange on Oldham Street. He also insists on having the window open, even in the middle of winter.

Frances is not in either. Tall, stick-thin Frances with the permanent dark shadows under her eyes, who talks incessantly about anything at all the moment anyone enters the room. I have long suspected that when no one is in she talks to the empty office. With Frances, every action demands a reaction. She is one of those people around whom it is impossible to relax.

I also pass Patience's desk, Sellotaped to which there is a single piece of paper with 'Patience's desk' written on it. There is nothing else either on, inside or near her desk. Patience is on long-term sick leave. I have seen her only once.

I sit down at my own desk, which I have attempted to screen off with large blue room-dividers. If anything, this has the effect of emphasising the presence of other people in the room rather than providing me with privacy. But now that I have got the screens, I can't bring myself to get rid of them. To make my corner of the room seem a little less like the set of Jacques Tati's *Playtime*, I have pinned up a few posters advertising academic conferences and readings in which I have taken part. Similarly, Will has stuck up a selection of covers of the how-to books he has written that have been translated into dozens of languages. Frances has just one poster, for the one-off read-through at the Bolton Octagon of a play she wrote fifteen years ago.

There is a knock at the door. I look at my watch. I turn sideways on to pass between two of my screens and navigate my way around the uncomfortable armchairs positioned around a coffee table in the middle of the room. I open the door.

'Hiya,' says Helen, an MA student I am supervising during her writing-up year.

'Hello,' I say as I hold the door open to allow her to enter the room.

I show her the way to my desk, as if she might have forgotten it, which is unlikely as she is one of the few students who make full use of their allocated number of one-to-one tutorials. Normally these students are the same as those who have trouble using correct punctuation around direct speech. Not so Helen, whose writing I regard as being close to publishable. In fact, given that it is more interesting than a great deal of the fiction that is piled high on 3-for-2 tables in Waterstone's, it is definitely publishable, but in my opinion she still makes the wrong word choice from time to time. I regard it as my job to help her see where she has made the wrong choice and to help her make the right choice instead.

Helen is a little shorter than me. She is about twenty-seven or twenty-eight with long dark-brown hair that she usually wears gathered in a ponytail. While talking about her work, she will pull the ponytail over her right shoulder and comb her fingers through it and not toss it back over her shoulder until I say something with which she disagrees. She will not say that she disagrees with me, but the tossing of the ponytail is a clear sign. She has chestnut-coloured eyes that somehow manage to seem both sad and happy at the same time, a small, delicate nose and lips that I have never seen without vivid red lipstick.

She is also direct. Most of the students are, whatever the standard of their work. They are paying for the privilege of being taught by myself and my colleagues and some of them like to remind us of that whenever they perceive that they are not getting value for money. Helen is not like that, but she can be very direct.

'What did you think of my short story?' she asks. 'Is it any good?'

'I think it's pretty good,' I say, pulling a typescript from out of a pile of papers and newspaper cuttings to the left of the PC that I never turn on because I would rather bring in my

Mac and connect to the university email system that way, wirelessly, and without having to choose between right-click and left-click. I find it hard to distinguish between right and left, east and west, on and off. When I lived in London I often had to use the Central Line. I would walk down the steps towards the platforms and I would stand for a moment in front of the maps that showed the two entirely different routes, one going east and one going west, and I would still sometimes choose the wrong one, ending up on a train bound for Hainault when I should have been going to Holland Park, or en route for West Ruislip when my destination was Mile End. It would take me two or three stops to realise my mistake.

'Cool,' says Helen, her eyes definitely looking happy rather than sad.

'Yes. It's very bold.'

'But?'

I take a moment. 'It's bold in context. Would it seem bold taken out of context? If you weren't you and I wasn't me? If you weren't studying for an MA in creative writing here and I wasn't your supervisor. Would it seem bold then?'

'I don't know. You tell me.' She levels her gaze at me like a challenge.

'It's interestingly metafictional—' I begin.

'But only in the context of this situation,' she interrupts. 'But then doesn't that make it even more metafictional?'

I think about how to answer. 'Metafiction isn't one of my specialist areas,' I say. 'But we do have a PhD student doing research on it. I'm just wondering if it gets a bit Grand Guignol?'

'But nothing happens,' she says, taking hold of her ponytail, drawing it over her shoulder. 'It's all implied. Nothing happens on stage, as it were.'

'But if it were to happen, as implied, wouldn't it be a bit Grand Guignol?'

She looks at my bookcase. If she looks hard enough she will see my small collection devoted to Antonin Artaud and the Theatre of Cruelty. She might even spot my copy of Richard J. Hand's *Grand-Guignol: The French Theatre of Horror*. She might wonder why I've implied that Grand Guignol is a bad thing.

'Are you a bit creeped out by the thought of me walking down your street and checking out your place?' she asks.

'That would be a very predictable response.'

'You wouldn't want to be thought of as predictable.'

'Of course not.'

'Did I at least get the commas in the right place?' she asks with her head on one side.

I smile. 'It's a good story,' I say. 'It's publishable.'

'Where could I send it?'

'I keep a list of magazines up to date on my machine. An increasingly short list. I'll email that to you with one or two suggestions.'

'Thanks. Maybe there's one that specialises in Grand Guignol?'

I don't take my eyes from her.

'What about you?' she asks. 'What are you working on?' Once again, she has been very direct.

'Bits and pieces.'

'A novel?'

'Maybe. Bits of journalism. Restaurant reviews.'

'Cool.'

She looks away again. I am not sure whether I should say what is in my mind. Either I say it or I don't. Either it turns out to be the wrong thing to say, or it leads to something. I wonder if she really has read my novel, as suggested by her story.

'I'm writing about south Manchester, too,' I say. 'Using real places, actual locations.'

'Really?' That she doesn't look back at me immediately as she says this tells me she is more interested than she appears.

'Well, it's very early stages. I'm not really writing, just researching.'

'How do you research?' she asks, finally turning back towards me.

'I hang around the airport, watch the planes, talk to pilots. Drive around Cheadle and Heald Green at night. I find it very fertile ground. Stories grow there. Industrial areas that change character after dark. Business parks with one or two poorly paid security guards nodding off over their screens and car parks full of Mercedes and Audis.'

'Sounds fascinating,' she says, deadpan.

I try out a little laugh and she smiles.

'I'd best be off,' she says.

At the door, she turns and says, 'Maybe I should check out Cheadle? Get more of a sense of place.'

I wait. We both know I can't be the one to suggest it.

'I could go with you,' she says at last.

'Good idea,' I say. 'I'll email you.'

After she has gone I return to my desk and pick up Helen's typescript. I put it back on the pile of papers next to the PC and leaf through what's there. There are several cuttings from the *Guardian*. More writers' rooms. Here's Michael Frayn's. Some reference books on the desk, a German dictionary. The same one I have at home, I see. The same typeface on the thick spine. I wonder what he uses his for. I remember buying Michael Frayn novels for Veronica after she had read and enjoyed *Headlong*. I had thought of him as a playwright, primarily, before *Headlong* came out and was shortlisted for a prize or won a prize, but then I would come across his earlier novels in second-hand bookshops while browsing to add to my Penguin shelves. I remember buying one novel in particular and giving it to Veronica and her saying, 'I've read this one. You bought me this one in hardback,' and I remembered I had picked up an ex-library edition, very cheap, somewhere. Perhaps in a library.

I carry on through the pile of cuttings. Sarah Waters. Not a book in sight. Instead she has a map of the world and a poster on the wall with a wartime motto: 'KEEP CALM AND CARRY ON'. Hilary Mantel's room is also book-free. She writes in the main room of her flat in a converted Victorian asylum in Surrey. There's no stuff or clutter. She has the same desk as Andrew O'Hagan and Antonia Fraser. A. S. Byatt's room looks more like my own with its 'purposeful disorder', a glass case of large insects and another German dictionary. There's a row of books on the window ledge, where they will spoil in the sun, their titles only half visible.

I sit at my desk in my study at the top of the house. The laptop is open but I am not writing. I had been looking at websites of office furniture suppliers, but the screen has gone dark through lack of use. I am actually looking at the seven pieces of red moulded plastic lined up on the desk next to it. These came out of the mound of rubble and crap in the back garden. They are all obviously from the same source, originally part of some coherent object that has been broken apart. The temptation is to try to fit them together, as if they were part of a jigsaw puzzle, but I have tried and it is clear that many pieces are missing. Three of the seven fragments I have are flat, four are curved. There are no markings or patterns, no scraps of any other material present. I have washed them in warm soapy water to remove any trace of the various other substances found in the landfill.

'What do you think, Cleo?' I ask the cat curled up in the armchair behind me. 'What do these come from? What are they? Eh?'

I pick up the biggest piece and slot my thumb into its curved hollow. I get up and move away from the desk. Cleo stirs, but remains where she is.

'What about you, Mr Fox?' I look at the stuffed fox's head as I stroke the red plastic with the pads of my fingers. 'What do you think? What do you have to say?'

I remember being in the back of a car, my parents' car. It was late, dark outside. My father was driving slowly, then speeding up, then slowing down again. He was leaning across my mother to see out of her window. They were trying to read house numbers in the darkness, looking for a particular address. He would slow down, they would both rake their eyes over the porches and doorsteps and brick walls and pebbledash and either see a number or not see one, and the car would roll slowly forwards, then my father would step on the accelerator once more, always a second or two before returning his gaze to the road ahead.

I saw it first. The golden flank, white underparts, face turned towards the oncoming car. Imprinted on the Kodak paper of the suburban night by flashgun headlamps. And then my father put his foot down again. I cried out, too late. The impact rocked the car, my father standing on the brake pedal. He got out and picked the animal up and laid it across my mother's lap. Her face was white. I watched in rapt silence as a trickle of dark blood escaped from the corner of the fox's mouth.

I knew the animal was dead, but the gentle motion of the car gave it the illusion of life.

And then, every time my father turned a corner, the fox's head lolled and swung on its broken neck.

A week later, my father presented me with the fox's head on a mahogany mount. I called him Mr Fox.

That evening, I am returning from Tesco with a loaf of bread and a bottle of milk, thinking about the student who came to see me after Helen. His name is either Lawrence Duncan or Duncan Lawrence. Either or. I can never remember which. There will be a list somewhere with his name on it, but probably accessible only from the PC at work and not from my Mac. His email address doesn't help, since it includes neither of his names. I have asked him once or twice to remind me, pleading forgetfulness, but it is not forgetfulness that is to blame. It is rather that I know that both variations are possible and so I find it impossible to distinguish between them. Like hot and cold. Sometimes I will look at the taps on a washbasin, even ones affixed with a blue or red spot, and I don't know which one to turn.

Like on and off. Televisions have become so complicated, having so many external devices. Standby, remote on/off, hard switch-off. Sometimes I don't know whether it's on or off.

Life and death is another. There are numerous well-known public figures who could be alive or may be dead. Members of the royal family. Is the Queen Mother alive or dead? Sometimes I know she is dead, at other times I think she may still be alive. Film actors. Directors. Sam Peckinpah. Is he alive or dead? Joseph Losey? Jazz musicians. Gerry Mulligan? Is he dead? I think so, but I'm not sure. Herbie Hancock? I might have said dead, but I saw he made a new record and was touring recently, so presumably still alive. Even members of my own family. Cousins. Aunts, uncles. My wife.

It's not that I think there is little difference between being alive and being dead. It is that I cannot distinguish between the two. Almost as if I cannot choose.

Lawrence Duncan – or Duncan Lawrence – is in his first year on the MA. He is a promising student. He and Helen and others like them are easy to teach. Mostly what you do is encourage them, give them the confidence they need. Every time I see Lawrence Duncan – or Duncan Lawrence – I remember what he was like in his interview. He was so nervous he was shaking and stammering. Every time he opened his mouth to speak, he blushed to the roots of his hair. He was about twenty-three and had spent two or three years since graduating, in English, doing various jobs and reading a lot, he said. The portfolio he had submitted with his application, however, had been outstandingly good and when he started work on his novel and submitted chapters to be workshopped, the reaction from his fellow students and from myself had given him that confidence. He was writing about a group of young people in a very contemporary idiom and was doing so with a certain flair.

He'd been due to come to see me earlier today, however, about the First Novels unit that I run alongside the workshop for the MA as well as the BA. While waiting for him, I had moved my chair away from the desk until it was facing one of the room-dividers. I was sitting forward in the chair, having lowered it slightly, until my spine was curved over and my elbows were resting on my knees. I pictured myself as a graphic on a piece of laminated card stored in a seat pocket. I placed my hands over my head, one on top of the other, unclasped. I felt the rough fabric of the room-divider where it grazed the front of my head. On a plane, that would be the back of the seat in front.

It was at this point that there was a knock on the door. I waited for a moment or two then pushed back the chair and crossed the room. I opened the door to allow Lawrence Duncan – or Duncan Lawrence – to enter.

'Hey,' he said.

'Hi,' I said, as I led him across the room to my corner.

'Why,' he asked, after a minute or two of small talk, 'has Philip Pullman's first novel never been reissued? I mean, he's mega. A reprint of *The Haunted Storm* would clean up, wouldn't it?'

'Of course it would. That's one of the things we'll discuss in the group,' I said, fiddling with the lever on my chair to raise it to the correct height. 'Why do some writers go to such lengths to keep their first novels out of the hands of readers? In Pullman's case, he refuses even to talk about it. If you manage to get hold of a copy and you ask him to sign it at a reading, he refuses. So I'm told. I haven't tried. But copies of the first edition go for a grand. With his signature even more.'

'Cool. That explains why I've not been able to get hold of a copy.'

'The paperback is a little easier to find, but only a little. You can pay a hundred quid for a copy on eBay.'

'Dude, *you* can, perhaps. I can't,' he said with a laugh.

The nerves Lawrence Duncan – or Duncan Lawrence – had shown in my first encounter with him had not reappeared since then. They had been interview nerves. Nothing more. Once on the course, he was as relaxed and informal as students tend to be these days.

'I have an idea to get around this problem,' I said.

'What? The photocopier?'

'That would be against copyright law.'

He shrugged and raised his hands palms upward as if to say, 'What copyright law?'

'I have two copies,' I said. 'It's a small group.'

'You loan it out.'

'Exactly.'

'And we take great care of it.'

'Precisely.'

'Coolio,' he said, then: 'Dude, I'd like to read *your* novel but I can't find a copy anywhere. How about you do the library thing with that?'

My thoughts about the tutorial with Lawrence Duncan – or Duncan Lawrence – are interrupted by the sound of someone calling from out of the darkness on the other side of the street.

'Paul,' the voice says again as its owner crosses the road. 'I thought it was you. *Ksssh-huh-huh.*'

He stands in front of me, as if barring the way, smiling.

'Yes,' I say.

'Come and have a drink.' He indicates the pub on the corner.

I glance at a figure who walks past us. Untidy shock of white hair, green anorak unzipped, suit trousers at half mast – Polling Station Man. On polling days he sits behind a desk in the local primary school and crosses voters' names off his list. At other times he is seen walking with long strides and carrying a single white plastic carrier bag. I remember standing in the polling booth not knowing where to place my cross, unable to choose. Either this one or that one.

'I've got to get back,' I say to Lewis, showing him the milk I've bought.

'Come on. All the lads are there. AJ's not there, but Jon and Chris and Gary. Kelvin—'

'Kelvin?'

'Yeah, you know, the pilot. Wasn't my idea, but still. *Ksssh-huh-huh.*'

I look at the shopping bag in my hand.

'I don't know,' I say. 'Maybe a quick one.'

'*Ksssh-huh-huh.*'

The pub is noisy and smells of damp bar towels. I accept a drink from Lewis and sit down in the only free seat next to a man I don't know who is telling a story about a football match.

'. . . and this guy's constantly shouting out that he's a cunt.'

'The linesman?' says Gary, whom I have met before, somewhere.

'Yeah, this guy behind me is shouting out in a really miserable voice that the linesman's a cunt, like, every time he misses an offside. "You're a cunt, liner. You're a cunt, liner." On and on and on. And then the linesman does raise his flag. He does give an offside, and an ironic cheer goes up from the crowd and a round of applause. And this guy, he times it perfectly. He waits a moment, until the noise has died down, and then in this, like, moment of quiet you hear his voice, really kind of morose but still timed to perfection, aware of the effect he was about to create: "You're still a cunt, liner."'

The story prompts laughter in the group. I raise my glass to my lips. The lads say hello to me and we exchange small talk. As soon as there is an opportunity I move around and take a seat next to Kelvin. I remind him where we've met and he says he remembers.

'You're obviously not flying tomorrow,' I say to him, looking at his pint.

'They're very careful,' he says. 'Random testing. It's not worth it.'

We sip our drinks as another story is begun in which I have no interest.

I turn to Kelvin.

'Is it true,' I ask him, 'what they say about brace? About the brace position?'

'What?'

'I heard that the brace position doesn't save lives. Isn't intended to save lives. It's designed to ensure that you die instantly by snapping your neck. Because it's cheaper for the airlines to pay out for wrongful death than lifelong disablement. So if the plane's going down, they'd rather you die than survive with terrible injuries. Also, it handily keeps all the body parts together in one place.'

'Where did you hear that?' he asks.

'Two guys on a train,' I say. 'So, it's true, then? I mean, I can see it would make the job of cleaning up considerably easier. From the point of view of identification and so on.'

Kelvin looks up from his pint. 'Conspiracy theory,' he says. 'The brace position does save lives in the event of a crash. Kegworth proved that. Remember Kegworth?'

I remember Kegworth.

'All right,' I say. 'Last question. Is it true that the engines on an airliner are designed to fall off if something goes badly wrong?'

Kelvin places his pint on the table. 'The engines on a Boeing 747 were designed to break away in the event of catastrophic failure, but it didn't work out the way they planned. In one or two cases, the engine that broke free, instead of dropping safely to the ground, smashed into the other engine on the same wing. You can imagine the consequences. Amsterdam, for example. You remember Amsterdam?'

I remember Amsterdam.

I go to the bar to buy a round and when I rejoin the group, I find myself sitting next to Lewis. He looks at me and grins as I pass him a pint of bitter.

'All right?' he asks.

I nod.

'*Kssh-huh-huh.*'

I look away. We sit in silence for a few moments. I put my hand in my pocket and take it out again.

'What's that?' he asks, looking at my hand.

I see that I'm holding one of the pieces of red plastic, the one into which my thumb slots neatly, and I'm caressing it with my fingers.

'It's from my back garden. I've dug a whole load of it up. I don't know what it is or where it's come from.'

He holds his hand out.

I hesitate momentarily, but then drop it into his palm.

He holds it up close and studies it. He pulls a face that says he doesn't know either.

'Some years ago,' he says, 'there was a plane crash in South America.'

'In the Andes?' I ask. 'The Uruguayan rugby team? The *Alive* story.'

'No. Much later.'

'That story had a profound effect on me as a child,' I say.

'On a lot of people, I'm sure, but this was twenty years later, maybe more. A passenger aircraft was flying over a mountain range – maybe it was the Andes, maybe not – and it went off radar. Just disappeared. They sent out military jets to search for it and everything. Nothing. Nada. *Kssh-huh-huh.*' He sips at his pint before continuing. 'Then they discovered the wreckage, I don't know, a year later or summat.' He looks at me. 'On the wrong side of the mountain.'

'What do you mean?'

'Exactly what I said. They knew where the plane was when it left the radar. They knew what direction it was flying in. They knew where it must have experienced what they call an "uncontrolled collision with terrain". But when they performed a fly-past, there was nothing to see. And then, a year later, they discovered some wreckage, on the wrong side of the mountain.'

'The plane must have travelled some distance after leaving the radar,' I say. 'Gone around the mountain, changed direction.'

'Then why, shortly afterwards, did they finally find some wreckage on the right side of the mountain as well?'

'What are you saying?'

'I'm not saying owt. All I'm saying is what I read in the paper. After they spotted the wreckage on the wrong side of the mountain they sent out search teams, which found debris from the plane on both sides of the mountain.'

'Near the summit, perhaps?' I try. 'It hit the mountain near the summit and part of the plane flipped over the top.'

'Nice idea, but no. Five hundred feet from the top and no easy way round either.'

He lifts his pint. A trickle of bitter overflows at the corner of his mouth and drips on to his patterned shirt. I am reminded of Mr Fox on my mother's lap.

'Seen Carol lately?' he asks.

'No, I haven't seen Carol. Or AJ.'

'You know what they say about Carol?'

'What? What did you say?' I look at the grin that cuts open the lower half of his face like a wound.

'You know what they say?'

'No.' Not 'No?', but 'No.' I didn't want to know.

'Cars,' he says, regardless.

'What do you mean?'

No one appears to be listening in. Group conversations underway. Pub hubbub.

'Apparently, Carol likes to have sex in cars.' Lewis looks at me intently, as if it is an important piece of information, something I have been waiting for.

'With AJ?' I ask in spite of myself.

Lewis shrugs. 'With or without AJ, is what I hear.'

'Really?' I mean it to sound as if I am indifferent, but the way it comes out, it's more like I don't believe him.

'See for yourself.'

I frown at him.

He taps the side of his nose like a cartoon lech.

'Video,' he stage-whispers. 'DVD. Apparently.'

I curl my lip.

'I mean, there's definitely some footage. It's just hard to say who it is.'

He raises his half-empty pint glass and seems to want me to do the same.

'Here's to Carol,' he says, 'whoever it is on the DVD.'

I drain my glass, then ask him, 'When was that plane crash? When did you read about it in the paper?'

'I can't remember,' he says. 'I've tried going online and can't find owt about it. I mean, it's not a lot to go on. Plane – crash – mountain. You get a gazillion hits.'

'They're not called hits.'

'Whatever.'

'What about adding "wrong side"?'

'Nothing.'

Lewis gets to his feet and points across the bar.

'Piss,' he says. 'And when I get back I want to ask you about how you write. Your routine, discipline, all that.'

As Lewis makes his way to the Gents, I sense Kelvin's eyes on me. I turn to look at him. His expression is unreadable.

'I need to get this home,' I say to Kelvin, showing him my bottle of milk, and while an argument about different interpretations of the offside rule is occupying the other members of the group, I quietly leave the pub.

The Writers' Rooms series kicks off with Beryl Bainbridge. What makes them pick her rather than Michael Frayn, I wonder, who appears in week two? Strangely, on the *Guardian* website, the order is reversed. Beryl Bainbridge has books on her shelves, but they are some distance away from the lens, and the glare of sunlight makes it difficult to read any titles or authors' names. Of more interest to the photographer, Eamonn McCabe, are the pistol and old typewriter on the table in the foreground.

Michael Frayn has a high-backed chair with a neck support of the kind that is good for bad backs. There are a number of similar chairs. Sarah Waters, David Lodge, Esther Freud, Simon Gray and Al Alvarez all have similar chairs. Geoff Dyer, Alain de Botton, Siri Hustvedt and Francesca Simon all have exactly the same chair as each other: it has a wide curved back and sturdy arm rests and several controlling levers. A surprising number of writers – David Hare, J. G. Ballard, Margaret Drabble, Colm Tóibín, Louis de Bernières, Martin Amis and many more – get by without castors. I imagine their chair legs scraping and dragging awkwardly on rugs, carpet, sisal matting and varnished floorboards as they sit down at their desks. William Boyd accessorises a rattan chair with some cushions, but it can't be good for his back. Most of his books are at too tight an angle to the camera for the spines to be easily read. Those that aren't are piled with the spines facing away. Any one of those could be of interest, but how would you know?

The only books visible in Ronan Bennett's room are behind glass, obscured by reflection, but pride of place is given to a vast collection of chess pieces also in a glass case. Penelope Lively's books are too far away in an alcove and all the stacks in the foreground reveal is a taste for Seamus Heaney. In the attic room of his house in Dublin, Seamus Heaney writes under the glass-eyed gaze of a stuffed yellow bittern in a bell jar. A short-haired cat tiptoes across Joshua Ferris' desk, a tabby occupies the corner of Julie Myerson's and a dog called Watson squats on Nicola Barker's chair. Barker has some orange-spined books, but they're easily identifiable as A-format Penguins.

Eric Hobsbawm, Elizabeth Jane Howard and Al Alvarez all have some larger-format orange spines with black writing, but they're too far away to make out. The photographer's job is to get as wide a view of the room as possible, not to allow you to read the spines of the books on view, which is what I am trying to do. Anyway, what could ever have motivated Eric Hobsbawm, Elizabeth Jane Howard or Al Alvarez to pick up a copy of a novel published in a limited edition by a tiny independent imprint in the early 90s?

A wooden artist's figure with articulated joints strikes a ballet pose on John Banville's desk, close to a neat pile of three Moleskine notebooks. His bookshelves are full of reference volumes and books on Bill Brandt and Koudelka. Siri Hustvedt keeps *Gray's Anatomy*, *Principles of Neural Science* and *The Norton Anthology of Poetry* to the left of her desk. Most of her other books are just slightly too far away to read the titles or authors' names. There is one orange and black spine that looks promising, but it's impossible to say. Though why would a copy have crossed the Atlantic? It was barely distributed in the UK, never mind the US.

In Martin Amis' room, in a separate building at the end of his garden, light pours in through a glass ceiling and there are numerous books scattered in an apparently random pattern on the floor: a huge book on Vladimir Nabokov and two or three spiral-bound manuscripts. On a table in the foreground, a paperback edition of J. G. Ballard's *Cocaine Nights* with a yellow Waterstone's 3-for-2 sticker showing that he didn't blag a copy, he bought it. The shelves seem to house mainly non-fiction: books on Hitler, Islam, cultural amnesia. Amis' own books are lined up on Catherine O'Flynn's shelves in a large photograph appearing in another newspaper, the *Independent*: *London Fields*, *Other People*, *Night Train*. Hilary Mantel is there too with *Beyond Black*. James Ellroy, Kurt Vonnegut, David Foster Wallace, Camus, Kafka. But there appears no order, alphabetical or otherwise. Still, I can see that the book I'm looking for is not there. Or not in shot, at least.

Julie Myerson is photographed, also in the *Independent*, in front of, or rather sitting below, a shelf of first editions protected by plastic covers. You can see the light glinting off them. Murdoch, Updike. When it's her turn in the *Guardian*, it's strikingly domestic: cat basket, baby photo, a tiny pile of books to the right of the desk. Joanne Harris, in the *Observer Magazine*, reveals that she collects French books, the Livre de Poche colophon and distinctive spine recognisable even across the room. Also in two separate *Observer* supplements, plastic covers are in evidence in different shots of, again, Siri Hustvedt, photographs clearly taken on the same day, unless she wears that black and white striped cardigan and dangly earrings for every photographer that comes to the house. In the background a wall-mounted bookcase, lines of serious-looking volumes in plastic sleeves. An olive-green leather sofa. In one shot, Hustvedt stretches out her long legs across the wide cushions; in the other she is sitting on the floor in front of the sofa leaning on the coffee table in the foreground on which are stacked various large-format books: *Conjunctions 49: A Writers' Aviary*, a monograph of René Char, *L'Oeil de Simenon*, a visitors' guide to New York City and *The Nancy Book* by Joe Brainard. To the right of the sofa is another bookcase on the adjoining wall. It contains a number of orange-spined books that could be Penguins but equally might not be.

Both Marina Warner and Simon Armitage have music stands.

Sarah Waters, Charlotte Mendelson and Sebastian Faulks all have the same poster on the wall, the wartime slogan 'KEEP CALM AND CARRY ON', in white on a red background.

Will Self and Sarah Waters have maps of London hanging on the wall. Robert Irwin has a map of the Middle East and North Africa. Esther Freud has an etching by her father Lucian, J. G. Ballard a copy of a painting by Paul Delvaux. Hanif Kureishi has a picture of Kate Moss above his desk. Kate Mosse has a photograph of sunrise in the Pyrenees.

William Boyd, Jacqueline Wilson, Adam Thirlwell, Anne Enright, Blake Morrison, Jonathan Bate, Sebastian Faulks and Deborah Moggach are all Mac users.

Simon Gray, John Mortimer and J. G. Ballard have all died since appearing.

Michael Holroyd and Margaret Drabble, husband and wife, have both been featured, separately, in the *Guardian* series. His room is much untidier than hers. Claire Tomalin's room is caught in the photographer's lens three months after that of her husband, Michael Frayn. Hunter Davies, still using an Amstrad PCW9512, is scarcely more technologically evolved than his wife, Margaret Forster, with her fountain pen and A4 paper. Joanna Briscoe and Charlotte Mendelson live together in north London; their respective rooms appear almost a year apart. Mendelson's temporary lodging in the downstairs front room is dominated by children's toys, kitchenware and an improvised barrier against the life of the street – a huge mountain of boxes blocking out the view of Dartmouth Park – while Briscoe's beloved top-floor book-lined 'tree house' study is destined to become a bedroom.

Among the reference volumes on Briscoe's bookshelves is an edition of the *Time Out Film Guide*, not recent enough to include Andrew Davies' adaptation of her novel, *Sleep With Me*. *Halliwell's Film Guide* sits on Marina Warner's shelf; had he still been alive on its release, it's doubtful Leslie Halliwell would have liked – or even included – Iain Sinclair and Chris Petit's film *Asylum*, in which Warner appears as herself. Martin Amis and Siri Hustvedt each have a different edition of Ephraim Katz's *Film Encyclopedia*.

Siri Hustvedt's husband, Paul Auster, has not been included in the Writers' Rooms series, but I doubt very much that it's because he hasn't been asked.

I have another look at Siri Hustvedt's half-page in the *Guardian*. Top shelf, slightly to the left of centre. Orange spine, black text. With her long legs she'd be able to reach it without needing to stand on that chair – the same chair as Geoff Dyer, Alain de Botton and Francesca Simon. I imagine her lifting her left foot off the ground and standing on the toes of her right, extending her right arm and stretching her calf and trapezoid muscles, questing fingers latching on and extracting the book, taking it down, opening it, sniffing the pages.

Has she read it? Is she intending to read it? I don't know, but I'd like to find out.

I have never read Siri Hustvedt. I think maybe I should. I will start with her first novel, *The Blindfold*.

I am invited to read at a new monthly live literature event in town. This is an event that in a few months has become unexpectedly popular. The first night was in the basement of a bar in the university district. The venue was tiny and it was packed. If you weren't standing by the bar there was no way you could get a drink. The organiser was a young writer who had just won a two-book deal with a fashionable publisher, but he was so modest and self-effacing in his skinny jeans and crumpled shirt, no one was anything but pleased for him. Plus, he could write, which helped.

They held the second evening in the upstairs room at the same venue, which was much bigger with a proper stage, decent seating and a disco ball hanging from the high ceiling. Still, the crowds kept coming, creative-writing students mainly, but also each successive month seemed to draw in more and more characters from the north-west writing 'scene'. Bloggers, debut novelists, literature professionals. Lecturers in creative writing. Across town, science-fiction writers and crime novelists soldiered on in readings at local libraries where they and the sad-eyed staff easily outnumbered the few people who had dragged themselves in off the streets to ask where the writers got their ideas from and how they had found their agents.

As I sit waiting to go on, I listen to the other readers. Girls with dyed hair and low-slung jeans read rough poems about sex and alcohol. Boys with pipe-cleaner legs and Converse trainers, and bookshelves back home full of Richard Brautigan and Charles Bukowski, tell stories about pool tables and girls and lonely men and failed sexual encounters and alcohol.

I go on and look out at the sea of faces twenty years younger than mine, their owners lifting expensive bottles of beer to their lips or rolling spliffs to stick behind their ears for later on, and I wonder for the first time if these reading nights have encouraged the formation of a particular school of writing marked by whimsy and flippant jokes and throwaway lines about sexual inadequacy. I wonder, if that's the case, how my own stuff will play. But as I stand thinking, the murmuring falls away and the room is filled with a tense, electric silence, in case I have dried.

But I begin. I read an extract from my novel-in-progress. It's a scene set in a pub. Dialogue between the narrator and two other characters, one more important than the other. While I read, I am aware of my attention wandering. When this happens, I am always surprised by my ability to stick to the script. Like flying by wire. Some back-brain function keeps the reading going while my mind fills up with unrelated thoughts. I look up frequently and at a table near the front I see Elizabeth Baines, her silver-blonde hair cut in a flattering new style, the lights reflected from the disco ball flashing in her spectacle lenses. I think of the barbecue at AJ's. I briefly picture Lewis. Even that doesn't put me off my stride.

When I have finished I leave the stage and the organisers call a break. Before I have a chance to sit down, I notice someone walking towards me. A woman, tall and angular, with heavy eye make-up and dark bobbed hair beginning to go grey. She's familiar, yet I cannot place her. She offers her hand and I take it hesitantly. Her handshake is firm but brief. When she introduces herself I realise I've seen her photo on a book jacket. She lectures in creative writing at one of the other universities.

'Nice reading,' she says as she touches my arm and smiles from under her hair. 'I just wanted to give you a heads-up.'

I realise that she is quite drunk. She goes on to say that the scene in the extract I just read – about the brace position and whether it's intended to save lives or curtail them – had sounded very familiar to her and her friends.

'Around our table,' she adds, gesturing vaguely towards the back of the room. 'We looked at each other and we said, "That's familiar. That's *Fight Club*."'

I raise my eyebrows. At the same time I become aware of someone, another woman, standing close by, as if she wants to speak to one of us and is waiting for an opportunity.

'I'm not saying you lifted it, of course. We're not saying that. But it's similar. I just, I suppose, I just wanted to let you know, in case, you know . . .'

'That's very thoughtful of you,' I say.

'In case, you know, anyone says, anyone else. You'll know, you know.'

'Yeah.'

She touches my arm again.

The other woman, whoever she is, will have seen that. I glance towards her, but that hand is still on my arm and I look back at its owner.

'The book, I mean,' she continues, 'not the film. Definitely the book.'

'Well, that's good. I haven't even read the book. I've seen the film. Everybody's seen the film, haven't they? But I haven't read the book.'

'It's in the book, I'm sure it is. I just thought. We just thought. You should be aware of it. In case.'

'Thank you,' I say and I can see that she is finally backing off and as she does so I realise how close to me she had been standing. She smiles as she turns away to face the direction in which she is walking, with exaggerated care.

I look at the other woman properly for the first time. I recognise her, but I don't know from where. I smile at her. Too late I realise it's Grace.

'She was winding you up,' Grace says.

'You think?'

'She was definitely winding you up.'

'She said she was just letting me know so I could check it out, so I'd know, you know. I'd be prepared should anyone else make a similar remark. I'd have had a chance to figure out what to say. Or I could cut the scene.'

'Exactly,' says Grace. 'She's playing with you.'

'Either she is, or she isn't.'

'Believe me. She wants you to cut the scene, or to be uneasy about it.'

'Or spend time and money checking to see if she's right,' I say.

'Exactly. And you will, won't you?'

'Either I will, or I won't.'

I experience a sudden wave of tiredness and glance towards where I'd been sitting. Grace seems to sense my need and nods at the table. I don't invite her to sit down, but she sits down anyway. I take a long drink from my glass. I wonder how many more readers there will be. I wonder how long the break will last before they start again. I wonder how long Grace will sit there giving me her basilisk stare.

'What did you think of what I sent you?' she asks out of the blue.

I have to think before I know what she is talking about.

'It was good. I liked the setting,' I say. 'Very vivid. I've never been to Zanzibar – never even been to Africa – but it felt authentic. And the detail about low flying and very low flying. I liked that too.'

'Was there anything about it you didn't like?'

'No, I don't think so. I think I liked it all.'

'What about the ending?'

'OK, the ending. I wasn't sure about the ending.'

'Wasn't sure about the idea or that I'd got it right?' Grace's persistence lacked the charm of Helen's. 'You can see what I'm trying to do there?'

'You are suggesting that his head is taken clean off by the undercarriage of the Hercules and you ambitiously have the POV switch to the severed head as it hits the ground and rolls across the beach. You describe what the eyes see as this happens, picking up on an earlier point about consciousness surviving for a certain amount of time after beheading.'

'Yeah. What's not to like?' she says, her eyes glittering in the reflected light from the disco ball.

'I like it. I like it very much. I applaud the ambition. I'm just not sure the impact of the plane would sever the head.'

'Isn't that a little pedantic?' she sneers.

'Isn't it my job to be pedantic?'

'With punctuation?'

'Luckily you don't need that level of hand-holding. Wouldn't whatever part of the plane strikes the head just deal it a terrible blow, take a chunk out of it?'

'Well, I don't know. I can't very well set up a controlled experiment.'

'Mmm. A blind experiment.'

'Is that a joke?'

'I probably am being a little pedantic,' I say. 'You take a leap of the imagination and the momentum of the story, the boldness of the conceit, should take the reader with you.'

'Yeah, but if that doesn't happen, it undermines the whole story. That's what you're saying.'

'But that's the beauty of the form. Of the short story. You can take risks that you wouldn't in a novel. How much time have you lost writing it? How much time has the reader lost reading it? And if we get it, if our suspension of disbelief is unbroken, it's all worth it.'

'Hmm.' She looks agitated.

It is my job to encourage the talented students, not discourage them. Grace is clearly talented, but there is something about her that makes me uncomfortable.

'How's your novel coming along anyway?' I ask her.

'The story is part of it,' she says, her jaws snapping shut like an insect's.

'Great. That'll work.'

'How?'

'I don't know; you tell me.'

She laughs a rustling, almost metallic laugh. 'We'll see,' she says, placing one large hand over the other on the tabletop.

I drain my glass.

'I'm going to head off,' I say, getting to my feet.

'Don't forget to check out *Fight Club*,' she says, a slight jeering tone reminding me either of what she thought of my passivity in dealing with the drunk novelist, or of what she herself thought of the drunk novelist.

◆

Following Flynn's death on Uroa beach, Ray struggled to carry out his full range of RAF duties. He gave it six weeks and then applied for medical discharge, which was granted. He wondered if it was granted in the hope that it would buy his silence. He had answered all questions put to him in the internal RAF inquiry that took place immediately after the 'accident' and he assumed that the two nurses who had been present in the Hercules had answered just as truthfully. He had no idea what Dunstan himself had told the inquiry and he didn't ask. But he suspected that the outcome of the internal investigation would be either hushed up or massaged into ambiguity if it wasn't the desired outcome and he knew that normal procedure dictated a full and open inquiry would have to be held at some future point according to the laws of the United Kingdom. He preferred to return to the UK as soon as possible to be ready for that, whatever he might choose to say when the time came.

Ray flew into RAF Northolt and caught the Tube to London and then a train to Manchester. He took a bus from Piccadilly Gardens to Hyde and felt mildly alienated – although he wouldn't have used that actual word to describe the feeling – to find himself walking down the streets of his childhood after three years spent living thirty miles off the coast of East Africa.

'It's our Raymond,' his father said when he opened the door to him, offering a slightly awkward handshake.

Ray's mother appeared and hugged him, not without warmth, then led him into the morning room, which had been transformed. It had been repapered and a new carpet had been put down. A playpen formed a square enclosure on the floor and in it sat a three-year-old boy playing with a wooden train set.

'Is this . . . ?' Ray asked.

'This is Nicholas,' Ray's mother confirmed.

'Hello Nicholas,' said Ray, bending down beside the playpen.

'Nicholas,' Ray's mother said, folding her arms under her bosom, 'this is . . . this is your father.'

Nicholas looked up briefly, turning startlingly big blue eyes on the newcomer, then returned to his train set.

'Nicholas . . .' said Ray's mother.

'It's all right, Mam,' said Ray. 'He's not set eyes on me for three years.'

'And he may not for another three either,' grunted Ray's father from the doorway.

'Me dad's right, Mam. Looks to me like you're doing right by the little feller.'

'Aye, well,' said Ray's mother, moving some knitting off a chair so she could sit down.

'You'll not be stopping long,' Ray's father said.

It wasn't clear to anybody, possibly even to Ray's father himself, whether this was a statement or a question.

'I've got to go to Newcastle,' Ray said.

Nobody asked why.

He took a train from Victoria. Three hours later he stepped on to the platform in Newcastle. He caught a bus to Whitley Bay. North of the white dome of Spanish City, the seafront was windswept and bleak. He walked a little way on the links, then turned inland under the shadow of a tall block of flats. He checked the name of the building – Beacon House. He was going the right way. Leaving Beacon House to his left, he entered a new estate comprised of two or three long, looping roads and numerous dead ends. Modern, boxy, flat-roofed houses constructed out of brick, tile and wooden boards. When he reached Granada Place, he turned in. It was a short cul-de-sac, houses on either side, a white wooden fence at the end. On the right, a man with a bald head and tufts of curly grey hair above his ears was cleaning a red Beetle. The door to his house was standing open and from within could be heard the sound of scales being played on a piano. The man smiled at Ray, who smiled back once he had spotted the number on the house, an even number.

Number 7 was at the end on the left. A grey Morris Minor stood on the short concrete drive in front of a yellow garage door. Ray took a deep breath, held it and let it out. He looked towards the white wooden fence that marked the edge of the property. Beyond it lay a green space bounded at the far side by a wooded gulley.

Ray stepped up to the front door and rang the bell. A two-note tone could be heard from inside the house. Ray took a step back and swallowed. He heard footsteps within and then the door was opened by a thin woman of about forty in a simple nylon dress with a pattern of blue and green pebble-like shapes. Her face looked tense under carefully applied make-up, large grey-green eyes wary beneath blue-shadowed lids.

'Raymond Cross,' he announced.

'Hello, Mr Cross. June Flynn. Please come in.'

June Flynn led Ray into an open-plan lounge/dining room that ran from the front of the house to the back. A wide wooden cabinet stood in the middle, two pot plants trailing upwards into a trellis-like structure that formed a subtle division between two distinct areas.

'Please have a seat, Mr Cross,' said June Flynn.

'Thank you, Mrs Flynn. Please call me Ray.'

June Flynn offered a weak smile. 'Then you must call me June. My husband will be down in a moment. You have had a long journey. Would you like some tea?'

'Tea would be lovely. Thank you.'

June Flynn left the room. Ray could hear her heels crossing the tiled floor in the hall and entering the kitchen. He heard the opening of cupboards and a fridge, the boiling of a kettle. Otherwise the house was silent. Eventually, June Flynn returned carrying a tray. She put it down on the coffee table in the centre of the lounge area. There was a pot of tea, a small jug of milk and three cups and saucers.

The tea was poured. Ray noticed that June Flynn placed her husband's cup on its saucer, but poured neither milk nor tea into it.

'Would you like sugar, Ray?'

'No, thank you, June.'

She passed him his tea and he thanked her again.

'You have a lovely house,' he said, 'in a very nice setting.'

'Thank you. Yes, Briar Dene is lovely.' She indicated the common land next to the house. 'Russell used to play there when he was little.'

Immediately her eyes glittered and she turned away.

'Excuse me,' she said, getting to her feet and going to the wooden cabinet for a box of tissues. 'I'm so sorry, Mr Cross.'

'Please, June,' Ray said, moving forward to the edge of his seat. 'I'm sorry. I didn't want to upset you by coming.'

'I'm very glad you've come. Very glad.' June Flynn dabbed at her eyes, trying not to smudge her make-up. 'The RAF sent someone, of course, but that was because they had to. It was official.'

'Yes.'

There was silence for a few moments and then they both started speaking at the same time.

'I'm sorry,' said Ray. 'After you.'

'I was just going to ask how well you knew Russell.'

'Well, as you know,' Ray began, clearing his throat, 'Russell had not been in Zanzibar very long before he . . .' Ray paused, spotting the trap he had unwittingly set for himself.

'Before the accident.'

'Yes, before the accident. Mrs Flynn. June. I wanted to come and see you and your husband to express my condolences in person and to say that Russell was a fine young man, an excellent addition to the squadron and a real credit to you.'

June Flynn suddenly spasmed and coughed explosively as she leant forward. The cough turned into a brief but horrifying moan and a flurry of tears fell on to the coffee table. Ray leant across and gently pushed the box of tissues in her direction. After a moment, she recovered her composure.

'I'm sorry. I didn't want to do this,' she said.

'Please,' said Ray. 'There's absolutely no need to apologise.'

'Will you excuse me for a moment?'

Ray got to his feet as June Flynn left the room for a second time. He crossed to the mantelpiece over the gas fire, where there were two framed photographs. One showed Russell and his parents when the boy could only have been about thirteen or fourteen. June Flynn looked happy and relaxed, not as gaunt and serious as the woman who now lived in the same house. Her husband stood slightly behind her wearing a pink button-down shirt, a thin black tie and a narrow-lapelled tweed jacket. He wore glasses that reflected the sunlight so that Ray could not see his eyes.

The other photograph showed Russell Flynn wearing his uniform with obvious pride, his blond hair combed back from a wide, clear forehead. Ray returned the photograph to its original position as he heard June Flynn coming back into the lounge. He stepped away from the fireplace and turned to face the room, assuming that she had perhaps gone to get her husband, but she had returned alone.

'My husband and I would like you to have this,' she said, holding an unidentified object out towards him.

Ray took a step closer and saw that she was holding a shell in the palm of her hand. It was a conch or a whelk – Ray was no expert – in perfect condition about three or four inches long.

'May I?' Ray said.

'Please do.'

He took the shell and brought it up to his nose. It smelt only faintly of the sea. He held it up to his ear and gave his head a little shake, trying out a small, friendly smile.

June Flynn smiled too.

'It was among his things,' she said. 'His personal effects. There wasn't much, but there was this, and there was a diary, which I'm ashamed to say I read from cover to cover. I don't think it contains anything he would not have wanted his mother to read.'

'I'm sure,' Ray said.

'He wrote in his diary that you gave him the shell and that he liked you. It seems you looked out for him.'

Now Ray remembered picking the shell up off the beach and handing it to Flynn. He felt a sudden tightness at the back of his throat.

'Thank you,' he said. 'Do you mind if we sit down again?'

'Of course. Sorry.'

'But I can't accept this,' Ray said, offering the shell back.

'I would like you to. I have his diary. When I reread it, as I will many times, I'm sure, it will remind me of the shell and it will make me happy to think that you have it.'

'If you're sure?'

'I'm sure.'

There was another silence, more comfortable this time.

'I should go, June. You've been very kind letting me come to see you. And thank you for the shell.'

'I'm very grateful to you for coming,' she said.

They both stood up.

'I'm sorry about my husband,' she said. 'He finds it very hard.'

'I understand.'

She showed him into the hall and opened the front door.

'Thanks again, Ray.'

'Thank you, June.'

They shook hands and he stepped on to the drive, hearing the door shut behind him. As he drew level with the front bumper of the Morris Minor, he turned and looked at the house. A movement caught his eye. The bedroom window. The corner of a lace curtain.

At the end of Granada Place he turned right instead of left and found his way, via a small sheltered car parking area clearly intended for local residents, on to the field at the side of the Flynns' house. He walked across it towards the stream – Briar Dene, June Flynn had called it – at the far side. A path led down through a copse. He imagined the younger Russell Flynn playing here. An only child, he would have relied on his imagination, playing one-sided games involving battles with various different enemies, making bivouacs and secret hiding places for sacred artefacts.

Ray thought about Russell Flynn's father sitting in his bedroom throughout Ray's visit. Either his own bedroom, or possibly his son's. Maybe he had been too upset by the official visit from the RAF to be able to stomach another one, albeit unofficial? Maybe he blamed Ray for his son's death, since it was known that Ray had been a passenger on board the Hercules at the time of the accident?

Ray climbed out of the shallow gully and looked back across the field towards the house at the end of Granada Place. He hoped that, whatever the reason had been for the boy's father's reluctance to come downstairs, he and his wife were now sharing each other's company rather than remaining isolated in their own private grief.

He proceeded down to the road and crossed it to get to the links. Then he walked the short distance over the links to the beach. He took off his shoes and socks and rolled up his trousers and walked on to the sand. A cold wind blew in off the sea. To the left was a lighthouse that could be reached by means of a causeway, which looked as if it would be inaccessible at high tide. To the right, a few miles to the south, lay the mouth of the Tyne. He kept on walking until he felt damp sand beneath his feet. Zanzibar had been somewhat warmer and arguably more beautiful than this, but he knew he had done the right thing by coming back. The sea, when he eventually felt wavelets washing over his bare feet, was icy cold. He put his hands in his pockets and found the shell that June Flynn had given him. He closed his fingers around it.

Life was short and unpredictable and Ray decided he would not spend a single second of it living in regret.

The house possesses a particular stillness. It is the stillness of a house you are not supposed to have entered. I think back to the time when Lewis mentioned that he habitually leaves certain doors unlocked and wonder if his mentioning it was deliberate. Did he want me to pick up on the line; did he want me to remember it? Or was he simply boasting that life here is like that? You can leave your door open without worry – who is going to come in? Or was he suggesting that he has nothing worth stealing? Since he has already lost what was dearest to him, what would it matter if burglars nicked his TV, his DVD player, his collection of Smiths albums? Actually, with regard to the latter, I might suggest they would be doing him a favour, although, as I'm always having to remind my students, since my opinion of the Smiths is irrelevant here, I have no business including it. It doesn't buy its way into the piece.

Although maybe it demonstrates character, my not liking the Smiths? Perhaps it's designed to show that I'm an outsider, a Mancunian in his forties who doesn't like the Smiths.

I close the connecting door to the garage quietly behind me.

There is a low hum from the fridge, a dripping tap. Beyond these noises lie the stillness of empty rooms, the tension of untrodden stairs. I move out of the kitchen into the hall. At the other end of the hall is the front door. I am about to cross the hall to reach the living room when I hear the clatter of the gate and then through the stained glass of the front door I see a dark shape approaching the house. Adrenaline surges to aid flight, yet I know that the slightest movement will betray my presence. The figure bulks up in the stained glass, bulging and distorting as it reaches the door. There is a pause during which everything is still. The shape of the shadow alters slightly, then the letter box is shoved open with a brassy clang and something is thrust part of the way through. A final push and a piece of twice-folded glossy paper falls to the floor. Splashes of colour; distended typefaces; pornographic photographs of what would pass for food only among the starving.

The takeaway menu delivery guy retreats down the path and I hear the gate snap shut.

The next sound I hear is the breath rushing out of me. I look at my hands. They will take a moment to be still. To my left is the lounge. I am like a concert pianist waiting in the wings, trying to shake the tension out of my arms, before walking unsteadily through the open doorway.

I immediately clock the large framed photograph on the wall above the hearth and recognise it as the work of Neil Roland, a local photographer who has built a successful business on giving the public exactly what they want: tasteful images of their immediate surroundings. Stained glass, gateposts, doors; the colour red, the colour blue. Lewis' TV, digibox and DVD player are in an alcove to the left of the Neil Roland picture. I look around and see a shelf of DVDs in the matching alcove on the other side of the hearth, which features a gas-fed coal-effect open fire. On the mantelpiece is an isolated photograph of Lewis' wife and daughters in an expensive frame.

As I cross the room, someone walks past outside the house in the opposite direction. The downside for me in this being a neighbourhood where Lewis feels able to leave his door unlocked is the possibility that anyone passing by might know Lewis or me and suspect that I have no right to be inside his house. Yet it seems that the best course of action to avoid attracting attention is to act normally. So I stoop to check out his DVDs.

My eyes flick from one case to the next, reading the titles. It is the collection of a man who appears to wish to be perceived as somewhat adventurous in his taste, the titles of films by Almodovar and Wim Wenders (later years). Quirky Euro fare – *Amélie*, *Delicatessen*, *Run Lola Run*. A copy of Park Chan-wook's *Oldboy*, still shrinkwrapped, because I would put money on Lewis having bought it only *after* it was linked to the massacre at Virginia Tech perpetrated by creative-writing student Cho Seung-hui. As my gaze drifts over the spines, it's not images from these films that flash across my mind, but imagined frame-grabs from the home movie I think I'm going to find here. Our mutual acquaintance, Carol, on the back seat of a luxury car in Wythenshawe Park, her face grainy in the near-darkness of the car park. If I do find it, who will she be with? AJ or some unknown dogger? Lewis, even? (In my nightmares.) I picture her with her hair down, as she was at the barbecue. I picture her with her top down. This is what I'm looking for, what Lewis – deliberately or otherwise – has allowed me to believe not only exists, but might be found here, in his house, among his collection of digitised images.

He'll have a computer somewhere, of course, a PC rather than a Mac, a laptop probably, but my guess is he'll have burned the footage on to a DVD so he can watch it on the plasma screen with the lights out and the curtains pulled to.

Prompted by this thought, I go over to the DVD player and press eject. The tray slides out. *The Motorcycle Diaries*. I check the shelves of the unit that houses the various machines and there, finally, I find what I'm looking for: a blank case containing an unmarked DVD-R. I am certain he would not identify the contents.

I think about slipping it into the machine to check, but I'm acutely aware of how long I've already been inside the house. Lewis could come back at any time. It's one thing responding to a perceived invitation to sneak in and help myself, but quite another to be so gauche as to hang around until the house-holder returns. Assuming I've interpreted Lewis' devious signals correctly, that is, and I'd only give myself fifty-fifty on that.

I stuff the DVD case into my jacket pocket and as I'm about to leave the room I notice a small bookcase against the wall near where I came in. I bend down for a brief inspection: his collection seems to be comprised exclusively of British crime writers. John Harvey, Steve Mosby, Michael Marshall, Mick Scully, Robert Edric. No women. Together on an otherwise empty shelf are seven copies of a book called *Straight to Video* by Lewis Harris. I take one off the shelf. The design is slightly off, with ugly typography and poorly used images. The publisher, Strangeways Books, is one I've never heard of. I turn to the author biography: 'Lewis Harris lives in Manchester. He has worked as a shelf-stacker, bingo caller, gravedigger and security guard. This is his first novel in a projected series.' One of *those* author biographies. I flick through the book, holding it up to my nose. It has no smell. I put it back on the shelf and leave the house the same way I entered it.

Five minutes later I'm inside my own house, kneeling down in front of the DVD player, when I change my mind and eject the disc. I take it upstairs and open the MacBook, sliding the DVD-R into the slot on the side of the machine that gives it a gentle tug as I let go.

I'll admit that I was in a state of heightened erotic tension as I sat crouched over my laptop in my study at the top of the house. And that when the images appeared, it took a few seconds for that tension to dissipate. The first shot, unmistakably the product of CCTV, as banal as it is ubiquitous, showed a woman walking away from the camera holding the hands of two little children, one in a red dress, the other wearing shorts and a little yellow hat. The woman was slim, mid-thirties, otherwise nondescript only because of the quality of the picture. In the next shot, you saw them walking past a horizontal windsock towards a man – balding, slight paunch, weak in the shoulder – standing by a plane. It was a small plane in a field with several other similar craft. In the background as they walked towards the man, another plane, a two-seater, could be seen taking off from a grass-covered runway.

Shot three was intermittently affected by some form of

interference, but it was possible to see the woman walking purposefully away from the plane, still holding the hand of one of the children, while the other had turned back to the man and appeared to be listening to something he was saying. He had his hand outstretched towards the departing group. There was a break. The screen was dark for a few seconds before the final shot appeared, apparently from a different camera. It showed a plane – a four-seater, clearly the same one the man had been preparing for flight – moving down the runway. Initially it wasn't clear to me whether it was taking off or landing, but then, as if a magic trick were being performed, it suddenly lifted from the runway and climbed into the air. In two seconds it was level with the camera, which swivelled a couple of degrees as if to follow it, but then the plane slid out of frame to the right. It had not been a great shot, the runway being distant from the camera, but it had been clear that there were four people on board, the pilot and three passengers.

I think I knew as soon as I started watching what it was I was seeing. Once I was certain I had seen all there was to see, I closed the machine and now I'm sitting here staring out of the window, watching the sky slowly darken. Did I pick up the wrong DVD? Is there another disc somewhere in Lewis' house showing Carol having sex in a car at Wythenshawe Park? Or somewhere on the Ringway Trading Estate or around the back of Somerfield? Or is Lewis shrewder than I gave him credit for? Is this what he wanted me to find, this glimpse into the past, and if so, why?

I stand in the back garden looking at what's left of the ivy and the fence it has partially destroyed. I poke around in the soil to see if I can uncover any more bits of red plastic. Most of the rockery has gone now, carted off in the skip, and the garden looks bare, desolate. At least the rockery gave it some definition. A bit of shape.

The garden on the other side of the fence is completely out of control. I wonder if the current residents have any knowledge of the history of the house before it was converted into flats. I wonder if they know in which room the former owner committed suicide. If his action has left some kind of trace – a disturbance in the air, a shadow on the wall. I think of Pompeii. Hiroshima.

I approach the fence. It's clear that the residents don't use the garden at all; nor does it receive any attention. It seems unlikely that anyone has penetrated the thick growth on their side of the fence in years. I stick my head through one of the large holes created by the removal of the ivy. Brambles, nettles, privet; the remains of the ivy, now dying, cut off from its roots. I notice a splash of colour deep in the undergrowth off to the left. Further along I get a slightly better view, but can't tell what I'm looking at, only that it's red in colour.

I get the shears and secateurs from the cellar and return to the fence. I break off half a panel and climb over. Even with the tools and a thick pair of gardening gloves, it takes me twenty minutes to work my way to the heart of the thicket. Inching closer to the object of my labours I realise that it is a model aeroplane, badly damaged, that must have been abandoned here a considerable amount of time ago. It takes me a lot longer than twenty minutes to extricate it and get the plane back into my own garden without causing it too much further damage.

I lay it down on the lawn, then immediately pick it up again and take it inside the house. I put it down on the kitchen table and study it. The pieces of plastic on the desk in my study are from the nose cone, one of the wings and a central section of the fuselage. I could go and get them and fit them into place, but there's no hurry. The plane is not going anywhere. There are obviously other bits somewhere else in either my garden or theirs, because the damage to the plane is fairly extensive.

With a wingspan of about three feet, the model would have stood almost a foot off the ground with its undercarriage intact. A serious model aircraft, then, complete with engine, propeller, authentically detailed cockpit. An enthusiast's much-loved toy.

I remember talking to Lewis in the pub about the pieces of red plastic.

I hear the cat flap and moments later Cleo jumps up on to the kitchen table and sniffs at the model plane.

'What do you reckon to this, Cleo? What does Lewis know about this, eh?'

Why don't you ask him?

'Why don't I ask him? Because I'm not sure I like the way this is developing. That DVD of his wife and daughters getting into that plane, which I think he wanted me to find. And now this, which I also can't help thinking he wanted me to find.'

You won't know for sure unless you ask him.

I stroke Cleo, from the top of her head, pressing back her ears until they lie perfectly flat, to the tip of her tail. I tickle her under her chin and, as usual, she lifts up her head and starts purring.

'I don't know.'

I arrive outside Lewis' house. There's a slight bite in the air, the sky clear. I'm wearing a little white cotton beanie. The

DVD is in my pocket. I have been to a photo lab and had a copy made, which is now in my study.

I stand in his drive, still not sure what I am going to do. Either I tell him or I don't. About the DVD. And about the model plane. Either he is in or he is not.

I take my hat off and stuff it in my pocket.

I knock on the door and wait. Someone walks past behind me. I turn around. Wearing a dirty raincoat and a flat cap and carrying a big striped laundry bag, it is Laundry Bag Man. He will deposit his bag on the pavement after twenty or thirty yards and go back for the other one. Laundry Bag Man always has two identical striped laundry bags with him, but seems unable to carry both of them at the same time. I don't know what he keeps in his bags, but I doubt that it's laundry.

I knock again.

I walk slowly to his garage door, open it and slip inside. I hear my heart beating faster as I approach the door to the kitchen. It, too, is unlocked. I enter the kitchen. Everything looks the same as before. I cross the hall to the living room and get down on my knees in front of the TV unit. I quickly remove the DVD-R, in its blank case, from my pocket and return it to where it had been when I found it.

As I am getting back to my feet I hear the clatter of the gate.

Without stopping to think, I scuttle back across the hall to the kitchen, rising to my feet once I can no longer see the front door. I cross the kitchen on my toes and wait to open the connecting door to the garage until I can hear Lewis' key rattling in the lock of the front door. As he moves into the hall, I negotiate a route from the side of the garage to the front and take care to lift the main door on its hinges so that it does not scrape against the tarmac of the drive as I leave.

Walking home, heart still thumping as I overtake Laundry Bag Man, I reach into my pocket for my hat, but it is not there.

At home, even though it's probably the last thing I should do, I watch the DVD again. The red dress, the little yellow hat. The woman walking past the windsock holding the hands of the children. The balding man with the paunch and the weak shoulder. The woman walking away, holding the hand of the child in the red dress. The other child, in the yellow hat, looking back at the man, undecided, torn. He seems to be offering some kind of promise. You wonder how much of an enticement it could be, looking at him. He doesn't look as if he has a great deal to offer. But the child in the yellow hat is considering it. Maybe that's all it takes? One child's hesitation. The woman walking away, the child in the red dress. Shall we say the girl? The woman and the girl walking away. The other child, in the shorts and the yellow hat. Shall we say the girl in the case of this child as well? The woman walking away, the girl in the red dress. The girl in the yellow hat looking back. The balding man's outstretched hand. His offer, promise, enticement. The outstretched hand.

The woman walking away from the camera, the first camera, holding both girls' hands. They walk slowly. As if relaxed? As if obliged? Either or. Compliant? Reluctant? Either or. The girls hold her hand, trusting. They will follow her anywhere. Do what she says. She walks away from the camera, holding their hands. Past the horizontal windsock towards the man standing by the plane. His plane? Has he hired it? Does he own it? Can he even fly? Maybe he's just showing it to them? Maybe all four will eventually leave together, on foot? Maybe the woman and the two girls will leave and the man will stay? Maybe he's still there, waiting, the woman and the girls somewhere else, not coming back?

The woman walking away from the man, her mouth a straight line, eyes tiny black dots. The girl in the red dress holding her hand, compliant as before, but struggling slightly to keep up, perhaps? The skirt of her dress – and the dress of the woman – caught in the wind that tugs at the windsock. The girl in the yellow hat looking back. The man's outstretched hand. The man's slight paunch. His jeans belted beneath his little round stomach. The knees bagging out. One shoulder dipping slightly. The shoulder that carries the arm that connects to the hand that is outstretched. Maybe it's lowered by the action of stretching out the hand? Maybe the stretched-out hand is too aggressive, the dipped shoulder the man's way of compensating? He wants them all to come back but doesn't want to coerce a small child. Doesn't want to be seen to coerce a small child. The woman walking away. The child will join her. The three of them will walk away. He will be left standing there by the plane.

The plane, the four-seater plane moving down the runway, the grass runway. The wheels turning and turning. The plane moving down the runway. The wheels turning. The plane lifting, suddenly suspended, the wheels ceasing to turn. The plane moving forward, away from the camera, all of its seats apparently occupied. Is it the same plane the man had been standing beside? Is there an obvious gap in the field where his plane had been? Is this definitely the man's plane? The four-seater plane moving down the runway. The wheels turning on the flattened grass.

The sudden lift, the rise into the air, as if on a string. The careful steadying of the wings. The gradual ascent.

The phone rings. I pick it up.

'Hello?'

Even to me, on my end of the phone, my voice sounds disembodied, alienated, suspicious.

'*Ksssh-huh-huh.*'

I don't have anything to say, so I remain silent.

'So listen,' Lewis says, 'do you want to go on a walk or what?'

'What do you mean?'

'Let's go out walking. We've got stuff to talk about.'

'Have we?'

'Yeah. Free tomorrow morning?'

'I don't know.'

'I'll pick you up at nine.'

'Make it ten.'

'Whatever.'

The moment I put the phone down it rings again. I pick it up.

'*What the fuck is it now?*'

'Paul Kinder?'

I don't recognise the voice.

'Yes?'

'Delivery. I'm outside your house.'

I apologise and hang up. I run downstairs and open the door.

There's a man on the doorstep wearing a blue driver's uniform jacket over a Manchester United shirt. He has dark hair going grey cropped to the length of his stubble. A gap between his two front teeth and a bigger gap in the bottom set where he's lost a tooth and not replaced it. A tattooed spider's web crawls up the side of his neck from under the United shirt. He's holding a bulky electronic device with a keypad, a little screen and a stylus attached by a curly plastic flex.

'Sorry about that,' I say.

'No worries, mate. Expecting a chair?'

'Er, yeah.'

'Sign here.'

I sign and he steps aside to reveal the chair standing on the path behind him.

'All yours, mate,' he says.

'Thanks.'

I carry the chair into the house and stand it in the hall for a moment. I get a knife from the kitchen and cut through the strong plastic wrapping. It is a black office chair with a wide curved back and sturdy armrests. Connected to the shaft under the seat are a number of controlling levers. It's quite heavy and an awkward shape, but I manage to carry it upstairs without crashing into the wall or having to take a break. I wheel it into my study. I pull my old chair away from my desk and slide the new one into place. Finally, slowly and with a certain amount of ceremony, I lower myself on to the chair and feel it gently sigh at it takes my weight.

It offers my back lots of support and is extremely comfortable. As it should be, given how much I've paid for it.

It is a Herman Miller Aeron chair.

It is the chair that Geoff Dyer, Alain de Botton, Francesca Simon and Siri Hustvedt all use.

◆

Since coming back from Zanzibar and then shortly afterwards visiting Russell Flynn's family in Whitley Bay, Ray had spent most of his time living in a small flat in Whalley Range,

Manchester, trying to decide what to do with his life. He visited his parents in Hyde. With Ray's blessing they adopted Nicholas. The boy called them his Nana and Grandad; Ray was Daddy, and Mummy, if Nicholas ever asked, was in heaven. Ray felt a little uneasy about this, but he accepted that it had to be his parents' choice what they told the boy since they were giving his son a home and an upbringing, and in any case, Ray couldn't think of a better alternative.

Ray read a lot – poetry, mainly – and applied to university with a view to perhaps taking teacher-training qualifications in due course. He was aware of England winning the World Cup at Wembley – it was hard not to be – but football had never been among his interests and the way the RAF had handled the death of Flynn had dealt a blow to his sense of national pride.

William Dunstan's trial was set for September at the Old Bailey. It meant missing the start of university, but Ray had no choice. He would be called as a witness. Even if he hadn't been required to attend, he would have done so. He owed it to Flynn and he was curious about Dunstan.

Over the summer he listened to a lot of jazz at home and went to concerts in Southport, Stockport and Manchester. He was living on a small pension from the RAF, which he thought of as blood money; he supplemented it with a few shillings earned collecting glasses at pubs around Ardwick.

The RAF offered to find him accommodation in London, but he preferred not to have to rely on their help and sorted himself out with a bedsit in Earls Court. He visited some of the local pubs, which appeared to be favoured by either Australians or homosexuals. Either way, the company was overwhelmingly male.

On the opening day of the trial, having been told that he

might be called on the first day but equally might not be, Ray was led to the witnesses' room. There were two other people present. One, a stocky man wearing a blue suit with his red hair shaved up the back of the neck, was sitting with his back to the door. Ray had only ever seen Henshaw in his engineer's overalls, but he was easily recognisable from behind. The other man, a court usher, exchanged a few quiet remarks with the woman who had escorted Ray, before she left again.

Ray found his thoughts escaping from the room like smoke and drifting into another part of the building. He pictured Billy Dunstan, sat in profile in the dock. Composed, erect and alert, impeccably turned out in his squadron leader's uniform, he would cut quite a different figure from the dashing individual in his leather flying jacket and white silk scarf. His dark reddish-brown hair, glistening with Brylcreem, would be combed straight back from his forehead, with a severe side parting. Ray tried to imagine Dunstan's barrister, and his opposite number, but found that he couldn't.

Which of them, Ray wondered, would he end up doing battle with? It depended which version of the truth he told. How important was it to mention, for example, the sexual attraction between Dunstan and the nurses he was trying to impress? It only had to be mentioned and it would stick. It would help to convict. All Ray had to do was stay away from that angle. The nurses were on the plane because they had been invited by Flight Lieutenant Campbell. With Campbell having been drawn away to Pemba Island, Dunstan had merely sought to avoid the nurses' disappointment by still allowing them on board. He was a kind man, a gentleman. What happened to Flynn was a terrible accident, a tragedy.

It would depend on what Frankie and Joan, the nurses, said on oath.

And on what Ray said, too.

Ray had never seen justice operate at first hand, and while he understood it and knew how it was meant to work, he felt anxious. What if the defence barrister wasn't as persuasive as the prosecutor? Supposing the defence had the balance of evidence slightly in their favour, but the prosecuting barrister was the more accomplished orator and cross-examiner? An innocent man might easily go down. Or a guilty man get off. It all rested on the intelligence of the jury, on their ability to see through all the arguments, specious and otherwise. They had to be able to see through, say, the prosecutor's efforts to establish a defendant's guilt even when it was clear to everyone in the room that the man was not guilty.

In the case of Dunstan, Ray was still undecided.

Ray's reverie was interrupted by the sound of the door opening. He looked up and saw the two nurses, Joan and Frankie, entering the room. He caught Frankie's eye, but she immediately looked away, first at Joan and then down at the ground. Joan didn't look in his direction. Together the two women sat in a similar position relative to Ray as Henshaw, although several seats away from the engineer, and Ray was left to contemplate the backs of their heads as they leaned close and whispered to one another.

The first day was adjourned and Ray was yet to be called. He decided to walk back to Earls Court. His route took him through Covent Garden into Soho, where he stopped for a drink in the Golden Lion on Dean Street. He got himself a half and sat at a table on his own, but it wasn't long before a man came and sat opposite him, without asking if the seat were free. The man was wearing a denim jacket, a T-shirt bearing an illegible slogan, and a pair of jeans. The newcomer launched into a conversation that seemed as if it had already been started earlier. He asked Ray if he liked the pub and if he thought he might want to come there again. Ray didn't know what to say and he kept his replies short, but there was something in the man's appeal Ray found hard to resist. Possibly it was nothing more than the fact that the man clearly wanted something – and wanted something from Ray.

Ray couldn't deny he felt pleased to be wanted.

After a while, the man asked fewer questions, but they became more pointed. Encouraged by Ray's answers, the man gave him some directions. Eventually the man got up and left the pub and Ray walked out behind him, following him to a public toilet just off Shaftesbury Avenue. Ray waited for a moment while the man went in and then he went in also. The light in the toilet was completely different from that outside. There were skylights, but they were of thick glass and the air inside was damp and gloomy. There was a smell of disinfectant and pools of water on the floor. The attendant's heavy wooden door appeared locked. On the right-hand side were four cubicles, faced by a urinal on the left. Ray walked up to the third cubicle along, which was shut. He gave a short double-knock and immediately heard a bolt being drawn back within. The door was pulled open and Ray stepped inside. The man, whose semi-erect penis was poking out of the fly of his jeans, pushed the door shut behind Ray and locked it.

Without speaking, the man sat on the pulled-down toilet seat and placed his hands on Ray's belt. His eyes swivelled upwards to seek approval. Ray felt incapable of voluntary movement and imagined – hoped, even, although he would have not liked to admit it – that his lack of any signal would be taken as acquiescence.

The man unbuckled Ray's belt, unzipped his fly and lowered his trousers, followed by his underpants. He started to rub and stroke Ray's penis, which responded by becoming stiffer, longer, heavier. The man glanced up at Ray, who was looking down on what was taking place with something close to disbelief. The man might have thought that the expression on Ray's face was a smile. It might even have actually been a smile.

The man put Ray's penis in his mouth and started to move his head backwards and forwards, backwards and forwards. His left hand alternately encircling Ray's penis at the root and lightly squeezing his testicles, the man moved his right hand down to his own penis, which Ray could see was now fully engorged. The man moved his right hand quickly up and down the shaft of his own penis while continuing to suck on Ray's and to fondle his balls. After a few moments, the man convulsed and jerked backwards as he ejaculated. He stopped rubbing himself, but his penis remained hard and erect and white in the greenish underwater light of the cubicle as he continued to do what he was doing to Ray, who was trying to shut down the workings of his own mind so that he might relax enough to achieve the same kind of release. Suddenly into his mind popped an image of himself on the beach at Whitley Bay, the damp sand under his feet, the hard convolutions of the shell in his hand, the tall white lighthouse rising out of the sea. The feeling – the conviction – that life was short and unpredictable. The promise that he would not live in regret. And he suddenly exploded with the very opposite of regret, with joy, a great, spontaneous, shocking rush of joy.

And the man grinned as he wiped his face with the back of his hand.

◭

In the morning, just before ten, there's a knock on the door. I open it.

'*Ksssh—*'

'Yeah, yeah,' I say, interrupting him, although I notice he's not looking as annoyingly chipper as usual. The annoyingly chipper look, though, is, I suspect, paper-thin.

'Shall we go for a drive?' he says.

'I thought we were going for a walk.'

'Summat I want to show you. We can go in your car.' It wasn't a question.

'I thought you were picking me up.'

'My car's fucked, mate.'

'Right. Hang on.'

I go back inside for the keys. This is a bad idea, I can tell. It doesn't take a clairvoyant.

'Come on then,' I say, locking the front door behind me and opening the car.

Lewis sits with his legs far apart, so that I keep knocking his right knee with the gearstick. He neither apologises nor makes any effort to move his leg.

'Where are we going, then?' I ask him.

'Get on to the M60,' he says. 'Westbound.'

For some reason I'd expected us to be going in the opposite direction.

'Are you going to tell me where we're going or what?'

'I'll direct you,' he says, adding, '*if that's all right.*'

It's my turn to say 'Whatever'.

The motorway is pretty quiet, unlike Lewis.

'All that teaching you do,' he says, 'do you enjoy it?'

'Depends,' I say.

'On what?'

'On how good they are, or how willing they are to take advice.'

'Which ones are willing to take advice? The good ones or the others?'

I see the gilt domes and trashy cupolas of the Trafford Centre coming up on the right-hand side.

'Generally,' I say, 'the worse they are, the more resistant they are to accepting any advice at all, whether it's from me or the other students.'

'Take the next exit,' he says. 'What about the good ones?'

'Now and again,' I say, indicating to leave the motorway, 'you get someone who's very good and knows it and doesn't really see the point in listening to what anyone's got to say about their stuff. Left or right?'

'Left. Maybe they're right?' he says as I change down into second and my hand knocks his knee.

'In one or two cases, maybe, but then what are they doing on the course? The best ones might know they're doing something right but they're keen to take on board any advice, whether it's from me or anyone else in the group.'

'Straight on,' Lewis says. 'Anyway. It's not like anyone buys books any more.'

We drive in silence for a while. Salteye Brook is on our left – the old course of the River Irwell – hidden behind a long line of redbrick houses with white PVC window frames and the shortest front paths in Manchester.

'It does sometimes seem,' I say finally, in response to his last comment, 'as if there are more people studying creative writing than there are people buying books. Even some of those who want to write can hardly be bothered to read.'

'Turn right here,' Lewis says, pointing across my chest.

I turn into the car park and pull into a free space at the end, killing the engine.

'Ta,' says Lewis as he opens his door and gets out.

'You're welcome,' I mutter as I open my own door.

Barton Aerodrome was opened in 1930, the first purpose-built municipal airport in the UK. It was intended to be *the* Manchester airport but within a short time it became obvious that the boggy terrain would not support the heavier aircraft coming into service, and plans were drawn up for Ringway to the south of the city. Renamed City Airport Manchester in 2007, it remains a busy airfield for general aviation. Some eighty or so private owners keep their Pipers and Cessnas there, paying fees to the airfield authority for the privilege.

Lewis leads me through the little gate on to the airfield itself. No security here. Apart from the CCTV cameras that I see bolted to the brickwork of the control tower and affixed to a couple of free-standing poles.

To our left, fifty or sixty planes are parked in neat rows, all facing the same direction – west. Ahead of us, the grass runway that I recognise from the DVD runs from left to right, west to east. And to the right, a few more planes, scattered more randomly than the larger group.

I experience a strange sense of temporal displacement as I scan the endless green for a glimpse of the red dress or the little yellow hat. I realise I don't know what colour dress the woman was wearing. I can picture her walking away from the camera – I look up for the right camera to orient myself within the field of that shot – but I can't remember what colour dress she was wearing.

Lewis is a little way ahead of me. I catch up with him.

'His plane was just over there,' he says, pointing to the right. 'She will have parked where we parked and walked in here through the gate we came through. She probably looked around, wondering where to find him. Although, knowing him, he'd have given her very precise directions.'

He stands upright, his head thrust slightly forward. There's a breeze, sufficient to fill the orange windsock. Then he turns to look at me. I almost look away, but I know this is a challenge, so I hold his stare. His eyes are cold, red-rimmed. It could be the wind, but it might not be. He hasn't shaved in a couple of days. There are lines around his mouth I've not noticed before.

'*Ksssh-huh-huh.*'

'Then what happened?' I ask him.

'You've seen the DVD.'

'It's not conclusive.'

'She walked towards the plane with the girls,' he says, as he takes a step in that direction himself. 'He was standing by the plane, as you know.' He looks at me at this point, a slight curl to his lip.

'And the next shot,' I say, taking up the narrative, 'is of him standing by the plane looking beseechingly, imploringly back at the woman and the two girls, although mainly at the girl in the little yellow hat, because the woman and the girl in the red dress are walking away. They have their backs to him.'

'They're walking away,' he agrees. 'And they should have carried on walking away.'

'But the girl in the little yellow hat stops and looks back,' I say.

'Anna,' he says with a hairline crack in his voice.

'And because he looks so pathetic, because he looks like a broken man, she takes a step back in his direction.'

'She used to cry over dead birds,' Lewis says. 'In the spring, when you'd occasionally find fledglings in the garden fallen out of their nests, she'd be in floods of tears. She couldn't bear anything dead or broken. She felt exactly the same when she looked back and saw that cunt extending his fucking hand to her. She couldn't walk away like Mel and Emily. She had to go to him.'

'Mel was your wife.'

'And Emily was my other daughter. She was a bit harder. Not hard. She was just, you know . . .'

'Older?' I guess.

He shakes his head as he watches a small plane flying overhead, presumably taking a pass over the airfield before coming in to land.

'They were the same age,' he says.

'Twins?'

'Not identical.'

The plane turns in the distance and describes a wide semicircle with the airfield at the centre of the diameter. Having reached a certain point, in the west, it turns again and comes in on a straight line towards the airfield. I remember Lewis using the phrase 'extended runway centre line' at Carol and AJ's barbecue.

Lewis has walked away from me. He stops by a plane thirty yards away. I see him touching the fuselage with his hand. I walk over to him.

'This is not . . . ?'

'*Ksssh-huh-huh.*' He looks at me. 'You've not been paying attention,' he says.

He's wearing a linen shirt, similar to the one he wore at the barbecue, but without a pattern. A simple white linen shirt with an open neck. Grey hair emerges in little tufted spirals at the throat. I can see his chest rising and falling beneath the material.

'They went up in the plane,' I say.

He doesn't reply. I don't know whether to push it. Either I push it or I leave it. Let it drop.

'These small planes,' he says after a while, 'there are two main types. Cessnas and Pipers. This is a Cessna. Cessna 172. It has a high wing. See, the wing joins the fuselage at the top so that you can see the ground when you look down from the cockpit, when you're doing *navs*, as they call them. *Navs*.'

He looks at me and I raise my eyebrows.

'Navigation flights,' he says. 'It would seem to make sense, wouldn't it, sticking the wing up there so that you can see down, see what's beneath you?'

'I suppose so.'

'Piper owners disagree, of course.'

'What did he fly?'

'What do you think? A fucking Piper Cherokee. Piper owners are like Mac users. Absolutely fucking convinced their more expensive, cooler machine is somehow better than the more commonly used alternative. Cessnas are like PCs. Reliable, safer – given the position of the wing – the obvious choice. They're the standard. Maybe if he'd been flying a Cessna 172 like this . . .'

This is all new to me and sounds suspiciously like bullshit. 'How is the Piper different?' I ask him.

'The wing is lower, so it's harder to see the ground. The wing comes in below where you're sitting. It's so fucking *obviously* fucked up.' A tiny bubble of spittle flies from his lips on the final plosive. 'When did you ever see a low wing on a bird?' His hand forms a fist and I wonder if he's going to take out his bitterness on whatever's to hand. Me, for example. Or this Cessna 172. More quietly, he repeats the line: 'When did you ever see a low wing on a bird?'

His fist opens like a flower on a passage of speeded-up film and he turns away from the plane.

'Take me back,' he says and walks past me, close enough that I smell his sweat.

I watch him walk back towards the control tower. Beyond him, the plane that had taken a pass over the airfield is now coming in to land. I watch its wings dip one way and then the other as it approaches the runway. Finally the pilot levels the wings as his undercarriage touches down and twenty yards later he drops the nose and the front wheel also meets the grass. The plane is travelling very slowly now. There is not that sense of something travelling far too fast that you get as a passenger on a jet touching down. The plane is always too fast, too heavy, the runway too short.

This looks much easier, much safer. The plane weighs nothing, is barely moving. It's hard to imagine how it could go wrong.

I catch up with Lewis in the car park. He's sitting in the car waiting for me, staring out of the window. I wonder how he got in. Surely I locked the car. I always lock the car. It's a reflex.

I get in and stick the key in the ignition, but don't turn it for a moment. I swivel in my seat and look at him, but his whole upper body is angled in the other direction. I start the engine and as I engage first gear I give his knee a good hard knock with the gear stick.

He fails to react.

We drive back to the M60 in silence. Even when we both look up at the sound of a small plane passing over the car, even then nothing is said. It does occur to me to ask him if it's a Piper or a Cessna, but I keep schtum.

It's not far from junction 11 back round to south Manchester, but when no one is speaking, motorway time gets stretched. We travel in the inside lane, doing a steady sixty-five. There's a regular *vroom* as cars overtake us in the middle lane. The exit signs become generic designs, blue boards covered in meaningless white symbols. The colours of the other cars correspond to a randomly generated pattern dominated by silver, red and white. Every other vehicle is a van or a truck. I switch off and enter a kind of semi-trance. The car drives itself.

After we had sex in her Golf GTI at Hatton Cross Underground station car park, Susan Ashton and I agreed that while it was fun, it was a one-off. Indeed, we said, that was why it was fun. We exchanged remarks along these lines in comically breathless voices as we panted to get our breath back and huge planes continued to thunder over our heads as they came in to land just a few hundred yards to the west.

After disengaging, I had moved back to the passenger side and allowed myself to sink back into the expensive leather seat. Susan Ashton had reached a hand under her own seat and passed me a box of tissues.

'Well prepared,' I said and we both laughed.

'That was nice,' I said.

'Very nice,' she agreed.

She busied herself with a tissue and I belted my trousers and she pulled down the sun visor and adjusted her make-up in the mirror and I pressed the on/off switch on the cassette player and 'Everybody's Gotta Learn Sometime' by the Korgis squirmed synthetically out of the loudspeakers. I looked at her and we both burst out laughing. We tried to sing along, but we got the giggles. At the end of the track, she switched it off and we sat there in silence for a while, occasionally smiling to ourselves.

'It'll be all right, you know, with Tony,' I said.

'And you'll be fine with Veronica,' she countered.

'Everything will work out,' I said.

'It'll be like this never happened,' she said.

And I said, 'Well, I don't know about that,' and I laughed and after a moment she laughed too.

She offered me a lift.

'What, to Feltham?' I said. 'You want to introduce me to Tony?'

She smiled, then the smile quickly vanished and a look of worry crossed her face for the first time.

'Sorry,' I said.

'This can't happen again,' she said.

'I know. I know it can't,' I said. 'Veronica wouldn't hear of it.'

She looked at me with the kind of look a parent gives a naughty child.

'Sorry,' I said again. 'I'll get the Tube. You gave me a lift to the Tube, that's all.'

'Go on, bugger off,' she said and leaned over towards me.

I tilted across to meet her lips and her rebuttoned blouse gaped in front of me and just at that moment a 747 flew over the car, making it vibrate. We lingered on the kiss for a moment, then parted and I caught her looking at me. It was a look that suggested to me that this whole one-off thing was not necessarily going to work. Not because I was so irresistible or anything. I didn't have any illusions about that. But there was something in the look, something I'd noticed at several points during the staff development weekend. A mixture of panic, abandon, desire. It almost felt like a dare.

As I reluctantly pulled away, I reached into the rear of the car and caught hold of her bra.

'Don't forget this,' I said.

She smiled and I reached for the door handle, grabbing my bag from the footwell.

'See you.'

'See you.'

On the Tube back into London I sat opposite a young mother and her two small children. They were too young to be fighting with each other and causing her problems of that kind, but they were hard work all the same. She wiped their noses and checked their nappies and gently admonished them when they tried to climb on to my seat. By the time the train reached Acton Town, she looked worn out and I was experiencing a full-blown attack of remorse. I felt that my guilt was stamped across my forehead for everyone to read – this woman, the other passengers, even the woman's tiny innocent children. How would Veronica not see it there the moment I walked in the door?

I got off the Tube at Hammersmith and phoned home from a call box. The conversation was a little strained, almost as if she already knew. But this was silly. She was just reaching the end of a long weekend's solo childcare and wanted me back to take them off her. She needed a break. 'Where are you?' she said.

I wondered that myself.

The pact that Susan Ashton and I had made, such as it was, lasted about a week. I struggled through the days, feeling guilty about what had happened when I was at home and watching Veronica feeding the twins, and guilty about the fact that, whenever I saw Susan Ashton at work, I wanted it to happen again.

Above all, I felt depressed by the predictability of it all, by the fact that it was such a terrible cliché. I was a weak male, easily tempted. I had spent a weekend away from the company of my wife, leaving her to look after our very young children, and I had succumbed to the oldest temptation in the world. And then I felt guilty that I was more upset by its being a cliché than I was about the fact that I had cheated on my wife and that I wanted to do it again.

I watched Veronica while she slept and I knew that nothing had changed, really, between the two of us. I still loved her and I felt she probably still loved me, but we had allowed the stress of childcare to obscure that love, to get in the way. We had reacted to perceived injustices in the division of labour in a tiresomely predictable and destructive way, bitching and sniping at each other, sometimes at home just the four of us, but also on the few occasions we got to go out and be with other people. We bitched about each other when we were out separately with our own friends and we bitched about each other when we were out together with mutual friends. We'd see them looking at each other, perhaps in recognition, but more likely in grateful realisation that someone's marriage was in a worse state than their own. So they thought.

Susan Ashton stopped by my desk in a crowded office on a spurious errand and typed out a message in the document I had open on screen.

Do you want to go for a drink after work?

I thought about it for two seconds and then typed a reply.

Go on, then.

She walked off and I watched her go. When she reached the doorway, she didn't look back.

I deleted the messages and met her after work.

We sat in an alcove in a basement bar sipping halves of lager.

'What a cliché!' I said.

'What do you mean?' she asked.

'I just . . . Nothing,' I said, since I could see that she didn't know what I was talking about.

She caught my hand under the table and held on to it. I could feel a pulse where the tip of my finger pressed against the base of her thumb, but I didn't know whose it was. I could smell a powerful scent coming off her and I didn't think it had come out of a bottle. She was wearing a blouse, as she had been at the weekend, and again it was unbuttoned a little further than you might expect it to be. I imagined her unfastening a button or two as she stepped down into the gloom of this empty bar (we had left work separately and she had arrived first) and I felt both excited in a visceral, animal sense and overwhelmingly tired at the same time, and not just physically. I didn't want this to happen. All I had to do was explain that to her, briefly, remind her of what we had agreed, and leave, walk up the stairs into the sunlight and not look back. Quit the job if necessary, get another. It wasn't like I was wedded to my employer like I was wedded to Veronica. There were a dozen jobs like mine available at any one time.

And at the same time I did want it to happen. A part of me wanted it to happen. Something in my stomach wanted it to happen. Something in my trousers wanted it to happen. But also something in my brain. Something in my brain both wanted it to happen and wanted it not to happen.

Either it would happen or it wouldn't happen. And if it happened, either it would fuck everything up or it wouldn't. And if it fucked everything up, either I would end up having to kill myself or I wouldn't.

We finished our drinks and I let Susan Ashton leave first. I got another drink and sat in the semi-darkness brooding, worrying, flipping coins in my head.

When I got home, Veronica was in the kitchen with the children. She was hovering with a cloth while they spooned food into their mouths, occasionally missing.

'Hello honey,' she said, getting up to kiss me.

'Hello darling,' I said. 'How's my favourite girl? Oops, I mean how are my favourite girls?'

Laura giggled. She didn't necessarily know what was funny, but she had learned to laugh at the joke.

'Have you been for a drink?' Veronica asked.

I looked at her quizzically.

'I can taste it.'

'Yes,' I said. 'A few of the lads were going out. Someone's birthday.'

Veronica smiled and I leaned in to wipe some food away from Jonathan's chin. I saw the tiny round scar at the corner of his eye, caused by his sister having accidentally caught him with a pencil. At least, we hoped it was accidental.

Although I stayed in the kitchen and helped clean up and then cooked our food, I felt as if I wasn't there, as if I had already moved out into some miserable bedsit where I would barely have enough shelf space for my copies of my own book, which had been published to widespread apathy the year before, never mind my library. I knew what I had to do. I just didn't know if I could do it.

At the weekend, I told Veronica a despicable lie and took a train from Waterloo to Feltham. I walked the short distance from the station to the address Susan Ashton had given me, my stomach churning not so much with butterflies as with unknown lacy-winged insects, patent-leather beetles and hairy moths like winged cigars.

We had sex in her bed with sunlight slanting in through the slats of the silver venetian blind. I could hear the planes coming in to land a mile or so to the north, but the noise was too faint. It lacked detail, character, specificity. The deep bass rumble of a 747 was inaudible at that distance. I couldn't feel the vibration in my bones. In purely mechanical terms it was good sex, but the tenderness was simulated. We didn't talk, or if we did what we said meant nothing, like the sex. Susan Ashton was beautiful, but the connection between us was an illusion, an accident of time and place. The artificiality of the previous weekend. The car park. The expensive leather seats of her Golf GTI. The planes. Most of the time it seemed to me that she was switched off. Now and then she would flicker into life and you'd see it in her eyes and you'd want her, or you'd want some small part of her. You didn't really want her and she didn't really want you.

Nevertheless.

'That was nice,' I said.

'Very nice,' she agreed.

'Of course, it must never happen again,' I said.

'Of course not.'

But I meant it this time.

I took the train back to Waterloo and switched to the Tube. When I got home, Veronica and the children were out. I filled a bucket with warm soapy water and cleaned the bathroom. I scrubbed the surfaces until they shone. I went through the kitchen cupboards and threw out everything that was past its sell-by date. I ran out to the shops and bought new stuff. I filled the fruit bowl and arranged some flowers in a vase. I didn't question whether Veronica would see through all of this. I just did it. By mid-afternoon I had finished and was beginning to get a bit twitchy. No note had been left. We didn't generally do much on a Saturday, just tended to hang around the house. I had thought the only place they were likely to be was the park, but not for this long. By the end of the afternoon I was checking in Veronica's wardrobe and in the kids' drawers to see if there were any unexplained gaps. I sat in my tiny box-room study. I switched the computer on and switched it off again. I sat on my swivel chair and spun around. The dummies made the room seem even smaller than it was. I had a full-size female dummy and two child-size mannequins that I'd picked up from second-hand shops on the Holloway Road. Veronica didn't mind them, she said, as long as they stayed in my room.

They weren't going anywhere.

'You're not going anywhere, are you?' I said, my voice loud in the empty house.

I looked at the bookcase. At the end of one shelf at eye level was a row of orange spines with black lettering. Bigger than A-format, slightly larger even than B-format, but not quite C. A somewhat awkward size, in other words. My novel, published the year before. Out of print, forgotten by the few people who had bought it and read it or been sent a review copy and never opened it. I took one out from the row, held it up to my nose and flicked through the pages. It had never had a smell, so I don't know why I expected it to have acquired one over time. I looked at the publisher's name at the bottom of the spine. A one-man operation whom few people had ever heard of publishing a book no one wanted to read. That was fair enough. If a book was rejected by all the publishers in town, that was generally thought to be a sign that it was either no good or it could not be imagined that anyone would want to read it. Or not enough people, anyway. Smaller publishers existed for the more marginal stuff and somehow they survived on subsidies or by having the odd surprise success. Most of these, too, had rejected my novel. I didn't blame them for it. I was grateful to the publisher who had taken it on. He'd done a couple of books before. He was smaller than the small presses. He would not have been expecting to have the odd surprise success.

I'd been toying with ideas, writing experimental passages, when I'd met Veronica. Meeting her had seemed to galvanise me and I'd written the book in a couple of years, in snatched moments, late at night, early in the morning, finishing it when the twins were about a year old. Veronica wasn't sure about it. It was macabre, she said, as if that were a criticism, which I guessed it was if you didn't like the macabre. I understood why she didn't really like it a great deal, and I didn't pretend it was just because she was a lawyer and didn't read a lot of fiction. She thought it was all a bit close, uncomfortably so. The female character in the book could be her, she said. The children could be ours. It wasn't, and they weren't, but I understood the objection.

When I'd started sending it out, the reactions of publishers had shown a degree of consistency. It was overwritten, it was too weird, it was unlikely to gain a mass audience.

I heard the door and quickly slid the book back into the row of identical volumes, aware that in my haste I had caught the bottom corner and it would now be folded over.

Veronica seemed happy and the children were excitable. They had been to a museum and had ice creams and come back on the Tube. I thanked Veronica and she smiled her acknowledgement.

'I'm knackered,' she said before collapsing like a rag doll on to the settee and making the children explode into fits of giggles.

'Do you know what time it is, children?' I asked in my giant's voice.

They looked at me wide-eyed and waited.

'BATH TIME,' I roared and ran to scoop them up, one under each arm as usual.

There were more giggles as they fought to escape and I heard Veronica faintly saying, 'It'll end in tears,' as I headed for the stairs with the children.

They eventually quietened down enough to be sat in the bath and given a good clean. Downstairs I heard Veronica opening a bottle of wine and then the clink of glass. As I played with the children, a number of thoughts drifted through my mind. This was what I treasured. Again it was a cliché, but a good cliché. This was what was important to me, not a fling with a colleague. I wondered vaguely if I would be saying the same thing if the sex the second time, in Susan Ashton's bedroom in Feltham, had been as good as the first time, in her car at Hatton Cross Underground station car park. But this wasn't a helpful thought. I was glad the second time had not been as good. It had helped me realise sooner rather than later that I was making a colossal mistake.

Ray's day in court finally came. From the moment he heard his name called in that great dark echoing chamber of a courthouse he felt as if he was outside himself watching the proceedings. He heard his own voice answer the questions that were put to him, whether they came from the prosecuting or the defending barrister, truthfully. His answers betrayed no suggestion of bias or preference. Here was a man, they seemed to say, who was present when the event took place and who has come here today to tell us, in his own words, what happened. He neither invented nor embellished. He offered not his impression of events, but his record of what took place. Where any gap in the narrative existed he did not try to fill it with conjecture or fantasy.

When all of the questions had been asked, he was thanked and dismissed and as he left the stand he felt a strange, almost visceral reconnection with himself. No longer was he observing himself from above. There was no doubt in his mind that he had done the right thing. There would be moments of sorrow, he sensed, but he would not allow them to consume him. They would not define him. He would rise above them and move on.

From the dock, Squadron Leader William Dunstan turned to look at Ray, but Ray felt no guilt, only a twinge of regret that this man, this beautiful man, would be beyond his reach, not only for the length of his sentence, but for ever.

From the Old Bailey, Ray walked to Soho and entered the Golden Lion on Dean Street. The man was not there, but other men were.

Later, he bought a cheap bound notebook from an oriental supermarket in Chinatown and sat in a noisy café writing notes, ideas, scraps of poems. When he was asked later, years later, when had he started writing, he always said it was that night. It was months before he produced anything he thought was worth sending off. But when he did start writing decent stuff, as he thought, he didn't allow rejection to stand in his way. He kept on writing and typing and sticking stamps on envelopes. His first offer of acceptance came from a relatively new magazine called *Ambit*. The editor, Martin Bax, wrote Ray a short note saying the editors had enjoyed his poem very much and would like to include it in the next issue. He was offered a small fee and encouraged to send in more work as and when he produced it.

Ray never did take up his university place in Manchester. His attendance at Dunstan's trial meant he missed enrolment and his simultaneous entry into London's homosexual subculture reduced his desire to return to live in Manchester, where he imagined the opportunities for experimentation and exploration would be thinner on the ground. The poetry magazines were mostly based in London, which was also where the more interesting live events tended to be put on. The Royal Albert Hall had been full to hear Allen Ginsberg perform at the International Poetry Incarnation a couple of years earlier. Because of his success with *Ambit*, which continued to publish his poetry, Ray took part in a reading that the magazine organised at the ICA with a new writer called J. G. Ballard who was making waves in science fiction. Ray let his hair grow down to his shoulders; a moustache appeared. The poems kept coming and they featured in a growing selection of magazines: *London Magazine*, *Bananas*, *Samphire*. Alan Ross even lofted the idea of a collection from London Magazine Editions. Ray demurred, not wishing to appear presumptuous. He had not been writing long, he said, and wasn't so sure he had a collection in him. He had been reading widely and making new discoveries all the time. Peter Redgrove, Ted Hughes and Sylvia Plath were writers whose work he admired. At the same time he found himself brushing shoulders with the likes of Christopher Logue, Michael Horovitz and Lee Harwood at readings and launches. His name started appearing on guest lists and if you had been invited into his humble Earls Court bedsit at any point from the turn of the decade you would have seen a number of invitations on stiff card leaning against the mirror above his mantelpiece. He was the first person to suggest, in a series of poems published in *London Magazine*, that Mark Rothko, the abstract expressionist, was perhaps not so abstract after all. The large black and grey paintings of 1969 and 1970 were pictures of the moon, Ray argued. The poems were well reviewed in the *TLS* and Ray began to feel as if he belonged, although he had yet to broach the subject of sexuality in his work.

In 1971, feeling restless, he requested permission to visit Dunstan in Pentonville Prison, but this was denied. Instead he took the train to Manchester. He had continued to make regular trips to the north-west to see Nicholas. His parents were entering their sixties yet still seemed more than up to the job of rearing his son. They appeared neither to enjoy life nor find it an intolerable burden. But that had always been the case. Ray tried to raise the subject of Nicholas' continued care without being overly explicit. Partly he feared offending his parents by suggesting that they might like to offload the responsibility. Yet he knew that taking over parenting duties would hardly sit well with his lifestyle. The status quo persisted by default.

An only child with elderly guardians, Nicholas was a bright and reasonably self-sufficient eight-year-old. He had been told the facts about his mother and he knew who his father was.

At the end of any one of his visits, Ray would stand at the gatepost and look back. Nicholas would be standing just in front of his grandparents on the path by the front door, his nana's hand resting on the top of his head.

Returning to London, Ray would throw himself into the life he was living with even more gusto, enthusiasm and hedonistic abandon. He divided his time between the Tate Gallery, the Cross at Vauxhall and the cruising grounds of the West Heath. At the same time, the work seemed to pour out of him. Someone from one of the magazines had a word with a small independent publisher and almost without Ray having to lift a finger a collection appeared in the next catalogue. As publication neared, Ray needed to be around more. The gaps between the trips to Manchester got longer until it was little more than an annual visit at Christmas. Nicholas' birthday was difficult for Ray. For all his living life to the full as a single man, Ray was still and would always be a widower. That pain never went away. It just became duller and then would flare up again at certain times or when prompted by events.

Ray's debut collection, *The Beach*, was published in autumn 1978. Ted Hughes was among those present at the launch party. Ray was introduced to the future Poet Laureate and he shyly confessed that without Hughes' example he might never have attempted to marry nature with humanity. He said that his poem 'The Mynah Bird' had been intended as a tribute to Hughes' 'Crow'. During a lull, Ray found himself at the drinks table taking small gulps from a glass of champagne in readiness for another that was in the process of being poured when a man in a wide-lapelled velvet jacket and flared jeans approached him, placing a hand on his arm.

'Don't you think you've had enough?' said the newcomer.

'I certainly don't, no,' said Ray as he turned to look at the man, whose reddish-brown hair was styled in a wiry bouffant that had been fashionable a year or so before. The straggly moustache had never really been in vogue. Ray himself had shaved off his own moustache when he had acquired a crew cut in 1977. It was the man's eyes that struck Ray. They were deep-set, wary, suspicious, even hostile. This was a man who had had good looks and lost them, a man who had deliberately shed them. Good looks in prison were a burden.

'Squadron Leader Dunstan,' said Ray.

'Just Bill nowadays,' said Dunstan.

'Bill.'

'So, you seem to be doing well for yourself, *Corporal*.'

'Bill, I . . .'

'What? You're sorry? You don't know what came over you?'

'How long have you been out?'

'A while.'

Dunstan took the glass of champagne from Ray's hand and downed its contents in one. He held it out to the waiter to get it refilled, then sipped at his second glass.

'How did you find me?' said Ray.

'Don't flatter yourself, Cross. I go to all the launch parties.'

'Was it hard?' Ray asked.

'What, prison? You get used to it. If you don't, you go under.'

'That boy had his whole life ahead of him,' Ray said, pre-empting Dunstan.

'I didn't tell him to climb on top of that truck.'

'You were flying the plane that cut off his head.' Ray stared hard into Dunstan's dark, quick little eyes. Emboldened by drink, he went on. 'All for your own entertainment and to impress a couple of nurses.'

'I seem to remember you being present,' Dunstan said, adding slyly, 'with your own unsavoury agenda.'

'Bollocks.'

'Quite the poet, aren't we?'

'If you'll excuse me . . .'

'*If you'll excuse me*. You'd never have lasted in my squadron if I'd have known your dirty little secret. You'd have been out on your ear.'

Ray was aware of a gap having opened up between the two of them and the rest of the celebrants, almost as if a space had been cleared in which they would fight.

'There was no *dirty little secret*, as you put it. I had just lost my wife.'

'Your family. That's an interesting topic of conversation. How interested would they be in the sordid details of your so-called lifestyle?'

'You know nothing about me or the way I live my life.'

'It's amazing how chatty some people get when you're maintaining their habit.'

Ray stared into the black holes of Dunstan's eyes.

A third person joined them. Ray's editor brought an immediate calming influence.

'Everything all right, Ray?' asked his editor with a smile.

'This gentleman was just leaving,' Ray said.

'He's right,' said Dunstan. 'I was just leaving. I've got what I came for.' From the pocket of his velvet jacket he slid out a copy of Ray's book.

'I hope you signed it, Ray,' the editor said, placing his hand on his author's shoulder.

'His signature's all over it,' said Dunstan before turning his back and walking in a straight line towards the exit.

'Funny chap,' said the editor. 'Friend of yours, Ray?'

'Not exactly, no,' Ray said, watching the space Dunstan's disappearing back had filled. 'Someone I used to know. Or thought I used to know.'

The encounter with Dunstan at the launch party had left Ray troubled, in particular the former squadron leader's mention of Ray's family. To reassure himself more than anything, Ray took the train to Manchester and followed the by now familiar route out to Hyde.

Everything appeared normal in the Cross household. Nicholas, now fifteen, was as tall and broad as Ray and took a bigger shoe size. Ray suggested a game of snooker in Gee Cross, where he bought his son a half of bitter. Nicholas surprised him by buying the next round. It seemed to Ray that they were more like uncle and nephew than father and son, but there was no denying their actual relationship. It just wasn't a subject for conversation.

The idea that Dunstan might show his face around Manchester and seek to cause trouble was a worry, but in the end it was the *TLS* that broke some difficult news to Ray's parents.

They were sitting in the lounge. The television was on but no one was really watching it. Maybe Ray's parents were, but neither Ray nor Nicholas were paying it much attention. Nicholas was finishing off some homework on the floor – he was doing well at school – and Ray was missing London. From his position on the settee, at the other end of which his mother was sitting, he could just reach the magazine rack with his feet. He pulled off his sock and went fishing among the contents of the rack with his toes. *Radio Times, Manchester Evening News, TLS, Woman's Weekly.*

TLS.

What were his parents doing with the *Times Literary Supplement*? Where had they even got hold of it? In other circumstances a proud son might have sent his parents a copy of the issue containing a generous review of his first collection of poems, but the reviewer in this case had interpreted a number of the poems in terms of the author's presumed sexuality. Presumed around literary London, perhaps, but not in east Manchester. And even then only presumed or guessed at. Ray had never publicly acknowledged his sexuality, but he wasn't a fool. He had known that people would talk and that talk had a way of spreading from one community to another. But from Bloomsbury to Hyde? He had feared the intervention of an embittered ex-con, but Dunstan had been beaten to it – at least as far as putting Ray's parents in the picture was concerned.

Ray turned to look at his father, ensconced in the armchair across the narrow room. His face didn't leave the television, but he gave what Ray interpreted as a tut of disapproval.

Ray returned to London the following day without having had that conversation with his mother and father. He imagined they would have said nothing to Nicholas and he also guessed they would have removed the *TLS* from the magazine rack and either used it to light a fire or – and here he knew he was pushing it a little – perhaps his mother might have hidden it away somewhere or, at the very least, used it to line a drawer.

◆

The way Veronica found out about Susan Ashton was stupid and regrettable and avoidable and all my fault. We were having a rather pointless conversation about dashboard displays in different makes of car. Particularly the colours used. We were bored with orange. The idea of getting a new car had been proposed some weeks earlier, since ours was not in great shape and we could probably just about afford to replace it. Each time the subject came up, we discussed a different aspect of design or specifications. On this occasion we were talking about dashboard design. I said I liked the red and the blue of a VW dashboard. I even used the phrase 'jazz-club blue and traffic-light red'.

Veronica asked when I had ever seen the inside of a VW and instead of quickly inventing this or that owner of a Passat or Polo whom I knew well enough for them to have given me a lift, or whatever other plausible explanation might have come to mind if I had been able to think a little faster on my feet, I hesitated, and that hesitation was what caught Veronica's interest. Maybe it was her lawyer's training, her hours of cross-examination, or maybe it would have been obvious to just about anybody that I had taken an unnecessary pause before answering. And then there was the answer itself.

'I don't know, someone gave me a lift once.'

'At night?'

'I don't know. Why at night? What do you mean?'

I could hear my voice getting whiny.

'When the headlights are on,' she said, 'the dashboard will glow.'

I could feel myself getting flustered.

'What's the big deal?' I said.

I could feel blood rising to my face.

She questioned me for an hour. Whose car was it? Where was I going? How many times was I driven in this car? I protested feebly, but with horrible self-righteousness, that I was not in a court of law, that I should be presumed innocent until proven guilty. But that clearly was another mistake on my part. I was in a hole and I couldn't seem to stop digging. We established an uneasy truce and slept on it, but in the morning she was cold and distant. She went off to work and I took the children to nursery and then I went to work as well.

When I came home I saw that, unusually, she had got home before me. She was in my study going through my desk drawers, picking books on the shelves and flicking through them before dropping them on the floor.

I didn't feel the hesitation had been sufficient to provoke this level of suspicion. I wondered what subtle changes to my behaviour there might have been during the week the affair lasted.

Perhaps I'd given the game away long before the hesitation over the VW dashboard, but Veronica had had no reasonable provocation. Maybe the mad cleaning session on the Saturday after returning from Feltham and finding that Veronica and the twins had gone out? Maybe that had sowed the seed?

'What are you looking for?' I asked her.

'Evidence,' she said. 'It'll be here somewhere. It always is.'

'Don't you think you ought to be picking up the children, not going through my private stuff?'

'You see, if anyone had asked me, I wouldn't have said you had any *private stuff*.'

'This!' I gestured at the mess she had made. 'My desk, my books. It's my property.'

'Oh don't be so fucking pompous!' she snapped. 'And why don't you get the kids, since they obviously mean *so fucking much to you?*'

I said I wasn't leaving her there to destroy my room, which she said was a further indication of my guilt. I did go and get them and once they were in bed she went to work again – on me. And eventually, under further pressure, I cracked. I knew, of course, that a confession at this stage was of very little value to me, but I felt a compulsion to be entirely honest now that the secret was out.

I told her about Susan Ashton, that it had started at the staff development weekend, and had finished a week later, and that during that period we had had sex twice.

Entirely honest, but not entirely forthcoming.

Veronica wanted details.

'Where?'

I stared at the floor; I held my head in my hands; I wanted to travel forward to a time however distant when Veronica might have forgiven me and we might have moved on.

I told her about the Golf GTI at Hatton Cross Underground station car park. I felt like a kid caught sneaking his first cigarette. And then I told her about the Saturday morning in Feltham and I felt even worse, because if the episode in the car had been spontaneous, the visit to Feltham had clearly been planned and executed with complete disregard for either the consequences or the feelings of Veronica, should she ever find out. I considered telling her that I had set out for Feltham with the intention of informing Susan Ashton that it was over, over almost as soon as it had begun, that I had felt I owed it to her to tell her in person rather than over the phone. But it was easy to see how that would be received. I was going out of my way to show respect and consideration to a woman who was virtually a stranger while I demonstrated nothing but contempt for the woman I had married.

I remained silent.

Veronica, too, fell quiet. Too quiet. She withdrew into herself. She continued to speak to the twins in a normal voice, determined to try to protect them from what had happened. She spoke to me only when absolutely necessary, but, after a week or so, without any detectable bitterness. There was, instead, a cadence of indifference in her tone that crushed my unrealistic hopes of an early rapprochement. I offered apologies; I didn't try to justify what I had done. I told her I hoped she would forgive me in time and not just for the sake of the children, but also because I loved her and I knew I had done a stupid thing and I regretted it.

'I don't know, Paul,' she would say in response to these approaches. 'I don't know.'

It wasn't until four or five months later that Veronica did know how she would react to my unfaithfulness – and it wasn't with forgiveness. Maybe she knew sooner and spent some time planning it? Or maybe it wasn't planned? Although it was hard to believe there was any spontaneity involved.

She started going on trips to the north-west, taking the children with her. I offered to look after the twins for the weekend if she wanted to get away on her own or with friends, but she insisted on taking them with her. The impression I formed was that I was so bad – or at least had done such a bad thing – that she didn't want them left in my sole charge for a whole weekend and preferred the inconvenience of taking them with her.

I didn't know what she was doing or whom – if anyone – she was meeting. I wasn't sure I had the right to ask. On one occasion I did ask and she told me to mind my own business.

'I have a right to know where my children are,' I said.

'*You gave up your rights to your children,*' she screamed at me, '*when you fucked that bitch in her car!*'

I recoiled from the venom of that attack and retreated to my study where I sat hunched over on the floor with my back to the door. In truth, I was a little frightened of her, and that made me feel less of a man – less of a human being – than she had already made me feel, in direct response, of course, to my completely indefensible act. I stared into the glass eyes of the mannequins. I gazed blankly at the books on my shelves, running my fingers over the spines. I would take out the odd volume and smell the pages and gently press the pads of my fingers against the covers, as once I might have touched a woman. Veronica, of course, but I even started to feel nostalgic for Susan Ashton, and that only served to make me feel worse.

For the first week, I had slept on the floor of my study with only the mannequins for company. There was not enough room even for a single mattress, so I folded up a double duvet and used that to lie on. Veronica had moved the twins into our room with her and on the only occasion that I suggested I be allowed to sleep in the twins' room she shot me a look that was perfectly clear in its meaning and intent. I was careful not to do anything – on top of what I had already done – that might push Veronica into leaving me and taking the children. I couldn't even raise the subject – I couldn't beg her not to – in case somehow it tipped the balance and what she had been holding in reserve as the last possible and most vindictive course of action suddenly seemed to become the only path open to her.

I didn't want to lose her. I still loved her and I harboured an increasingly desperate hope that we might one day reach some kind of neutral ground across which we both might walk, with predictably extreme slowness, until we met in the middle.

Above all, I didn't want to lose the children.

In my lowest moments, when I faced the prospect of never achieving reconciliation with Veronica, I concentrated on the twins. I held their tiny faces in my mind, their eyes as wide and trusting and innocent as ever.

Veronica and I were both from the north-west. We had met in London and come together as exiles. She had no family left up there, so I knew she was not visiting relations. I thought about following her. Hiring an anonymous saloon and trying to keep at least three vehicles between us on the motorway, on the occasions that she strapped the twins into the car seats and went by road. Sitting in the next carriage when she took them on the train. But just as both methods of pursuit seemed doomed to failure, so too I feared her reaction should I be spotted.

Then she started dropping his name into conversation. Trevor this, Trevor that.

'Who's Trevor?' I asked.

'An old friend.'

'Do you see him when you go to Manchester?'

'That's my business.'

'It's my business if you've got the children with you.'

'No, it's not. It's really, *really* not.'

These conversations tended to take place in front of the children and so were conducted in an uninflected tone. I doubted the children were fooled. At other times, she wouldn't talk to me at all. But the name-dropping was clearly deliberate.

Whenever I had the chance, I took the children out on my own. We went for walks using the buggy and I talked to them endlessly. I wanted them to remember the sound of my voice. I told them all about me and my life and my family, my background, which was their family, their background, I told them, and they should always remember that. Whether any of it went in, I didn't know. I took them to the London parks and to patches of waste ground by abandoned stretches of inner-city motorway. When they both slept at the same time, I sat and watched them breathing. The almost imperceptible rise and fall of the chest, the tiny tremor of the squiggly blue vein at Laura's temple. When Jonathan woke first, as he invariably did, I talked to him in a low voice until his sister woke too. I didn't try to poison their minds against Veronica and nor did I presume that she was doing that to them against me, although with regard to Trevor, I feared the worst.

Veronica tried to limit the opportunities I had to be alone with them and her trips to Manchester became more frequent. I decided I had to force the issue.

'I know you've told me it's not my business,' I said, 'but I would very much like to know – and I *do* think I have a *right* to know – what is going on with this Trevor.'

She tapped her cigarette on the rim of the ashtray. She had started smoking, or taken it up again, but was careful to do it only downstairs after she had put the twins to bed.

I had asked her if it was just to spite me and she had scoffed.

'Not everything is about you,' she had said. 'It's not the case that every decision I make is influenced by what you might think or say or do. You really are terribly self-centred, you know, Paul. You have this solipsistic approach to life that, really, is a little bit paranoiac.'

I thought about correcting her English, but decided against it.

Whenever she took a deep drag on her cigarette, her lips contracted around it creating a kind of Japanese naval ensign of tight little lines radiating out from the burning tip that I knew she would one day regret and blame me for. She also winced as she drew the smoke into her lungs. I wondered about the cost to her of this new habit, which she showed very little sign of enjoying.

'We fucked a few times,' she said.

I looked at her in shock. Although it had been obvious that something was going on, I was taken aback by the fact that she had used the past tense. It wasn't like it had just happened. This had taken place, on several occasions, some time ago and I hadn't known about it.

'A revenge fuck?' I said, feeling cold and bitter.

'It was a bit more than that, and like I said, it was a few times.'

'How many times? Are you still sleeping with him?'

'Do you honestly think you have any right to ask me these questions? Any right to an answer?'

I watched a vein throbbing at her temple, the same side as Laura's.

'I do wish you wouldn't smoke in the house,' I said weakly.

She immediately lit up another, closing her lips around it and sucking.

'I think he wants it to be a bit more serious than I do,' she said.

I couldn't tell if this was intended as a concession or a taunt.

Early in the new year, the visits to Manchester having become far fewer, she declared that she had told him it was over. She still had told me nothing about him, other than that he lived in south Manchester somewhere because it was handy for the airport. I had given up asking questions, renounced my spurious 'right to know'.

If he had ever called the house, I had been unaware of it. Occasionally, I entertained the possibility that while he probably existed she had invented the relationship between them. I had no evidence to back this up, but nor was there any proof that they had, as she had put it, 'fucked a few times'.

I was hopeful, then, that our marriage would survive. Whether the Trevor thing had actually happened or not, it didn't appear that anything was happening now, and perhaps this might mean we could get on with our lives. Was it hopelessly naïve of me to think in terms of us now being equal?

Veronica moved the twins back into their own room. She said it was so that she could get a decent night's sleep, but I couldn't help hoping that it might be the prelude to her allowing me to return to our bedroom. Since she was hardly likely to ask me, I dropped a hint by complaining of a bad back from sleeping on the floor.

'You should have thought of that,' she said.

I asked myself what I felt about her having slept with another man and I found that I felt a deep, dismaying sense of disappointment, if it was true, but that I was just glad it was over, if indeed it had ever begun. It would not be a bar, for me, to the resumption of sexual relations between the two of us.

And then she did get a call, not from Trevor, but from the police.

The effect of Trevor's suicide was like a bomb going off.

Two detectives came down from Manchester to interview Veronica at Paddington Green Police Station. The circumstances of the death were such that suicide was by far the likeliest verdict, but this still meant that the police were obliged to rule out every other possibility.

Trevor had been found hanging by a dressing-gown cord from a heavy-duty hook screwed into a false beam concealing an RSJ that ran across the ceiling of his bedroom. The RSJ had been there since the house had been converted into flats and the hook had been screwed into it by a previous tenant who had needed it to get a grand piano in through the windows (which had been temporarily removed for the purpose).

'Had the former tenant not been a concert pianist, Trevor might still be alive today,' Veronica said to me, before blowing her nose.

'He would have found another way. Suicides are extremely resourceful,' I said in an unconvincing attempt to comfort her.

'I don't think that's true,' she said. 'I think suicide is like robbery. Opportunity is as important as motive.'

Trevor had lived in a two-bedroom flat on the first floor of a converted Cheshire lock semi in south Manchester. A former pilot based at Manchester Airport, he had been fired for alcohol abuse. His first officer had raised the alarm when he had noticed, walking behind Trevor to board an early morning flight to Kalamata, that his captain appeared incapable of walking in a straight line. A failed breath test meant Trevor was taken into police custody and subjected to a blood test, which he also failed. He lost his licence, his airside pass and his job, exchanging them for a criminal record.

Trevor's life had suffered an immediate contraction and diminishment. He would ever after be found in only one of two places, either drunk in his flat or flying a model plane in the nearby park. It emerged that he and Veronica were not old friends, as she had told me, but had encountered each other when she had answered an ad he had placed in the personal columns. She felt sorry for him, she told the police, but of course the truth was somewhat different. She had been looking for a way to move back to Manchester with our children and at the same time had jumped at the opportunity for, as I had crudely put it, a 'revenge fuck'.

'I still don't understand why the police would send two detectives down from Manchester to interview you,' I said to Veronica, 'when everything about the case points to suicide.'

'Apparently,' she said, 'he was found in a locked room – his bedroom – and for a suicide verdict you would normally expect an upturned chair or a table or a stepladder. A window ledge if the rope is near the window, which it wasn't. It was nowhere near the bed either. They've got high ceilings those houses. They couldn't rule out the possibility of him having had help.'

In the end, the coroner recorded an open verdict.

Initially, his death seemed to bring me and Veronica closer to each other. I regained my place in the marital bed. We went out to places as a family. But Veronica suffered very black moods and we would have long, bitter arguments that started in various ways but always came back to the same thing – my affair with Susan Ashton. If I tried to argue that Veronica's relationship with Trevor had squared things up between us, she became quite violent with rage, throwing things at the wall and hitting me, her fists raining down on my chest like hailstones against a window.

A month later she informed me she had put the house on the market and had started divorce proceedings. In the circumstances – not least that the case would be handled by a friend and colleague of hers – she expected a swift settlement and there could be no doubt that it would be in her favour. Her retaliatory fling with Trevor would be portrayed as merely that, while my two sex sessions with Susan Ashton would be characterised as a premeditated affair, partly conducted in a public car park.

I asked her what were her intentions regarding the children and she told me that she was virtually guaranteed to win sole care of the twins. The most I could legally expect would be visitation rights, but that, just between her and me, she would do all she possibly could to make sure those children never had to see their father again.

I signal to leave the motorway, but Lewis, whom I had assumed to be asleep, suddenly speaks.

'Keep going,' he says.

'I tend to come off here,' I say. 'Otherwise I always seem to end up going the wrong way on the A5145. Before you know it you're halfway to the airport.'

'I meant keep going past the next junction as well,' he says. '*If* you don't mind. We've not been for our walk yet.'

I cancel the indicator and keep going.

'You've got a really funny way of getting people to do what you want them to do,' I say finally.

Lewis just grunts. I think I prefer him being annoyingly chipper.

When we reach junction 24 he tells me to get off on to the M67.

'We're going to the Peaks,' I say. 'How lovely!'

Half an hour later, somewhere on the A57 between Glossop and Sheffield, he advises me to pull over. I see a layby a little way ahead, so I coast down to that and turn in. The tyres scrunch on the gravel and Lewis opens his door and slams it shut. I can see something white sticking out of the door pocket on his side. I lean over for a closer look. It's my white cotton hat. I remove it and stow it in the glove locker.

'How far are we going?' I ask him once I've got out of the car.

He ignores my question and just says, 'This way,' leading me over a stile and on to a rough path.

We walk down towards a stream first of all, through a glade of deciduous woodland, and then alongside the stream until we come to another stile and a wooden bridge, which we cross. On the other side we start to climb. On our right is a pine wood; to our left, some way below us, is the river the stream was feeding into. The path diverts this way and that around boulders and rocky outcrops and becomes quite steep for a short distance and then levels off as the pine wood on our right falls away.

Lewis walks in front, not looking back. Presumably he can hear that I'm just a little way behind and keeping up with the pace. The ground vegetation begins to change, dominated now by bilberry and heather, signalling that we are getting on to the moor. The incline flattens out altogether and the path widens. Lewis stops and looks back. I draw alongside, breathing hard, and return his gaze.

'*Ksssh-huh-huh.*'

'What?' I ask.

He doesn't reply.

'Back at the airfield,' I say to him, 'how did you get into the car?'

'It wasn't locked,' he says.

'I always lock the car whenever I leave it for any length of time.'

'It wasn't locked,' he insists, his cold eyes staring into mine.

In the distance the drone of an aircraft can be heard, a jet executing a final turn to join the extended runway centre line.

'It's not much further,' Lewis says and starts walking again.

I sigh with theatrical exasperation and come alongside him. We walk in silence for two or three minutes before he starts speaking again.

'He was someone I knew,' he says, 'someone I trusted. He was older than me, almost a father figure. A pilot. Safe, reliable. So you'd have thought. So *I* thought. He said he'd look after Mel and the girls while I was away. I didn't think he meant look after in that way. It would never even have occurred to me to warn her. He didn't seem predatory. Mind you, I didn't know about his drinking.'

'He was a drinker?' I ask.

'A bit. Apparently. Not good news in a pilot. Anyway,' he continues, 'he must have exuded some fatherly protectiveness or summat, because it wasn't like he was a great catch. Whatever it was, Mel fell for it. They spent time together. The girls trusted him. Mel trusted him. *Ksssh-huh-huh. I* trusted him. Big mistake that was.'

Lewis' trousers make a swishing sound as he walks. Our boots push through the heather that encroaches at the sides of the path.

'She only slept with him a few times, he told me later. It annoyed me he couldn't be more precise. I wanted to know. Wasn't like it made any difference, obviously, but I wanted to know. I think it was *that* I hit him for, the imprecision, the not knowing, not caring presumably, rather than for the actual act of sleeping with her.'

Lewis looks across at me from time to time as he tells me all this, as if checking I'm listening and taking it all in. I'm listening, all right.

'How badly did you hit him?' I ask.

'Depends how you mean. I tried to give him a right good smack, but it was soft as shit. He went down, because there was nothing to him, streak of piss; most men would have stayed on their feet.'

'Did you hit him again while he was down?'

'What is this? Am I on trial?'

'Thought you'd be grateful if I showed an interest. You seem so keen for me to hear all this.'

This shuts him up for a while and we walk in silence. At one point the path narrows and he goes in front again. I look at the back of his head. His hair needs cutting. It's only half a centimetre long, but if you're going to keep it short you might as well keep it short, especially with male-pattern baldness. The regrowth emphasises the baldness, and straggles of curly grey hair run down his neck at the back in two lines towards his shoulders. Men who cut their own hair with electric clippers, as I assume he does, always seem to forget you need to take a wet razor to those lines. They grow quickly and become unruly and unsightly like epicormic growth on the trunks of lime trees.

'You said you were away,' I say in an attempt to restart the conversation. 'Where were you?'

'Just away.'

I remember him at AJ and Carol's talking about having been in the Far East. Did he go to the Far East and leave his wife and girls in Manchester? Or had he come back from the Far East and gone away somewhere else, somewhere closer to home? Was he away a long time or only a few days? The thing was, even if he told me, I wouldn't necessarily believe him. But his story lacked detail. It was imprecise, like the pilot's confession. What was his name, the pilot?

'What was his name?'

'Trevor something.'

'Trevor?'

'Yeah.'

Now I remain silent.

Trevor.

'Fancy losing your wife to a guy named Trevor, right? Just makes it worse, doesn't it? Fucking *Trevor.*'

I look at the ground as I walk, the name *Trevor* going around in my head.

'Look!' Lewis says, pointing towards a change in the land-scape in the distance. The moor starts to climb again and falls away on the left-hand side. 'That's where we're going.'

He starts walking again.

'She wasn't that into him,' he says, picking up his thread. 'She went to the aerodrome to finish it.'

As we continue walking, the topographical feature up ahead acquires more definition. A small hill rises from the plateau, which itself falls away, surprisingly, on one side.

'He told me he'd sensed she was losing heart and so he invited her to bring the girls to the aerodrome and promised he'd take them all up in his four-seater. As soon as she arrived, he said, she told him it was over. So he challenged her, asked her why she'd brought the girls if that was the case? Did she really think he would take them up if she'd just dumped him? She said none of them had any desire to go in his plane and that it had been over in her mind on the way out to the aerodrome and it was twice as over now.

'He begged her to change her mind, said he was in love with her and without her he didn't know how he would carry on. He told me all this. It was as if he thought by telling me, he was somehow making it better. But, you know, there was no making it better.

'He claimed he told her that if she didn't relent, he would kill himself and how would she like to live with that? She, at this point, according to him, told him to fuck off. I kind of admire that, whether in front of the girls or not. And she walked away – as you saw on the DVD. She's walking away holding Emily's hand. But Trevor sticks his own hand out and calls after Anna, because he's picked up on the fact that she's more sensitive than her sister. He plays on her emotions, making it look as if he's simply offering a spin in his plane, while subtly letting her know that if she doesn't help convince her mum to come back and at least talk to him, he'll be as broken as the dead birds he knows she cries over in the garden. That was Mel's fault for telling him that stuff.'

We're at the base of the hill now and there's a clear choice either to go around it or to start climbing. Lewis stops and stands with his hands on his hips.

His story is almost over.

'So that's how he tricks them into his plane. They take off and Mel is still telling him it's over, even as she's looking out and enjoying the view, or what she can see of it out of a Cherokee with the bloody wing in the way. He says he's not saying much at this point, whether that's because he's hoping the experience will do his talking for him or because he believes her and has decided upon his course of action. He told me the latter, but I wasn't convinced. I think he was trying to dig himself an even deeper hole than he was already in. Punishing himself as harshly as he could.'

'What do you mean?'

'They flew over the centre of town and then out here. Takes about fifteen minutes with a decent westerly wind behind you. He told me that he spotted this hill from two or three miles away and just made a beeline for it. Didn't deviate from his path for a second, even when Mel and the girls started screaming. The subsequent investigation suggested otherwise, that a couple of vital components failed at the same time and the crash was much more likely to have been a tragic accident. That was the official finding, anyway, whatever he said. The thing was, there was compelling evidence for both propositions, expert evidence on the one hand and possibly unreliable testimony on the other.'

'They crashed into this hill?' I ask him.

'On the other side. I come up here once a month or so.'

'He was the only survivor?'

Lewis gives a small nod.

'But they found the wreckage, presumably, and the bodies?'

'Of course, but I keep hoping, you know. Have you ever

read *The Bell Jar*? There's a line in it I find comforting. Gives me hope. "It worked around in the back of my mind like a needle in the body.'"

Lewis looks up at the hill, his eyes scanning the regular brush strokes of green grass blown in the same direction by the wind, looking for a glimpse of red or yellow. A scrap of material, a fragment of bone.

3

The Sniper

'If someone said the tragic will always be the tragic, I wouldn't object too much; every historical development takes place within the embrace of its concept.'

Kierkegaard

N icholas won a place to read languages at university.

At Queen Mary College, University of London.

He had talked to his nana and grandad about his desire to apply to London and they had said it was his decision. They were proud that he was going to university at all. He wanted to tell them he didn't want them to think he was rejecting them by going to college in the city where his father was living, but he didn't. He wanted to tell them that he loved them very much and that he appreciated all the sacrifices they had made for him. He knew that his father sent small amounts of money whenever he could, but he also knew that those contributions had been paid into a separate account to be made available to him when he needed it, and that all the cost of bringing him up had been borne by his nana and grandad. He knew that neither his nana's part-time position as a dinner lady at a nearby school nor his grandad's job working for SELNEC, one of the local bus companies, would have paid all that well, but he had never worn a dirty school shirt or a pair of socks with holes in them.

He was offered a place in an inter-collegiate hall of residence, Hughes Parry Hall in King's Cross, so that he found himself mixing with medics and dental students and civil engineers as well as arts students like himself. London was so big and so full of different sources of excitement and amazement and entertainment and enlightenment, he couldn't take it all in. Whatever he sampled, he knew there would be more of it and a hundred different choices besides. College was only part of what was on offer. He went to hear live music, to repertory cinemas that ran double bills and all-night shows, to exhibitions in art galleries you could have fitted his grandparents' whole estate in, never mind their house.

His attendance record at college was not the best, but he was still on site, hidden away in an office in the union building writing reviews for the arts pages of the college newspaper, having discovered that not only could he do this, but it was also a good way to get to see films for free – and before they came out. He sat looking at his first byline – Nicholas Cross – so hard and with such intense excitement that he was surprised the paper didn't ignite in his hands.

He arranged to see his father, who was now living above a shop in Camden Town. They didn't meet there, but on the South Bank in the coffee bar of the National Film Theatre. Ray looked at the newspaper his son handed over and he felt almost intoxicated with pride, but also humble as he knew he could take no credit for his son's accomplishments. He was grateful beyond words, however, that it was important to Nicholas to show him what he had done.

'And – Dad,' Nicholas said, becoming increasingly – surprisingly – comfortable with the nomenclature as he got older, 'I've met a girl. Liz, a medical student.'

'That's great, Nicholas. Tell me all about her,' Ray said, beaming. 'I mean, if you want.'

Nicholas' failure to turn up at college – for German lectures in particular – started to become a problem. He knew he should have done single honours French, but he'd wanted to impress his grandparents, wanted to pay them back, and foolishly opted for combined honours. His German was poor but he had a plan, to read all the set texts in English translation. Kleist, Kafka, Schiller, Böll – this stuff was relatively easy to get hold of. But the Goethe, surprisingly, was not available, and to make matters very much fucking worse, it was not available in roman script in German either, only in Gothic type.

He sat in his room one evening – the night before an essay deadline – trying to ignore the competing sounds of music playing in neighbouring bedrooms. The book lay open on his desk under the lamp. He stared at the bold, angular, spiky letters. The page looked like it had been created by someone in a secure ward with an italic fountain pen that was leaking ink. It might as well have been Arabic or Mandarin.

Maybe a drink would help?

He went down to the bar and stared at the range of drinks on offer. He was not a big drinker; he'd never really had the opportunity. The girl before him, a dental student from Guy's, ordered a vodka and orange. He asked for the same, but the orange failed to mask the taste of the vodka, which was like some kind of foul-tasting blunt horn trying to force its way down his throat. He tried a gin and tonic. How could something utterly colourless taste so sharp and unpleasant? A vodka and grapefruit worked a little better and a gin and lime – with lots of lime – seemed to be the answer. It was important to have enough lime to hide the taste of the gin completely. You needed enough lime that it – the lime cordial itself – caught the back of your throat and made you cough.

Nicholas went back up to his room and stared at the sticklebacks and spider crabs swimming across the pages of his book. The drink didn't help him make any more sense of Gothic script, but it made a nonsense of the looming deadline, which no longer seemed so important (or not until the following morning, at least).

Ray and Nicholas started to meet up more regularly, often on the South Bank or at the Tate or the National Gallery. Sometimes Nicholas invited Ray to come along to film screenings and afterwards they would get a coffee at Bar Italia and discuss the movie. They talked about Ray's work, which Nicholas had started to read. Ray wanted to hear what his son thought of it. Indeed, when he was getting together material for a second collection, Ray asked Nicholas if he would mind reading the manuscript and giving him feedback. Were there some poems that shouldn't make the cut? Was there too much of one type of subject and not enough of another? Nicholas said he was honoured to be asked, but that he felt inadequate to provide the kind of feedback he sensed was required.

'Bollocks,' said Ray.

Nicholas read the manuscript and he talked to Liz about it and then he read it a couple more times and arranged to meet up with Ray at Patisserie Valerie in Soho. Ray didn't show. Nicholas waited half an hour then phoned Ray's flat from a call box. There was no answer and his father appeared not to have an answer machine. He went back to Patisserie Valerie and waited a further half-hour. He called again later that day, but there was still no answer.

He kept trying.

Ray called the phone on Nicholas' floor at Hughes Parry a few days later. He apologised. Something had come up, he said.

'Don't worry about it,' Nicholas said, trying to keep the hurt out of his voice.

'Look, Nicholas, I'm sorry,' Ray said, sounding like he meant it. But still. 'I lead something of an unpredictable life. Sometimes it's hard to keep appointments.'

Nicholas wondered if that was what he was, an appointment. Like the dentist.

'I've got to go, Dad,' he lied. He had to get off the phone.

He went down to the bar, but it was shut, so he went to the pub on Marchmont Street opposite the Brunswick Centre and ordered a pint. He drank it swiftly, feeling nothing more than a slight unsteadiness, and so he switched to spirits. A vodka and grapefruit. A gin and lime. And another gin and lime, and another – asking the bartender to be generous with the lime. The bartender complied until he suggested Nicholas might have had enough.

All his life he had expected nothing of his father. He knew it was a mistake for that to change.

He went back to the hall and shut himself in his room and ignored people when they came knocking. He ignored Liz until she threatened to go and get the floor tutor to bring a master key.

'What the fuck is this?' she demanded. 'How often does this happen?'

'It doesn't,' he said. 'It doesn't happen. It happens very rarely. It happens very fucking rarely, OK? I'm very fucking surprisingly together, all things considered.'

He sat on the floor, pressed up against the wall, his hands clenched at either side of his head. He was trying to stop it from spinning.

The next message Nicholas got, to say that his father had called, he ignored. Liz managed to persuade him to call Ray a few days later, but there was no answer. He was aware that there would be some kind of deadline for getting his remarks about the manuscript back to his father. He wasn't conceited enough to think that his input would have any great value, but Ray had asked him and so, for all Nicholas' hurt pride, he was determined to finish the job. He didn't have his father's address in Camden Town, but the address of the publisher was easy to find. He parcelled up the manuscript with a hand-written note and dropped it off.

A few days later, Nicholas walked out of the hall. A familiar figure was leaning against the railings across the street.

'I got your package,' Ray said. 'I wanted to thank you.'

'No problem, but I'm late for college.'

'I'll walk with you – if that's all right?'

'Sure.'

Ray ended up taking the Tube with Nicholas over to the East End. He told him again that he was sorry he'd failed to turn up and he asked him to trust him – he said he knew there was no reason why he should – but he would have turned up if he'd been able to. From time to time, he said, there was a possibility he might fuck up with his timekeeping. It didn't mean he didn't want to see Nicholas, he said. It didn't mean he didn't—

At that moment the train hit a set of points and Nicholas didn't hear what his father had said. It was a shame because he had a sense it had been something his father had been building up to, but, partly because of that, it didn't seem appropriate to ask him to repeat it.

'It meant a lot to me,' Ray said, 'not only that you read the manuscript and commented on it, but that you went to the trouble of delivering it. You had to go out of your way and you must have been pissed off at me for letting you down. So, thank you.'

Nicholas smiled and Ray put an arm around him and pulled

him in for a hug, which Nicholas allowed him to do. It was the closest they'd been, physically, in years.

'You know, if you've got problems,' Nicholas said, looking at his shoes planted on the carriage floor, 'you can talk to me about them. Whatever it is.'

'Thanks, son. I will,' Ray said.

During Nicholas' second year, he continued to do well in French and badly at German. He worked hard on the college paper, attending press screenings – in the presence of broadsheet critics Derek Malcolm and Philip French and, on one memorable occasion, director Andrei Tarkovsky – when he should have been sitting in Professor Fowler's lectures on Brentano, Goethe and Tieck. His relationship with Liz deepened and that with his father survived one or two more instances of apparent unreliability on Ray's part. He waited on tables in the summer and got three weeks' work experience at *Time Out* magazine, where he did a lot of filing and was asked to write a review that didn't get used. But, more importantly, he got the bug and he knew what he wanted to do after graduating.

His third year was spent in Paris. Liz's course wasn't the kind you could dip in and out of, and Ray explained that certain circumstances prevented him from travelling, though he didn't elaborate on what they were. As a result, Nicholas came back to London as frequently as funds allowed. He told Liz he was worried about his father, concerned that he might be on drugs. It would explain a lot of his behaviour – the unreliability, the restrictions on travel.

'Maybe he's on a methadone programme?' Liz suggested.

'For all I know,' Nicholas said, 'he could be supplying. I can't see how else he makes a living, unless he has a private income. Which seems unlikely. There was an RAF pension, but I don't know if he still gets that.'

Liz shrugged.

'It could also explain the presence of that weird guy at the party,' Nicholas said.

He'd timed one of his trips back to coincide with the launch party for Ray's second collection, *Flight Path*, which was dedicated to the memory of Russell Flynn. At some point during the evening, Nicholas had seen a balding man in an unfashionable velvet jacket being firmly encouraged to leave by a couple of senior editors with a lot of literary lunches under their belts. He'd also spotted his father watching the ejection from a safe distance and visibly relaxing back into a conversation with a journalist and a publicist once the intruder had left the premises.

'And why he's so thin,' Liz said.

'Is he thin?' Nicholas asked.

'He seems thinner to me,' she said.

'So you think he's using rather than supplying?'

'He could be doing both. But he's definitely lost weight.'

'You see him less often than I do,' Nicholas pointed out. 'You're more likely to notice change.'

In his final year, Nicholas threw himself into German. A warning from the dean that he would almost certainly fail if he didn't buckle down seemed to be the catalyst. As for the language, a few days in West Berlin, taken at the last convenient moment before the exams, over Easter, when it happened to be snowing in that part of Germany, helped more than he would have imagined possible. Just being surrounded by the language, both spoken and written, made an appreciable difference to his understanding and ability to express himself. In the end, he got a decent result, an upper second, and like most of his fellow non-vocational students went straight on to the dole. He tried to get more work experience, but that wasn't happening either. He kept his hand in by contributing to fanzines. He and Liz, who was still studying, found a flatshare in Archway with two other medics. He saw his father on a fairly regular basis and came to agree with Liz that he was looking gaunt. Ray seemed as cheerful and positive as ever, offering words of advice at the same time as warning Nicholas he was the last person in the world who should be handing it out, particularly on the subject of careers. However, he was able to fix his son up with a week at his publishers – unpaid. Nicholas enjoyed it, but not as much as he had *Time Out*. He retained vivid pictures in his head of the ramshackle office, with its countless in-trays and bulldog clips, wire pigeonholes, sheafs of paper sliding off desks, dodgy swivel chairs. He loved the teetering towers of CDs, videos and books, the overflowing baskets full of old Jiffy bags ready for reuse.

The publishers' office, by contrast, was much quieter and more sedate. He didn't see any authors until his last day when a small flurry of activity greeted the arrival – and departure soon afterwards – of a first-time novelist.

Nicholas came off the dole to work a short-term contract at the National Union of Students as Information Officer. On the staff there he met another writer, Judith Meadows, whose first novel, *The Summerhouse*, had just been published. He proudly told Judith who his father was and she gave him an enigmatic smile. Over the next few weeks he realised all her smiles were enigmatic. He found a copy of *The Summerhouse* years later in a second-hand bookshop. On the back was a large photo of the author wearing an enigmatic smile.

The NUS contract terminated, Nicholas was sitting in the

flat in the middle of the day writing another round of job applications when the phone rang.

He left the applications unfinished on the kitchen table and took the Tube from Archway to Goodge Street, then walked the short distance to Middlesex Hospital. He found Broderip Ward without difficulty. It was not how he imagined a hospital ward to be, especially an NHS hospital ward. It looked more like a hotel. A posh one at that. The beds had duvets instead of sheets and blankets. There were telephones by the bed and potted plants dotted around and comfortable seating areas with magazines and coffee machines. He found his father sitting up in bed writing in a notebook, which he immediately closed and put to one side when he saw Nicholas.

'Hello, son.'

'Dad.'

'Sit down, sit down.'

'Dad, what are you doing here? What's wrong?'

Nicholas had learnt nothing in the initial phone call, only that his father was in hospital. He'd made the Tube journey in a state of suspended emotion, but with anxiety building up inside him. The sight of his father – thinner-looking, haggard even – was a shock. He had never before seen his father in pyjamas. There was a rust-coloured sore on his neck.

'Dad?'

'Nicholas. There's some stuff I haven't told you.'

'You're dying!'

'No, I'm not dying. I'm not very well, but I'm going to get better. Do you know where you are?'

'In a hospital. What are you talking about?' Nicholas felt himself getting angry. His father appeared to be playing games.

'This ward,' said Ray gently. 'You might have seen it on the news or read about it. It was only recently opened, by Princess

Diana. There's been a bit of fuss in some quarters. It's too nice, there's too much money being thrown at it.'

There was a silence, which Nicholas broke.

'It's the AIDS ward.'

'Yes, it's the AIDS ward. But don't worry, you are not at risk.'

'I'm not worried about being at risk,' Nicholas snapped. 'You've been sick for a long time.'

'Yes.'

'Why didn't you tell me? All those times you didn't show up, you were in here getting treatment.'

'I was getting tested. Prodded and probed. And treated for infections, yes.'

'Why didn't you tell me?'

'I couldn't tell you.'

'Why couldn't you tell me?'

'Because it would have meant telling you other stuff, too, that maybe you wouldn't have wanted to know.'

'You mean about you being gay?'

Now Ray was silent.

'Yes,' he said eventually. 'You knew? How did you know?'

'I don't know. I just knew. You're my dad.'

'I wish I'd known,' he said.

'That I knew?'

'Yes.'

'Well, I wish you'd felt you could talk to me about it,' said Nicholas.

'I didn't know what you would think. And I kind of thought it would be disloyal to your grandparents, in a funny way. Better to maintain the illusion.'

'Better to tell a lie?'

'A white lie.'

'Is that how you got sick?'

'Probably. Yes. Definitely. I mean, almost certainly.' Ray sighed. 'For a long time they didn't have a clue what was going on. With me and with lots of others. They've got more of an idea now.'

Ray explained about HTLV3 and HIV and AIDS.

'They're calling it a Gay Plague,' he said.

He explained about the haemophiliacs, about the worries over blood.

Nicholas said he'd seen the tombstone adverts and he'd read James Anderton's double-page rant in the *Daily Mail*, which had done the rounds at the NUS when he'd been there.

He took hold of his father's hand, which he was pleased to feel grip his tightly.

'Do you have AIDS?' he asked.

'No, I have HIV.'

'So why do you have to be in here? Will you get to leave?'

'I had a bad turn. My T-cell count went down, but it's already back up. I'll be out of here in no time. I may have to come back in, but then I'll get out again. That's how it's going to be.'

There was another silence.

'I wish you'd told me.'

'I wish I had, too.'

And that was how it was. Ray was in and out of Broderip Ward for years. Nicholas got to recognise many of the regulars on his visits. Sometimes Ray was sicker than at other times. He talked to Nicholas about his work, about poems he was struggling with. He would show him drafts and ask his advice and Nicholas would protest that his advice was worthless, but he liked being asked and he offered his opinions. Eventually, Ray started planning a third collection, working title *The Sniper*.

The title poem, over several pages, was set in a holiday resort on the Mediterranean. People having fun sailing, canoeing, swimming in the sea, doing laps of the pool. Playing tennis, water polo, beach volleyball. Socialising at the bar, making new friends, eating together in the open-air buffet-restaurant where they would queue for eggs in the morning made by a spatula-wielding Greek chef called George with a hat as tall as he was. And all the while, a sniper moves from one rooftop to another, from hotel to beach bar, trattoria to taverna, picking off victims one at a time with a high-velocity rifle. Efforts are made to find and eliminate the killer, but he always seems to be one step ahead. The holidaymakers, meanwhile, instead of deserting the resort or cowering in their rooms, carry on as before, intent on having a good time, just hoping it won't be them next. They take time out to attend the funerals of the dead, but life must go on.

Life for Nicholas and Liz turned a dark corner when Liz fell pregnant and while they were both happy about this, and started looking for a flat for just the two of them, the pregnancy did not proceed in a normal manner. After six weeks Liz developed an infection and had to be rushed into the Whittington Hospital. Not only did she lose the baby, but the infection left her sterile without hope of ever conceiving again. Before the pregnancy, babies had been a subject they had raised only rarely, but they had both known it was something they very much wanted for the future, once Liz was qualified and Nicholas was earning, too.

Dark times. Ray, feeling well and keen to do something to cheer up his son and his partner, threw a party in their honour at his flat in Camden. He invited his friends and theirs. Nicholas recognised one or two faces from Broderip Ward. His father introduced him to Oscar Moore, whose novel *A*

Matter of Life and Sex, he had just read, in floods of tears for the most part, and to David – just 'David', no surname – an architect in his late sixties. Watching his father with David – the ease and familiarity with which they negotiated each other's company and anticipated each other's needs – Nicholas wondered if they were long-term partners.

Nicholas got a job at *Time Out* and he and Liz did move out of the flatshare into a rented flat of their own, so to speak, in Finsbury Park. Over bowls of black pepper soup at the Jai Krishna on Stroud Green Road, Nicholas asked Liz to marry him and she said nothing would make her happier. When they met up with Ray for dinner in Islington and told him the news, Nicholas asked Ray to be his best man and Ray burst into tears. He said it would be the proudest day of his life. He then joked that they'd better not hang about, though. Nicholas found those jokes, to which Ray had become partial, rather difficult to take, but he assured his father that they were not planning a lengthy engagement.

They married at Marylebone Town Hall on Euston Road and took over one of the cheap Indian restaurants on Drummond Street for the reception. Nicholas' grandparents came down from Hyde, their first visit to the capital for longer than anyone could remember, including them. In a bid to keep costs down, Nicholas and Liz had not engaged a professional photographer, but had asked a friend of theirs, Simon, to do the honours. Nicholas asked Simon to make sure he got a shot of the family group on the Town Hall steps: Ray and his parents with the bride and groom. Liz's parents had emigrated to Australia and separated. She had lost touch with her father and the wedding was arranged too quickly for Liz's mother to be able to come. Nicholas remarked that he had never seen his father in a collar and tie before; wiping sweat from his forehead with a handkerchief, Ray agreed that it was the first time since he'd appeared in court that he had worn such attire. Ray gave a short speech that contained a couple of jokes and a handful of personal remarks that had many guests in tears for different reasons. As the evening wore on, Ray unbuttoned his collar and removed his tie. As he leaned across the table towards Nicholas to say something, a rust-coloured sore or scab could be seen on the side of his neck. Nicholas tried to ignore it and Ray pretended he didn't know that Nicholas had seen it.

Late in the evening, Simon the photographer entered the Gents to find Nicholas and his father in an embrace. Ray was clasping his son's head against his chest while Nicholas' shoulders rose and fell as sobs tore through his body.

Two weeks after the wedding, Ray was back on Broderip Ward. He told Nicholas he thought it could be a long stay this time. Nicholas gathered up an armful of unwanted review copies from the box under the books editor's desk at *Time Out* and walked over to the Middlesex.

He waved to a couple of faces on entering the ward. His father was occupying the same bed as he had the first time Nicholas had visited him. He smiled as Nicholas started unloading the books. A bound proof from Faber, *This Is the Life* by Joseph O'Neill; a collection of stories by Mark Richard, *The Ice at the Bottom of the World*; Adam Lively's *The Snail*. A handful of crime novels – a new blah blah mystery, an Inspector So-and-so novel – and one or two unknown quantities, first novels from new names put out by small presses, the sort of thing published more in hope than expectation and chucked straight in the charity boxes at books editors' desks across London.

'I'm sorry there's no poetry,' Nicholas said. 'The poetry

editor takes it all. There's the odd thing left, but believe me, I'm doing you a favour by not bringing it.'

'About that,' Ray said, 'I want you to do something for me. Look in that drawer. There's a key.'

Nicholas took a set of keys from the drawer by his father's bed.

'Keys to the flat,' Ray said. 'I wanted to get that collection sorted and delivered before I came back in here and I ran out of time.'

'You'll be out again soon and can do it yourself.'

Ray tried to smile. 'I don't want to waste any more time,' he said. 'I want it tidied up and delivered. You'll find it all on the machine in a folder marked "Sniper". All you need to do is make sure I haven't forgotten anything obvious, then print it out and post it. You'll find the address there, too, somewhere. Same lot, anyway. They've not moved.'

'I'll take care of it for the time being,' Nicholas said.

Ray was sweating a lot and tended to use the books Nicholas had given him to fan himself with rather than for reading. There was a rash of tiny pustules across his chest and more telltale Kaposi's sarcomas had appeared on his neck and at the top of his back. His bones were sticking out of his pyjama jacket, creating hollows where perspiration collected. He kept telling Nicholas to go back to work, that there was nothing to see here, move on, show's over. He managed to stretch a smile across his increasingly skull-like features. Nicholas did leave, but not to go to work. He hired a car and drove to the outskirts of Manchester and then around the M63 to Hyde and he knocked on the door of his grandparents' house. One visit to London in twenty-five years and now they were expected to go again for the second time in two weeks? Nicholas knew it wasn't the upheaval of leaving home or the effort required for travel that was putting them off. They had never accepted their son's sexuality. To them he was still the young Post Office worker who had married the bingo caller, for good or bad; or the young airman on the other side of the equator but still the right side of the sexuality divide; if not the innocent young boy they had brought up to embody the right values and follow the rules of normal behaviour.

'You may not have another chance to see him,' Nicholas advised them.

He went out for a walk to give them a chance to talk and when he came back his nana took him into the morning room, which had lost the paraphernalia of childhood but kept the brighter colours.

'I can't see your grandad going,' she said.

Nicholas decided to see this as encouraging and he called Liz to let her know he was stopping the night and would be back the following day. In the morning, he rose early, made a coffee and sat in the back garden listening to a blackbird singing. He wondered if his father had ever done the same. Tea instead of coffee, perhaps. When he went back into the house, his nana was putting her coat on and collecting her handbag from the telephone table in the hall.

'What about Grandad?' Nicholas said.

'I don't think so,' said Nana.

Nicholas paused, thinking hard, wondering what more he could do. His grandparents were proud people.

He shouted upstairs, 'We'll be leaving in a couple of minutes, Grandad.'

There was no answer.

'Come on, Nana.'

They left the house and Nicholas started the car. They sat in it for a few moments with the engine running and then Nicholas depressed the clutch and selected first gear.

'Just a minute, love,' Nana said.

Nicholas looked out of the side window, which allowed him to see the front of the house. Everything was still. Then he saw movement behind the frosted glass and the front door swung inwards and his grandad appeared. He closed the door, locked it and stumped down the path. He stood at the kerb by the passenger door, clearly expecting his wife to give up her space in the front seat for him. With a barely perceptible sigh, she opened her door and eased herself out of the car. Nicholas shook his head and stared out of the windscreen. His grandfather lowered himself into the front seat, leaving the door to be closed for him, and then Nana climbed into the back.

'All set?' Nicholas asked and didn't wait for a response.

When Nicholas saw the look on his father's face as the three of them walked on to the ward, he knew it had been worth it. Fearful, grateful, relieved, humble: all of these expressions guttered like dying candles in the recesses of his sockets. Nicholas watched his grandad progress slowly down the ward, every muscle contracted, making sure he came into physical contact with nothing that might infect him. Nana had cast her eyes on her son the moment she'd stepped through the door and she allowed his deep-set gaze to reel her in without any concern for her surroundings.

They sat around the bed. Nicholas had taken his father's hand and given him a hug, as much to show his grandparents there was nothing to fear as for the contact itself, but so far they had kept their hands to themselves. Nicholas went to get some drinks and when he came back he observed that Nana had moved closer to the bed and was holding her son's bony, cannulated hand.

Nicholas spoke to the consultant to ask if he should try to persuade his grandparents to stick around for a night or two.

The doctor said Ray was not in immediate danger, but that he was unlikely to be leaving the ward any time soon.

'If at all?' Nicholas asked.

'Your father is at the end stage.'

Nicholas drove his grandparents back to Hyde that evening. There had been a handshake between Ray and his father, and Nana had kissed her son and hugged him and cried. Nicholas saw them back into the house and turned down the offer of a bed. He embraced his nana and thanked her and shook his grandad's meaty hand, the old man's grip still fiercely strong, and thanked him too. Nana, in turn, thanked him for taking them and bringing them back; his grandfather remained silent on the issue, but Nicholas was confident he had done the right thing, at least by his father.

Ray died three weeks later, at 10.17 a.m. on 19 April 1992. Nicholas was with him, holding his hand, having gone to visit on his way into work. Ray had been conscious for the first hour of the visit and Nicholas had told him that just the night before he and Liz had taken the decision to do something they had been considering for some time: they were going to adopt a child. Nicholas said that while theirs might not have been the most conventional father–son relationship, it had ultimately inspired him to become a father himself.

'I don't know,' he joked to Ray, 'I get the sense you've enjoyed being a dad and I want some of that, too.'

In response, he felt the slightest increase in pressure from his father's grip.

Nicholas also reassured him that the publishers were very happy with the new collection and were pressing ahead with publication in the autumn.

'Thank you, by the way,' Nicholas said, 'for the dedication. It means a lot to me.'

This time there was no answering squeeze. His father had gone.

The funeral, at Highgate Cemetery, was well attended. Nicholas recognised a lot of people from the party his father had thrown for him and Liz at the flat in Camden Town. One or two patients from Broderip Ward came and the consultant was spotted at the service, too. Ray's parents both made the trip; Liz looked after them for the day.

'I'll be next,' said Nicholas' nana. 'You wait and see.'

'You're as fit and healthy as me,' Nicholas said. 'Healthier, I suspect.'

'I've got a line of tablets to take every morning as long as your arm,' she said.

'It's this new GP she's seeing,' said Nicholas' grandad. 'I think he's trying to keep the pharmaceutical companies in business.'

'I don't think they need much help,' Liz said with a laugh.

'Isn't there an argument that says they have to charge a lot for drugs to fund new research?' said Nicholas.

'There's certainly a lot of money being spent on research for HIV and AIDS drugs,' Liz agreed.

They fell silent.

As part of the service, Nicholas read an extract from the title poem of his father's forthcoming collection.

The Sniper was published in the autumn, as planned. Nicholas and Liz hosted a small launch party at the flat in Camden, which Ray had left to them in his will, much to their surprise as they had not known he even owned it. Nicholas discovered it had been a present to Ray from David, the architect. David, it turned out, had been providing Ray with financial support for years. They had had a long-term open relationship.

At the party, Nicholas said a few words on his father's behalf. He kept half an eye out for a balding intruder wearing a velvet jacket that might by then have become fashionable again, but there was nothing to worry about on that score. The party was well attended and some appreciative reviews followed in the poetry press, alongside respectable notices in the *TLS*, the *Guardian* and *Time Out* (by the poetry editor, who could be considered impartial).

Nicholas and Liz registered with the Adoption Agency and got the ball rolling there. They filled in a hundred forms and submitted to a thousand interviews, or so it began to seem to them. They took to observing certain parents when they were out and about – and Liz sometimes came across them in the NHS – and they wondered why such people were not subjected to the same rigorous testing they were having to go through. They read about cases in the news involving parents' abuse of children. They became extremely sensitive to the subject. Nicholas' own unusual upbringing was the subject of particular scrutiny.

'Anyone would think we were convicted murderers or rapists,' Liz said, aghast at the latest test of suitability.

'Or drug addicts who are going to leave needles lying around for their adopted children to play with,' Nicholas added, similarly disgruntled.

There were numerous false starts and delays and there were times when one or other of them started to lose the will for battle. But finally, in spring 1994 they had their first face-to-face meeting with Jonny, who was very nearly four years old. He was very quiet and withdrawn, uncomfortable meeting people and uncomfortable, it seemed and according to the reports, with himself – with his body, his intellect, his emotions. But he had been through some tough times, like a lot of children up for adoption. He had seen some trauma. Nicholas and Liz were put fully in the picture, but they didn't hesitate for a moment. Liz said later that she felt as if her heart jolted or shifted position on meeting him. She knew it was silly, she added, because it's not even in the heart that you really feel these things, but in the stomach or gut, but she insisted on the heart. She felt, she said, that when he reached out his little hand to shake hers, he didn't stop there but carried on somehow and his hand passed into her chest where it grasped her heart and gave it a squeeze.

They had more face-to-face meetings, completed further interviews with assessors and psychiatrists and all manner of folk and finally the handover took place.

'It's like Checkpoint Charlie,' Nicholas whispered. 'Or North Korea.'

Finally, in May 1994, they were a family. They were living, the three of them, in the flat in Camden Town. They didn't expect it to be straightforward.

And it wasn't.

Birthdays were difficult. Jonny's fifth birthday came around in May 1995. Nicholas and Liz felt caught. They wanted to listen to others and take advice, but at the same time they didn't want to. They emphatically didn't want to. They didn't want to do things the way they had been done before, because clearly that hadn't worked, so they wanted to do their own thing, but it had to be right. They couldn't afford to make mistakes. By 1995, children's birthday celebrations had already started to become much more elaborate affairs than during Nicholas' childhood, which admittedly had been far from typical.

They organised a party at the flat inviting children from

school. It soon got out of hand as Jonny refused to accept the result of any game in which he was not declared the outright winner. When the candles were lit on the cake he refused to blow them out, or to let anyone else do so. When one child did manage to blow them out, Jonny started screaming until Nicholas relit them and asked the other children to let Jonny blow them out himself. But again he refused. In the end, frustrated and embarrassed, Nicholas blew them out and Jonny focused on the dark coils of smoke rising from the blue and white candles, his face set like a mask.

The party went downhill rapidly. Jonny bit and scratched other kids and ended the afternoon wearing a dress he had somehow physically removed from one of the girls. Unusually for a little boy's party, most of the guests had been girls. Jonny had not asked for any boys to be invited, but Nicholas and Liz had tried to do what they thought was the right thing by insisting on a more balanced guest list. Parents who stuck around, hovering uneasily at the edge of the party to wipe food off chins or to check that little Sammy or darling Annabel was not given too many fizzy drinks, were quietly outraged at Jonny's behaviour, exchanging shocked expressions and openly glaring at the young offender while offering strained and patently false smiles to Nicholas and Liz.

Both parents thought it a good idea to try to involve grand-parents as much as possible. There was a vague plan for Liz's mother and her new partner to come over from Perth at some point, but it really was very vague. Nicholas encouraged his grandparents to increase the frequency of their visits to London, but his grandad disliked leaving the front room, never mind Manchester.

'What about you, Nana?' Nicholas asked. 'We could meet you at Euston and then it's just a couple of stops on the Tube.'

'I don't know, love. It's a long way and the GP says with my heart I shouldn't be going on long journeys.'

'Well, we'll just have to come up and visit you and Grandad.'

They went up on the train on a Friday. It was a tight squeeze in Nicholas' grandparents' house, Nicholas and Liz in the spare room and Jonny having a bed made up on the floor of the same room out of the cushions from the settee downstairs. They took these up at the end of the night, and transferred Jonny from their bed to the floor while he was asleep.

'Your grandad's getting quite frail, isn't he?' Liz whispered as they lay in the darkness listening to the night sounds – the pipes, the floorboards and general settlement.

'Is he?'

It hadn't occurred to Nicholas that this might be the case, but as he thought about it while listening to his son's regular breathing he realised it was probably true. The unwillingness to move very far from the front room was not just inertia or laziness; he moved slowly and unsteadily and even the shortest walk seemed to leave him out of breath. He was nearly eighty, after all.

'I wonder if, while we're here, we should offer to do some shopping for them or something?' Liz suggested.

'You're right. Good idea. I'll offer in the morning.'

At the breakfast table Nicholas watched Jonny eating. He seemed to concentrate intently on his bowl of cereal. Nana had been out and bought a selection pack of miniature cereal boxes, by some distance the most expensive way to buy cereals, but what child can resist those miniatures? His features seemed to sharpen when he was engaged in a task, as if absolutely everything in the world at that point was focused on his successful consumption of breakfast. His cheekbones seem to angle forwards, his lips reach out and actively seek the spoonful of cereal. There had been a question mark at one point over whether he might be on the spectrum for autism, according to the Adoption Agency, but this had been ruled out. There was nothing wrong with him that hadn't been directly caused by the trauma he had witnessed and experienced.

'Is that nice, love?' Nana asked.

She was sitting, arms folded on the table in front of her, across from Jonny.

'Yes, Nana.'

'Yes, thank you, Nana,' Nicholas corrected him.

'Yes, thank you, Nana,' said Jonny through a mouthful of Coco Pops.

Nicholas had suggested that Jonny call his adoptive great-grandparents Nana and Grandad, just like he did.

'What's all this about not going on long journeys, Nana?' Nicholas asked.

'It's my heart, love. I've got this heart-valve problem. You know about it.'

'Mitral stenosis,' Grandad's voice announced as he appeared in the kitchen doorway.

'Aye, well. It means I'm at high risk of blood clots.'

'Arterial thrombosis,' added Grandad.

'I know,' said Nicholas.

'And I used to take warfarin for it, but the GP says that can interact with my arthritis tablets, so he took me off it. Off the warfarin, you know. So I'm at high risk of blood clots.'

'To the brain, causing a stroke,' elaborated Grandad.

'Hmm.' Nicholas studied Jonny's empty cereal packet. 'You should have a chat with Liz, you know, Nana. Get a second opinion.'

'Can I have some orange juice?' Jonny asked.

'Can I have some orange juice, *please*?' Nicholas reminded him. 'I'll get it,' he added, addressing Nana.

He squeezed past Grandad in the doorway and took the orange juice from the fridge. When he had returned and poured Jonny a glass, he spoke again.

'Fridge is looking a bit bare, Nana. Why don't you let us do a bit of shopping for you while we're here?'

'All right, love. You can take the car. It needs a run out. I don't know when it last had one, to be honest.'

'Great. I'll just get His Lordship dressed. Come on, sunshine. Let's get cracking.'

Liz stirred while Nicholas was getting clothes for Jonny, who was in the bathroom.

'You have a lie-in,' Nicholas said, lying down next to her for a minute. 'Give us a kiss.'

'Mmm,' Liz said, pulling up the blanket and sheet, and adding sleepily, 'I wonder if we should buy your grandparents a duvet for Christmas.'

Nicholas got Jonny ready and they headed downstairs. Nana had produced the car key. It was sitting on the kitchen table.

'It ought to start all right,' said Grandad. 'There should be petrol in it.'

'Don't worry, Grandad.'

Nicholas took Jonny outside.

He unlocked the car and it was only at that point that he realised he didn't have any kind of child seat. He wondered if it would be OK to go ahead without one. But very soon it became clear that this was a side issue.

The moment he opened the back door of the car and encouraged Jonny to get in, the boy refused.

'Come on, Jonny. We're going to get some shopping for Nana and Grandad. You don't want them to go hungry, do you? And anyway, we're staying with them for the weekend, so if we don't get any shopping there'll be nothing for us to eat either.'

But Jonny turned his back on the car and crossed his arms.

'Come on, Jonny,' Nicholas said, trying to turn him around and push him lightly in the direction of the car.

His face wore that mask of concentration that Nicholas had seen at the breakfast table. He seemed quite determined not to get in the car. Nicholas released his pressure and knelt down in front of his son.

'What's up, mate? Why don't you want to get in the car?'

'No,' Jonny said, stamping his foot. 'No no no no no no no.'

'What's the matter?'

Jonny started screaming. 'No! No! No!'

'Look, this is ridiculous,' Nicholas said, getting cross. 'I think you're a bit old for tantrums, sunshine. You are five, remember. Five-year-olds don't generally behave like this. If they don't want to do something, they give you a reason and they do it without screaming. Also, if Daddy wants you to get in the car, I really think you should just, you know, get in the car, don't you?'

Jonny screamed.

Nicholas took hold of his shoulders and the boy squirmed and fought to get free. Nicholas tried to keep hold of him, but the boy bit his hand and managed to break away, running back to the front door and when he found it closed he tried to get around the side of the house.

'Jonny,' Nicholas shouted, 'Jonny. Stop it. Forget the car. I'm not going to make you get in the car, OK, but you have to stop screaming and fighting and especially biting. Right? You have to stop all that right now.'

The front door opened and Nana appeared.

'I don't know what's going on,' Nicholas said to her. 'I opened the car door and he went ballistic. I don't think we'll be going in the car.'

When Jonny saw that Nana had appeared, he ran to her and threw his arms around her legs. Nicholas caught his breath when he saw her rest her hand instinctively on top of Jonny's head.

Jonny eventually calmed down, but he stayed in the house with Liz and Nana and Grandad, while Nicholas drove off on his own, puzzling over what had happened and feeling depressed by the incident.

Later, when they were in bed and Jonny was asleep, Nicholas talked to Liz about Nana and her various tablets, those she was taking and those she was not.

'It's true what she says, that warfarin can interact with what she's taking for her arthritis,' Liz said, 'and it's also true that taking her off it increases the risk she'll get an arterial thrombosis. She could have a stroke. But she could have one whether she sits on a train to London or not. That seems a bit odd.'

'Really?'

'I suppose if she's got bad arthritis, she can't really be getting up for a walk around while on the train, so maybe it makes a kind of sense. But still . . .'

'Is it worth her asking for a second opinion?'

'It depends. I'm sure she doesn't want to get the GP's back up.'

'Yes, but how often do people die because they don't question the advice they are given? Because they don't ask for a second opinion?'

'Only once.'

'Very funny.'

'Sorry. I don't know, but not often, I wouldn't think,' Liz said. 'If you're worried I can ask around about him.'

'Thanks. Just to set my mind at rest.'

Liz did ask around – making a number of phone calls first

thing in the morning while Nicholas was getting Jonny up and dressed – and most of the feedback was good. The doctor was well liked by patients, maybe less so by colleagues, one or two of whom thought him a little odd. But these were people who didn't work with him closely, other Manchester GPs who did occasional locum work at the surgery.

They were due to return to London in the afternoon. Nicholas proposed that they drive out towards the Peaks and find a nice pub for lunch, but there was the question of whether his nana and grandad would want to, and, more to the point, whether Jonny could be persuaded to get in the car without another screaming fit. In the end, Nicholas' nana suggested that Nicholas and Liz take Jonny for a walk in the park while she prepared a salad for lunch.

The boy ran off and seemed to enjoy having the freedom of the place – a windswept scrap of land on the side of a hill. A couple of swings and a rusting roundabout. No railings.

While Jonny played, Nicholas and Liz talked. They decided there was no particular justification for questioning the judgement of the GP.

◆

The year turned: I was glad to see the back of 1992 but I had no cause to believe that 1993 would be an improvement. Veronica was no more than civil to me; the marriage was over, in all eyes but those of the law. She made no attempt to restrict my access to the children. She was too clever to present my legal team with useful ammunition. Legal team. A university friend specialising in conveyancing and operating out of storefront premises between a charity shop and a bookmaker's in Basingstoke.

I took the children to nursery and picked them up most days. I wasn't trying to rack up credit; I knew there was no point. I was just trying to maximise the amount of time I spent with them. I knew I would always have photographs, but I didn't want to forget what they smelt like. I didn't want to forget the touch of their skin. The sound of their breathing as they slept.

I kept up appearances, but when I was alone I couldn't concentrate on anything. I couldn't read or write. If I put a CD on, I took it off again before the end of the first track. I would put the radio on, but it could have been broadcasting static for all I took in. I went for long walks. I walked on different routes out of London, each time in a straight line – Uxbridge Road, the A5, the A1. I just kept going until exhaustion forced me to stop and then I would catch a bus or the Tube to get back. I thought about nothing other than the upcoming case and the twins. Their faces went round and round in front of my eyes until they started to blur and I had to get their picture out of my wallet to fix their faces in my mind again.

There was a chance, or so I believed at that stage, before the case reached the courts, that I'd get visitation rights. A good chance. But I felt that chance receding once the case began and Veronica's lawyer, predictably, went to town on the dogging angle. My own counsel just ended up sounding pathetic as he objected that we had not been dogging because we had not been deliberately performing for the entertainment of others.

'They had sex – let's not put too fine a point on it,' said Veronica's lawyer, 'they had sex in Ms Ashton's vehicle in full view of other car-park users and hundreds, if not thousands, of airline passengers coming in to land. Those with window seats, anyway.'

214

A titter ran through the courtroom.

The case did not reach a conclusion on the first day.

'I think we still have a good chance of visitation rights,' my lawyer friend said to me.

I looked at the defeated slope of his shoulders in his ill-fitting suit.

The following morning, Veronica left the house first. The idea that we should have travelled to court together was, of course, absurd. She was going to drop the twins off at nursery and I was to leave the house shortly afterwards. Instead I sat in the kitchen, staring out of the window at the brick wall that separated our house from our neighbours'. I made a cup of tea, but didn't drink it. A greasy film formed on the surface of the tea.

I got a bag from the cellar and packed it with a small number of items. I walked out of the house and placed the bag in the boot of the car. I returned to the house and walked up the stairs to my study. I sat at the desk and looked at the manne-quins – the woman and the two children. I got up close to each one and stared into their glass eyes. They looked real.

I looked at my books, my eye drawn by the repetition, numerous copies of the same book. The same title over and over again. The same author's name. The same colophon.

I got up and left the room. I went downstairs. I stood in the kitchen staring out of the back window. After an indeter-minate length of time I left the kitchen and walked through the hall. I closed the front door behind me and double-locked it. I got into the car and started the engine. I drove around the block. I parked again and switched off the engine. I started it again and drove to the nursery, where I said I had come to pick up the twins. We were going somewhere, I explained. The staff were surprised, but released the children. They were my children, after all. I led them out of the building and to the car, which was double-parked. It was a narrow road with cars parked on both sides and there was no way past my car. Three cars sat waiting. The driver of the first car was leaning on his horn. When he saw me he started to gesticulate. He wound his window down and shouted at me. It was just noise. I strapped Jonathan into his seat, then took Laura's hand and led her around the back of the car to get to the other side. I told the driver of the car behind to shut the fuck up. He got out of his car. I took no notice of him, even when he came very close to me and continued to shout abuse at me. I just made sure that I kept my body between him and Laura. I lifted Laura into her seat and fixed the straps. I closed the car door, aware of the man's breath in my face. He wouldn't stop shouting. I told him again to shut the fuck up and I felt a sudden buzzing in my ear and I fell against the car. My ear started to throb. I realised I had been hit. I opened the driver's door and collapsed into my seat. I managed to pull the door shut and lock it, despite the man's efforts to stop me. He stood alongside the car, his arms tensile bows, fists clenched, white knuckles. His body seemed to vibrate with fury and barely controlled energy. I looked away from him and felt a powerful thud against the door where he had kicked the car. I twisted the key in the ignition and pressed the accelerator to the floor, vaguely aware of another insistent noise just below the screaming of the engine. Because the man had to run to get back in his car, I reached the junction before he was able to catch up with me and there was no way out into the traffic for him to be less than several cars behind me. I tried to change out of first gear, thinking that the noise I could hear was the sound of the engine racing, but I wasn't in first gear and the noise I could hear was the children crying. I checked the rear-view mirror, but there was no sign of the man's car. I overtook a bus and negotiated a roundabout and headed out of London.

The children eventually cried themselves to sleep and didn't wake until I pulled into a service station on the M1, parked up and switched off the engine.

I turned to face them as they stretched and slowly came round.

'Daddy, why have you got a bleed?' asked Laura.

'Where?' My jaw ached as I spoke.

'On your face. You've got a bleed on your face.'

I turned to look in the rear-view mirror and saw that I had a cut above my cheekbone where the man's fist had struck me.

'It's nothing,' I said.

I took the twins with me into the services and bought sandwiches and crisps and drinks.

'Where are we going?' Jonathan asked once I had strapped them both in again.

'For a drive,' I said.

I started the engine and looked for the way out of the car park.

Jonathan asked a couple more times where we were going, but I just kept driving. I checked my watch. It was a little after half past eleven. I pictured the courtroom. The looks of worry, my lawyer's drooping shoulders. I pictured our empty house, a ringing phone. I took the exit for the M6. All the choices I was making seemed preprogrammed. They had nothing to do with me. I looked in the rear-view mirror. Jonathan had gone back to sleep and Laura had her head turned to one side and was gazing out of the window. I didn't know where I was going. I was just driving. I knew what was in the boot, but I wasn't thinking about it. I read the road signs, noticing how the distance to Manchester kept decreasing. Each time I read the name, I sensed a certain lightness on the horizon, which seemed incongruous. I left the motorway at the next junction. I didn't know where I was. I didn't want to know. I just wanted to drive and drive and never stop.

I drove automatically. I turned the wheel when I had to. I obeyed the rules of the road. In terms of where I was going, I simply headed away from everything. The light changed, became softer, yellower. The children made occasional noises, but slept most of the time, lulled by the motion of the car. I pulled off the road, into a field, parked in the lee of a high hedge, switched off the engine. I sat for a moment, hearing a gentle shifting behind me. I checked the mirror. Laura was moving about in her seat; Jonathan was rubbing his face with his fist.

I opened my door and got out. I stretched. I opened the rear door and leaned in. I kissed Laura on the forehead and squeezed into the space between the front and back seats so that I could reach Jonathan also. I kissed him on the cheek and noticed the little round scar at the corner of his eye. I caught a whiff of washing powder or fabric conditioner. I pulled back and exited the car.

I went to the boot and opened it. I took out the black bag and removed from it a coiled length of hosepipe. I put the bag back in the boot and closed it. There was a noise coming from somewhere, but I didn't know what it was. I got down on my hands and knees to affix one end of the hosepipe to the exhaust. This was difficult to achieve but after two attempts I got it in place. I wiped my hands on the grass and dried them on my jeans. I uncoiled the hosepipe and walked around the side of the car. I placed the pipe on the ground and it immediately started to recoil itself. I opened the rear door on

Laura's side and wound down the window a short distance. I picked up the hosepipe and threaded it through the gap, then wound up the window enough to trap the hosepipe without squeezing it too hard. I was still aware of a noise coming from somewhere. I didn't know what it was. I ignored it. I closed the door and got back into the car. I reached round the back of the driver's seat and picked up Laura's coat from the floor. I got out of the car again and stuffed the coat into the gap at the top of the window. I used one of the arms to plug the last bit of the gap, noticing a stain where Laura had spilt something on it. I got back into the car and closed the door. Jonathan was crying and trying to get out of his seat. Laura was watching him. I turned the key in the ignition. Laura was asking questions. I couldn't tell what she was saying. I climbed into the back of the car and squeezed into the space between their two seats. I told the children it was going to be all right. Jonathan's crying got so bad he coughed and kept coughing and I thought he was going to choke. But he was OK. Laura was still asking questions and I was still unable to process the sound of her voice. I could no longer hear the other noise that I had heard outside. I could now hear the chugging of the car's engine. I looked through the gap at the dashboard and saw that there was plenty of petrol in the tank. Now that Jonathan was calmer I undid his seat belt and he moved free of the straps. I leaned forward and around the driver's seat to engage the central locking. I undid Laura's seat belt and encouraged both children to sit in my lap. Laura kept talking and Jonathan was saying something as well. I hugged them both, pulling them into my body. *It's going to be all right*, I told them. *It's going to be all right.*

4

Lumb Bank

'. . . things happen only in the present.'
Borges

I t was either going to be all right or it wasn't. In fact, no,
it wasn't. It was never going to be all right.

It wasn't all right.

I woke up in hospital under police guard. Once the medical
staff informed them that I was good to go, officers removed
me to the police station where I was formally charged with
the murder of my daughter Laura and the attempted murder
of Jonathan, my son.

Some days passed.

I had been assigned a lawyer called Arnold, a tall, well-built
Yorkshireman with a gruff, friendly manner. He had dark hair
cut very short at the back and sides, just beginning to go grey
at the temples, and rimless glasses with red plastic arms. He
walked a difficult line between seriousness appropriate to the
alleged crimes and off-the-cuff jokey remarks, including dis-
respectful references to certain police officers. I asked him at
one point why no one had mentioned my attempted suicide.

'If they ignore the attempted suicide angle, it should be
easier for them to make the murder charges stick.'

'Murder charge.'

'Murder charge and attempted murder charge.'

'But how can there be any doubt?'

'We need to argue you didn't know what you were doing.

The emotional upheaval caused by the impending divorce and probable loss of your children upset the balance of your mind.'

'Temporary insanity.'

'It's our best shot.'

It took a long time for the case to come to trial. Jonathan had made a full physical recovery. I had requested permission to see him, which had been denied. According to Arnold, we could have challenged that decision, but it would not have looked good. A great deal seemed to rest on what looked good and what didn't.

'It's the way the law operates,' Arnold said.

Arnold also reported some chat that Veronica was coping very badly and that it couldn't be assumed that Jonathan would necessarily end up with his mother in the long term.

'Where would he end up in that case?'

'There are different options.'

'None of them involving me.'

'That would be unlikely, even given a good outcome.' Arnold looked at me. 'So how would you feel about Jonathan ending up in the system somewhere?' he asked me.

It was a strange question, coming from him. He had not previously asked me about my feelings. I told him I didn't have any.

He reminded me – he said he was reminding me – that when I had been informed of the charges against me, having been told nothing of what had happened prior to my arrest when I had regained consciousness in hospital, I had broken down and the investigating officer had suspended the interview. I was locked in my cell and a suicide watch was maintained. On the third day, by which time I was quiet and withdrawn, they made the decision to continue questioning me.

'Did you know what you were doing when you attached

the hosepipe to the exhaust of the car?' Detective Inspector Huxtable asked me.

'You don't have to answer that,' Arnold advised me.

'Either I did or I didn't,' I said.

'Do you feel any remorse over your actions and their consequences?' asked Huxtable, rubbing at the bags under his eyes with nicotine-stained fingers.

'My client chooses not to answer that,' said Arnold.

'Either I do or I don't,' I said.

Arnold requested a temporary halt to the interview and we ended up back in my cell.

'I strongly advise you to answer "No comment" to all further questions,' he said.

I tried to follow his advice, but the fact was I didn't care enough about the outcome.

The case eventually went to trial and despite Arnold's best efforts I was convicted and handed a life sentence for murder and a further five years for attempted murder, but given the nature of the case the two sentences could be served concurrently and the amount of time I had spent on remand would be credited to my account, as it were.

In 1993, I began my sentence, in prison rather than hospital, the temporary insanity argument having failed to impress the judge.

Arnold had asked me if I wanted to go on Rule 43 to protect me from other inmates. In prison, if you're a certain class of offender, they stab you with a knife in the showers first and ask questions later. I refused, saying either I'd be attacked or I wouldn't. But one morning in my second week I was standing on the upper landing in a line of men waiting to slop out, when I realised the man standing next to me had received a sharp nudge in the back once he had drawn level with the stairs. I watched him tumble down two flights of metal stairs, hitting his head several times on the way. Word had got out that he was in for the rape of a minor. I decided to try to take control of my own destiny.

People didn't tend to ask you straight to your face what you had done. They were more likely to ask someone else. My cellmate, Joel, who was known to be reliable in one way only, as a gossip, had told me what had led him inside: he had thrown a punch at a debt collector's chin and while Joel, who had apparently always been as thin as a reed, even before becoming addicted to smack, had dealt him a feeble blow it had caused the debt collector to take a step back, lose his footing and hit the side of his head on the sharp edge of a brick wall. Blood everywhere. So Joel told it.

One night, I waited for Joel to fall asleep and then threw a pen at the stainless-steel toilet bowl in the corner. The noise woke him up. Disorientated and flustered, he asked what was going on. I said I didn't know. Nothing. But that I was lying there thinking about what I'd done to end up in a jail cell with a man who'd murdered a debt collector by doing little more than breathe on him.

'No offence,' I said.

'None taken.'

I lay there in silence waiting for him to pick up the baton.

'So, what did you do?'

'I killed a man,' I said. 'I suppose you could say it was in cold blood, or you could argue it was a crime of passion, as my lawyer did, not very successfully.'

'Why did you kill him?' Joel's voice, with its strangulated Glaswegian accent, sounded vulnerable and needy in the dark.

'His name was Trevor.'

'Reason enough,' Joel cut in.

I grunted. 'He was an airline pilot who'd been sacked for being drunk on the job. Anyway, I found out my wife was having an affair with him. She tried to end it. She took my two daughters up to see him to end it, thinking that if he saw she'd got two little girls with her—'

'Twins?'

'What?'

'Are they twins?'

I hesitated. 'Yes,' I said. 'They were twins. She thought if she turned up with the twins and told him it was over he'd just accept it. He wouldn't make a fuss.'

'What do you mean "were twins"?'

'I'm coming to that.'

'Sorry, pal.'

'So, anyway, he made them go up in his four-seater plane. He was allowed to fly small planes. The plane crashed and they all died.'

'Except Trevor, right?'

'Yes, except Trevor.'

'So you killed the cunt.'

'I tracked him down and I killed him with my bare hands. I throttled him. Strangled him. Somehow I even managed to break his neck.'

'Fair play. The cunt deserved it.'

After the visit to the hill where his wife and children died, I don't see Lewis for a couple of weeks. The Residential is looming and I have to make certain preparations for it. The days will be structured, the mornings around exercise-based workshops, while the afternoons will be given over to one-to-one tutorials. During the evenings there will be readings.

Helen emails me and suggests we go on a research trip together, as previously discussed. Helen is from Bristol (I checked the information the department holds on file) and is renting a place in Fallowfield, so I suggest I pick her up one evening and we go for a drive. As we head down Kingsway, an Emirates flight passes over the road ahead of us from left to right. We come off at Cheadle Royal.

'So are we going to John Lewis?' Helen says. Playing with her ponytail, which she has pulled over her right shoulder, she looks very relaxed in the passenger seat of my car.

I smile, but don't answer, as I drive past the exit for John Lewis and past the exit for Heald Green before turning left into the business and leisure park. The plane is very low now, just visible in the distance, perhaps as it passes over Ringway Road.

'I guess that's where you play tennis, right?' she says, nodding at David Lloyd.

'*If* I played tennis, maybe I would play there,' I say.

'My dad plays at David Lloyd,' she says. 'A different one, obviously.'

I laugh. 'Do I remind you of your dad?'

'He's older than you.'

I negotiate the roundabouts and enter the parking area behind an office building of blond brick and smoked green glass.

'You like places like this,' she says.

I'm not sure if it's a question or a statement.

'Their anonymity is interesting,' I say. 'The very blandness that should make them boring makes them interesting. They could be anything. The people who work here by day could be doing anything at all.'

'What about the people who come here by night?'

'Security guards?'

'Isn't this the kind of place you write about where people go dogging and piking?'

'Do I?'

'You gave a reading at uni, remember?'

'What's piking?' I ask, looking at the bright white lights of an approaching plane in the darkening sky over the Stockport Pyramid.

'Isn't it watching? Dogging's doing it and piking's watching people do it?'

'Sounds like you know more about it than I do.'

'I doubt it,' she says, pulling her fingers through her ponytail.

A car enters the parking area and drives slowly by.

'What do you think they're up to?' she asks.

'I think it's a bit early – it's only dusk – but you tell me.'

Helen tosses her ponytail back over her shoulder.

I start the engine and we drive out of the car park and back into the network of wide empty roads and roundabouts that serves the business and leisure park. I take the road for Heald Green and slip the Rachel's CD into the CD player – *Full on Night*. I turn right into Ringway Road and slow down as we pass the Moss Nook. I try to spot another ponytail through the tiny square panes of the restaurant's windows, but there's a car behind us. I press my foot lightly on the accelerator, but the driver behind overtakes me with an angry sidelong glance. We're now beyond the restaurant, but, while there's no longer anyone behind me, I slow down again as we approach the layby on the left. I turn the wheel sharply and pull on the handbrake.

'What's this?' Helen asks.

I show her the runway lights and tell her how it would once have been a good spot to sit and watch planes landing.

I look over my shoulder to see the lights of an approaching airliner.

'If the police come by?'

'They'll move us on.'

'Just that?'

'Depends what kind of mood they're in.'

'Have you ever spent time in a cell?'

'Why do you ask me that?' I snap.

'All right, all right,' she says, palms in the air. 'I have, that's all. And I'm in no hurry to do it again.'

I turn to look at her.

'What did you do?' I ask her.

'I was on a demo. A load of us got rounded up and spent a night in the cells.'

I look out of the window. The plane is almost on top of us. I reach out my left arm and grab hold of something and squeeze.

'What the fuck?' she says.

'Sorry,' I say, withdrawing my hand just as quickly. 'Must have missed the handbrake.'

Helen seems to shrink back against the door.

'We'd better go,' I say.

On the way back up Kingsway I point out Tesco at East Didsbury and tell her about Richard Madeley.

'I don't suppose you've heard about that. You would barely have been born.'

'Very funny. I'm doing my project about book clubs, so I'm very interested in Richard and Judy.'

'In that case,' I say, 'there's somewhere we can have a quick look at on the way back.'

I turn left into Fog Lane and a couple of minutes later I'm turning right off Wilmslow Road into Old Broadway. This wide avenue, its only exit at the far end by foot into Fog Lane Park, is lined by large Victorian houses. Trees run down the middle. I drive up the left-hand side and stop outside number 23.

Helen looks first out of her window, then at me, eyebrows raised.

'They lived here,' I say. 'Richard and Judy. When they were doing their show from Liverpool.'

'Really?' She is impressed.

'Really.'

With her right hand she finds my left and gives it a little squeeze.

Grace emails and asks if we can schedule a tutorial. I tell her it's now so close to the Residential, we might as well wait until then. The truth is I have been avoiding Grace. If she has been happy to agree to a phoner instead of a tutorial in person, that's what we have done. I have tried to limit my feedback to highlighting clichés and any loss of verisimilitude in her dialogue. There are not a lot of problems with her work, but from time to time she fails to meet her own high standards.

I have no control over who attends the Residential; the departmental office handles such matters. Nor can I back out of it, having agreed to do it some months ago. I will just have to see how it goes. Invariably on these residential courses there is one nutjob. There is rarely more than one, but there is always, *always* at least one.

Lumb Bank, an old rambling house where Ted Hughes once lived, is located on the north side of a wooded gulley in a valley above Hebden Bridge. It is operated by a charitable organisation, which runs week-long residential writing courses with two tutors and a guest reader, all three published writers. Some weeks are set aside for groups from universities or other institutions with creative-writing schools, which hire the centre and its staff, and bring in their own students and writers.

My institution's Residential is one of those weeks.

In previous years our department has assigned two tutors to the Residential. But with staffing problems at the university, the department has decided to see if the week can be run by a single tutor. Either that or none of my colleagues wanted to spend a week at Lumb Bank with me.

I arrive on the Monday afternoon. Climbing out of my car, I am greeted by Nikki, one of the three administrators. She shows me around – the main house, the woodshed, the barn and the garden – and leaves me at the door to my room on the first floor of the main house. The room has a double bed, a chest of drawers, a writing desk and chair, and a view over the garden and valley. Below the house is a large field patrolled by a pheasant with a cry that is a harsh metallic squawk. There are also two rams and a heavily pregnant ewe. Beyond this field another one runs down to the river. The far side of the valley rises steeply and is thickly wooded. Here and there, criss-crossing paths can be made out. At the top of the valley side, fifty feet higher than my vantage point, a sandstone bluff stands proud of the mixed woodland; it and the scrubby ridge either side form the horizon.

The students begin turning up around 6 p.m. Grace is one of the first to arrive. Nikki brings a tray of tea, coffee and cake into the main room, a low-ceilinged, white-walled snug with an open fireplace and mismatched chairs and sofas. Grace perches on the edge of a low armchair in one corner where she can look through the poetry magazines and other journals stored on shelves in the alcove next to the chimney breast.

The silence is broken only by the sound of Nikki pouring tea. She hands a cup to Grace, who mutters thanks, and then we all hear the sound of more arrivals and Nikki bustles off to welcome them, leaving me and Grace alone.

'So,' Grace says after a moment.

'So,' I say. 'So.'

In the field below the house, the pheasant gives its industrial croak.

Within an hour, all the students are gathered in the snug. Every square inch of space on the sofas and armchairs is taken. Lawrence Duncan – or Duncan Lawrence – sits cross-legged on the floor. Helen sits at the end of the green sofa with her legs drawn up on to the cushion and her shoes removed. I know one or two of the other students – there's Kieran, who's writing an experimental novel about a bear that shaves off its fur and joins human society; Greg, an American student who has already published a collection of stories in the US and is now writing a novel; Geeta, whom I have advised to abandon her historical novel of Ancient Greece and concentrate instead on a voodoo mystery set in her native Trinidad – but several students I'm meeting for the first time because they are taught or supervised by my colleagues.

Nikki runs though her housekeeping announcements, then I remind the students how the week will be structured. I tell them I've made a grid on the flip chart in the dining room, dividing the afternoon sessions into half-hour slots, and I ask them to sign up for a one-to-one tutorial.

Grace asks if people can have more than one tutorial and I say that if everyone signs up, it's unlikely there will be enough time. She wears a look of slight disgruntlement and I add that I hope everyone will get all the face-to-face time they think they need.

The evening proceeds with drinks, dinner and more drinks. Before anyone gets too drunk I make my excuses and retire to my room, where I keep the light off and sit by the window watching the smokers who have gathered outside in the garden. Grace, who doesn't appear to be smoking and never seems to smell of cigarettes, sits with the smokers yet slightly apart from them. Her broad shoulders seem tense, hunched. It strikes me I have never seen her looking relaxed.

I pull the curtain and switch the light on. I am reading Siri Hustvedt's *The Blindfold*. Thirty pages in, I have a strange sense of déjà vu as if I have read it before and know what's coming next, and yet I'm certain I have never read it and in fact I have no idea what's going to happen. When I start the second part of the novel it takes me a while to accept that it does not follow on from the first part, yet it seems inevitable that the different parts are obscurely connected.

In the morning, I am sitting outside looking across at the sandstone bluff on the other side of the valley when Lawrence Duncan – or Duncan Lawrence – comes and sits next to me.

'Dude,' he says.

'Hiya.'

'How's it going, man?'

'OK.'

'Coolio. Nice view.'

'Yes.'

'You reading to us tonight, then?' he asks.

'That's the plan.'

A small bird with a red face and yellow and black bars on its wings alights on the railing in front of us.

'Do you know what that is?' I ask him.

'It's a bird, innit?'

I smile. 'It's a goldfinch.'

'Cool.'

'Not necessarily,' I say. 'They used to represent death.'

'Wicked.'

'Mind you,' I say, 'most birds have represented death at one time or another.'

'What about tomorrow night?' he asks.

'What about it?'

'Who's reading then? Who's, like, the guest reader?'

'Oh right. Lewis Harris. Writes crime novels. Independent publisher. That kind of thing.'

'Cool.'

After breakfast we all sit around the large table in the dining room and I get the students to do a couple of ice-breaker exercises. First some automatic writing and then I ask them to pair off and interview each other about their novels-in-progress and to be prepared to feed back whatever they've learnt to the whole group once we have reassembled.

'Pretend you are Kirsty Wark,' I say. 'It can be helpful for the interviewee to describe their own novel. Very often you find out stuff about your work you hadn't been aware of.'

When they come back I get people to make a little presentation to the group based on what they've discovered about their partner's novel. Greg partnered off with Grace and he comes back and announces that her novel is about a girl who kills a tramp and that it can be pitched as *L'Etranger* meets *The Bell Jar*. I glance at Grace and see that she is staring right at me.

'Is that all you found out about it, Greg?' I say. 'It doesn't sound a lot like the novel I've been supervising.'

One or two people laugh.

'Well,' Greg says, 'it kicks off in Zanzibar in the 1960s. Or should that be *on* Zanzibar? Like *Stand on Zanzibar*? Whatever.

It kind of tells the story of this kid, how she comes into the world and what happens to her in it and how she ends up trying to leave it.'

'What does that mean, Greg?' I ask him.

'Suicide attempts,' he says. 'Hence *The Bell Jar.*'

'Sounds pretty intense,' interjects one of the other students.

A few more people comment and we move on.

After the session, while people are getting lunch, I look at the flip chart and see that Grace has signed up for one of the afternoon tutorials. I get *The Blindfold* from my room and sit in the garden and read.

Grace comes to find me at 3.30 p.m. We stay outside.

'I like all this stuff about Ray's career,' I say, 'the way it develops. And I like the way you tell *that* story at the same time as telling the story of his relationship with his son, Nicholas. You interweave the two successfully. We're never in any doubt as to which is the more important, yet keeping the story of his career just as prominent helps to ground the bigger story, make it more believable.'

'Thanks.'

We're sitting on the step outside the barn. The garden is wide but shallow and it's just a few feet from where we're sitting to the railing and then there's the drop to the field with the pheasant and the sheep. I spend most of the half-hour tutorial staring across the valley at the woods and the sandstone bluff on the other side while talking to Grace or listening to her, very aware of her virtually uninterrupted stare drilling into the side of my head.

'Is it still a bit clichéd?' she asks.

'Not the set-up or the plot, no, but every now and then you let a line get through that's not really worthy of the rest of it. Like, er . . .' I flick through the manuscript pages in my lap. 'Or just a phrase, like this, "brushing shoulders", when you're talking about the other writers Ray encounters at book launches and so on.'

'Is "brushing shoulders" a cliché, then?'

I pull a face. 'I don't know. Is it? It struck me as one when I read it. Mind you, I'm not even sure if it's right, now I come to think about it. Is it brushing shoulders or rubbing shoulders? I'm not sure.'

'Well, whichever one is the cliché, I can use the other one, right?'

I laugh. 'I suppose so,' I say. I'm looking at the manuscript again. 'This, here. "This gentleman was just leaving." It's TV dialogue. *Casualty. Holby City.* You know, like "I'll see myself out." Phrases you never hear in real life, only on the telly. And not very good telly.'

'Very popular telly, though.'

'Yes, but your novel doesn't feel like a commercial novel.' I turn to look at her. 'And *L'Etranger* meets *The Bell Jar* certainly doesn't sound like it's describing a commercial novel.'

'Greg came up with that.'

'It's a good pitch for what sounds like a pretty serious novel.' We both look out across the valley.

'Meursault in *L'Etranger*,' she says, 'he kills an Arab.'

'Yes.'

'In my novel, it's a tramp rather than an Arab.'

I hesitate. Then: 'Like the workshop piece on campus, written by someone in your group. Was that your inspiration for that element of your novel? Did you borrow it, or was that your piece?'

She doesn't answer. I turn to look at her.

'I think my time's up,' she says. 'I don't want to keep you from whoever's next. Thanks . . . Paul.'

I note the hesitation.

That night we all gather in the snug after dinner. I read to them about the Moss Nook and the runway lights and the waitress with the ponytail and Erica and the Stockport Pyramid and the idea that this life is just a blink in eternity, that what really matters is some kind of eternal survival, if only on the outside, if only by appearance, that appearance is the same as reality, that there's no difference between the inside and the outside, if there's nothing inside, like in a stuffed animal where all the insides have been taken away, leaving only the skin and the appearance of the animal as it was before, how that's no less authentic than the alternative, how you can live a life without feelings, without thoughts almost, if you have to. I read to them about how you can live without regret if you lack the capacity for regret, how you can live without distinguishing between this and that if neither this nor that has any meaning for you, how you can be either alive or dead and it makes no difference, how something can be either true or false and it makes no difference, how a story can be either yours or somebody else's, how you can be either you or another person, how there can either be someone watching you have sex in your car or no one watching, how you can be either the man or the woman, or the man or the other man, or the woman or the other woman, how it can either make sense or not make sense, how you can be either male or female. I read to them about how you can watch either surveillance videos or amateur porn, how you can fly either a Piper or a Cessna, how you can travel either east or west, how you can go in either this direction or that direction, how you can choose either right or wrong, how you can either choose or not choose, how you can be either sane or crazy, how you can either go straight on at the junction without looking or stop at the white line, how it can all either be very important or not make a fuck of a lot of difference.

Though, arguably, most of that is subtext.

They clap when I'm done because that is the convention. I ask them if anyone has any questions and for a moment it looks as if no one has, but then someone asks me who is my favourite writer and I say I don't think I have favourites any more. I used to avoid saying writing was either good or bad and would just say instead whether I liked it or not, whereas now I don't know what I like and what I don't like, nor even if I have the ability or the capacity to like or not like someone's writing, and I think instead in terms of good and bad. There's good writing and there's bad writing. Someone either has it or they don't. This is a line I've heard myself use before – you've either got it or you haven't – in response to the perennial question 'Can you really teach creative writing?' If someone has it, maybe I can help them develop it and write a little bit better; if they don't have it, I can't give it to them or teach it to them and neither can any of my colleagues or any other creative-writing tutors anywhere in the world. If you can't write, you can't write, period. If your writing is bad it will always be bad. If it's good, it could perhaps get better.

There is a pause. Then Helen asks a question.

'We're all writing first novels,' she says, looking around for confirmation and receiving a few nods around the room. 'And we know you have a particular interest in first novels because you selected all first novels for the lit course. What is it about first novels that appeals to you so much? And,' she goes on, deadpan, 'why is your own so difficult to get hold of?'

A few laughs greet Helen's question; a smile seems to be in order.

'I suppose I think first novels are important because it's the first thing the author says about the world. People say they are autobiographical, and many are, but they're not all. Just as often I would say that they are a mistake, or are viewed as a mistake later in an author's career, retrospectively, either by readers and critics or by the author himself. Or herself. Sometimes they're the best thing an author will ever write. They don't know this at the time, of course, and in some cases maybe they'll never see it. In others, maybe they think their first was the best and they never manage to surpass it, but in fact they do. And as for my first novel, it was published by a very small press and it went out of print. Simple as that. I haven't done a Philip Pullman or a John Banville and either disowned or tried to suppress it. Few copies were sold and even fewer remain.'

Helen smiles and nods and then opens her mouth to speak again.

'Well, in that case,' she says, 'I'm even more pleased I managed to find a copy.'

From her lap she produces a trade paperback: orange, black and white on the cover, a stylised photographic image of an Egyptian mummy, a vague geometrical hint of a pyramid in the background. The orange spine with black type: *Rites* by Paul Taylor.

Her trick produces a reaction from the group. One or two jaws hang down; there are even small gasps. It seems Helen is not the only student who has been looking for a copy, but she is almost certainly alone in having found one.

'Would you mind signing it?' she asks, thrusting it forward.

I accept the book and study the cover. The bottom corner has been folded over at some point. The spine is unbroken, but the book looks as if it has been read. It has that slightly loose look about it, the edges of the pages not quite bookshop-sharp. I look at the front cover again, the crease on the corner. A picture enters my mind of my hand returning a copy of the novel to my own bookshelf, back in another life, and doing it too hastily and catching the corner. I open the copy that Helen has handed to me. There's no second-hand dealer's price pencilled on the first page. Copies come up for sale extremely rarely, in any case. Not that they're worth anything. Those that I have located and bought, I've tended to pay more for the postage than for the book itself.

I write 'For Helen, Lumb Bank', then sign and date it.

Her eyes widen as I hand the book back to her.

'Right,' I say, 'I need a drink.'

Wednesday morning, everyone is seated around the large table in the dining room. I announce that we're going to do an exercise about place. The importance of place in fiction. I tell them that I want them to imagine a place that's important to them. It could be somewhere they've known since childhood. Equally it could be somewhere they went for the first time only last week. But it must be a place that has a real resonance for them, for whatever reason. I tell them I want them to write a scene set in this place featuring themselves and one other character. It could be based on a real event or entirely fictitious. It's up to them.

While they're off working on their submissions, I sit outside looking *up* the valley, instead of across it. Rising out of the trees are two huge chimneys, evidence of the march of industry up the river valleys of this part of the world in the nineteenth century. I have walked along the wooded paths that go up the valley, but I don't remember seeing the bases of the chimneys, although I suppose I must have done.

We regather around the large table and Geeta reads first, a

haunting and ultimately very effective piece about attraction and jealousy set in Trinidad. Lawrence Duncan – or Duncan Lawrence – reads a short but powerful scene set in a club where he tells us he has DJ'd; the action takes place the morning after a big party and features the DJ and a traumatised clubber suffering from delusions. Helen sticks her hand up next. I stop doodling on the pad in front of me and sit back and fold my arms.

Dave picks me up in his car and we drive around for a bit. He points out this and that and I smile and nod like I think he wants me to. We stop and watch the planes landing, until we're moved on by the police, who make a big deal of searching Dave's car, saying, Remember the Yorkshire Ripper, we don't want to get caught out like that again. We turn into the car park of a fancy restaurant near the airport and I wonder what Dave's got on his mind. Carpaccio of beef or a roll in the back seat. But we just sit there while Dave's hand hovers over the gearstick and eventually he selects first gear and we are back out on the road.

It's a world of chain-link fences and tatty scrub, razor wire and gravel. The leonine roar of aircraft engines and screech of high-pressurised rubber on runway tarmac. A world of epaulettes and wheeled suitcases and aviator sunglasses and pull on the straps to inflate.

Dave's picturing all this as we drive slowly by, hugging the airport's perimeter. He's thinking ahead to the next workshop, formulating exercises. A sense of place. This is Dave's place. I want him to take me to mine, only I don't know what mine is. We drive north, away from the airport, pull in to the car park of a supermarket on the A34. Dave backs into a space away from the store, pulls on the handbrake and switches off the engine. The heat rising from the bonnet reminds me of a burning car I once saw in a supermarket car park, maybe this one, yes, it was this one, and it had only just caught fire because it had yet to attract a crowd of gawkers and the fire brigade were not in attendance and no one from the store was standing by speaking urgently into a mobile phone. As I watched the thick orange and yellow flames leaping from the windows of the car, windows that were either open or had blown out, flames that reminded me of graphics in a computer game, I saw an apparition through the heat haze rising from the bonnet of the vehicle. I saw a break-fast TV presenter standing alone on the far side of the flames, the only other person apart from me watching the burning car. I tried to see into the car to see if there was anyone trapped inside it, but the flames danced around too much, and when I looked up again, the TV presenter had gone.

Dave starts the engine and we roll out of the car park, heading north again. Wide roads, traffic, cars parked in driveways, stop lights, takeaways, bridges over dismantled railways lines. Nowhere that's ever been anywhere. Street lights come on. Night falls. We turn left, go right, turn second right. We stop outside a large semi-detached Victorian house. I see the number 23 on the gatepost. There are trees in the middle of the road, more large houses on the other side. At the end of the road is a park. It's a road of million-pound houses occupied by music producers, university professors, property developers, celebrity lawyers and TV presenters. I could live in this road, one day in the far future.

Dave puts his hand on my leg, moves it slowly up and down. I turn to look at him.

'It goes on,' Helen says, looking up from her notebook, 'but I don't want to hog the time. Lots of people have to read.'

There are murmurings of protest.

'Aw, what's going to happen?'

'Come on.'

'We want to hear all of it.'

'Great stuff,' I say, 'nicely done. But as Helen says, there are lots of people to read and not much time left.'

I silence the persisting grumbles and ask Kieran to share his piece with the group. Kieran opens up his laptop and prepares to read.

Once the session is over and people are helping themselves to lunch, I check out the grid on the flip chart to see if Helen is booked in for the afternoon. She is not. She has reserved a slot on Thursday.

Instead of getting lunch, I leave Lumb Bank, taking the path that leads up the valley. I pass through deciduous woodland, the path gradually drawing closer to the river on my left. All I can hear is the tumble of the river and the occasional snippet of birdsong. A packhorse bridge takes me across the river and I start walking downstream on the other side. The path climbs away from the river and soon splits. I stand at the Y-junction and consider my options. They are few. Either left or right. Down or up. Or back. I take the right fork that leads diagonally up the hillside through the forest. After ten or fifteen minutes I realise the path is petering out. I face another choice. Either

I go on or I go back. I check my watch: there should be enough time. I decide to go on. Straight ahead, the way looks difficult: outcrops of rock and increasingly dense tree cover with tangles of sharp dead growth low down on the pine trunks that would impede my progress as effectively as barbed wire. If I take a more direct approach to reaching the ridge, it will mean tackling a very steep slope, probably having to go on all fours at certain points. This is what I decide to do. Soon I am hauling myself up the steepest section by grabbing handfuls of tussocky grass and clambering the best I can. Eventually I exit the treeline and the gradient falls away. I am at the ridge. I walk for a further five minutes and I reach the sandstone bluff. I climb on to the top of this and look down across the valley to Lumb Bank on the far side. I shield my eyes; I can see a couple of people in the garden. It's a long way, but one is almost certainly a woman, with long hair in a ponytail. Is Helen the only female student who wears her hair in a ponytail? I don't know. The other person I'm less sure about. The size suggests it's a woman, but there's a mannish quality to the stance. I watch the two figures from this considerable distance, obviously without any idea what's going on between them, but they are standing on the little rectangle of lawn, close enough to each other that they must be talking.

The afternoon's tutorials pass off without incident and then everyone is waiting for the guest reader, who normally arrives some time between 4 and 6 p.m. Three students are in the kitchen on cooking duty; most of the others are scattered around the house and grounds writing or reading. I sit in the garden staring across the valley at the sandstone bluff, remembering standing on top of it only hours before. Out of the corner of my eye I see Grace enter the garden and immediately I slip my phone out of my pocket and hold it up to my ear.

I walk further down the garden pretending to be engaged on a call. At the end of the garden is a cottage, where the administrators are provided with accommodation, and beyond that a path leads off the property, through the woods and down the valley. As I step into the shade of the broadleaf wood, a large dark-brown bird takes off from nearby and flies away from me in a straight line between the trees going down-hill. I have heard owls here at night.

When I return to the garden, Grace has disappeared but a few of the students have started drinking. Geeta asks me what time the guest reader will be arriving and I check my watch, see that it's not far off 5 p.m. and say I'm surprised he's not already here. By six he still hasn't turned up and I walk up the lane to the main road with a couple of the more restless students, to see if we can see some sign of him. When we get back to the house, Nikki asks me if I have tried to call or text him. I tell her I don't have his number. Dinner is served a little bit late, the expectation being that he will show up while we are eating. He doesn't. By 8 p.m., everyone is gathered in the snug. It's clear Lewis is not coming. One or two people voice their dissatisfaction. Helen asks if any of Lewis' books are in the Lumb Bank library, in the adjoining room, and Stephen, who is writing a novel about vampires on Income Support in south Manchester, goes off to check. He comes back empty-handed and says there's no one between Joanne Harris and M. John Harrison.

'Shame,' says Helen, turning to me, 'you could have read to us from his work.'

There is some kind of inflection in her delivery, but it's hard to say what it is. A short collective discussion ensues about Lewis Harris and the possible reasons why he has failed to turn up. Soon small groups form and numerous conversations are held at the same time. While chatting to Stephen about his vampire novel I overhear Helen telling someone else she'd tried to check out Harris and get hold of one of his books but had been unable not only to locate any of his titles, but to find any evidence that a writer of that name existed at all.

Later that night I finish *The Blindfold*. I immediately go back and reread the first page and only then do I realise how clever and sly the author has been.

Thursday morning. I set the group an exercise that requires them to go off and find an object somewhere in the house or garden, or a view that they can photograph, that should inspire a scene in their novel-in-progress. We are to reconvene in half an hour, after they have written as much as they can.

I walk up the lane to the road. By the time I reach the top, my heart is pumping fast and there is a light sheen of sweat clinging to my forehead and the back of my neck. I look one way – the road winds off towards the moors – and then the other. If I started walking to the right I would be in the village in five minutes, and half an hour later I could be down in the town waiting for a train to Manchester. I look at my watch. There are twenty minutes remaining. My scalp prickles. I look down the road. A car approaches slowly. It slows down even further as it reaches the crest of the hill. The driver peers through the windscreen at me. He has a shaved head, a goatee. I swivel and hold the man's gaze while his car comes alongside and then passes me as he drives on towards the moors. I watch the car become smaller and smaller. It turns a corner and is gone.

I walk slowly back down the lane.

In any case, my car is parked by the house.

Once everyone is reassembled in the dining room, I ask who would like to go first. I look around the group. Helen is playing with her ponytail and sitting back from the table. Stephen is bent over his notebook. Grace has her elbows on the table and is either biting her fingernails or removing dirt from under them with her teeth. Her eyes flick up and lock with mine and she removes her fingers from her mouth. She is about to speak, to volunteer to go first. I look away quickly and see Geeta doing some last-minute editing to the page in front of her.

'Geeta?' I say, aware that Grace has raised her hand. 'Geeta, would you like to go first?'

Geeta hesitates as she looks at Grace, who is saying she wants to read.

'Geeta, you go first,' I say.

She collects herself, offers a conciliatory glance in Grace's direction.

'It's very short,' she says. 'And a bit rushed.'

'Please,' I say. 'Everyone's in the same boat.'

Geeta begins to read.

'The clock had stopped just after 9.15 a.m., just after my mother made a funny little croak. She lay back with her mouth slightly open. I had felt then as if a transparent butterfly or dragonfly had emerged from her throat, hovered for a second, then flew to a place where I could not follow. I felt betrayed that she would die just two months after I had come back. That she would not wait. I was just easing into things, trying to ask her about that time when I was sixteen, when I was abruptly changed into a woman, a woman who immediately sustained a terrible loss. I wanted to ask her why she didn't say something, why she would let her own flesh go to strangers. I wanted to ask her about the nature of shame and why was it so important to glue our faces together so the cracks won't show. I wanted to tell her that in Japan, they deliberately made beautiful porcelain with crackled surfaces. I took the clock in my hands and stared into its round face, the long hand just after a quarter past. I wondered at time being stopped for her. For me too.'

There is a hush around the table. Lawrence Duncan – or Duncan Lawrence – breaks the silence.

'That's well cool.'

There are murmurs of agreement.

Someone asks Geeta what her object was and someone else says it's the clock above the fireplace and she nods her agreement at this.

Grace anticipates my asking who wants to read next by raising her arm. The loose sleeve of her hooded top yields to gravity and then it seems as if everyone around the table is staring at the pale flesh of Grace's inner forearm criss-crossed with red weals. A battle between defiance and embarrassment is fought silently inside that strange, square head. Eventually she lowers her arm and pulls the sleeve back into place. She looks down at the pages on the table in front of her and I am not alone in inspecting the white trails of exposed scalp revealed by her somewhat stringy hair. They remind me of the paths visible in the woodland on the far side of the valley.

Grace starts reading: 'One occasion the following year, Nicholas and Jonny travelled to Hyde without Liz, who was on call and therefore couldn't leave London. Nicholas had tried to increase the frequency of their visits. It was important to him to give Jonny a real sense of his adoptive family, a firm grounding in its history.'

Grace glances up and has a quick look around the table before continuing.

As Nicholas and Jonny were arriving, slightly out of breath after the uphill walk from the railway station, a man was just leaving the house. He was short and stocky, thickening around the middle, with dark hair and a silver-white beard. He wore round glasses and a sleeveless, green quilted jacket and carried a bag. He seemed preoccupied and didn't reply when Nicholas spoke to him. With a distracted air he got into a Renault Espace that was parked outside the house and drove off.

Nicholas rang the bell, but nobody came to the door.

'Maybe Nana Grandad gone out,' Jonny said.

'They don't go out that much,' Nicholas said.

'Why?'

'I don't know. I suppose they're old. It's difficult. Maybe Grandad's gone out and Nana's asleep. Or the other way around.' Nicholas smiled at Jonny. 'Let's go round the back.'

They let themselves in via the kitchen door. The house was quiet. Nicholas could hear a clock ticking in another room. The kitchen smelt as it always did, of lemon curd and Bovril and potted meat and vegetables that were just beginning to turn. He opened a cupboard and found a bottle of orange squash so he could make Jonny a drink. The boy sat at the kitchen table while Nicholas went into the front room, but there was no sign of his grandad, who had perhaps nipped out for supplies, knowing that Nicholas and Jonny were due. There was a line of cards on the mantelpiece. Two weeks previously it had been his nana's birthday. He picked each card up in turn and read inside. Seeing his own handwriting made him feel self-conscious. He briefly wondered how old she was and worked out that she was eighty-six. He read his grandad's card, which said 'To my darling wife, with my love.' Nicholas swallowed as he stood the card back on the mantelpiece.

He returned to the kitchen, but the plastic cup sat unaccompanied on the table. From upstairs he heard a voice.

'Daddy?'

'Yes?'

He started walking into the hall and towards the foot of the stairs.

'Nana's asleep.'

'Well, don't wake her,' he said in a loud whisper as he climbed the stairs.

'She's sleeping with her mouth open.' Jonny's voice grew slightly shrill. 'She won't wake up.'

Nicholas climbed the stairs and entered Nana's bedroom to find Jonny holding her by the shoulder and shaking her. He grabbed Jonny's arm and pulled him back, roughly, too roughly. The boy started crying. Nana lay on her back, her bottom jaw hanging open. She looked small, doll-like. Jonny was still crying. Nicholas reached out and gathered him into a fierce embrace.

'I'm sorry, Jonny. I'm sorry.'

They waited downstairs and Nicholas didn't call anyone. He found something for Jonny to play with while he listened for the sound of the front gate. Instead, what he heard was the scrunch of tyres on gravel. He went to the door to see his grandad climbing effortfully out of the car.

'I went to fetch you,' Grandad said.

'I'm sorry, Grandad. You must have just missed us. We walked. Grandad?'

Grandad stopped and looked at Nicholas.

'Come inside.'

'What is it? What have you got to tell me?'

Nicholas took his grandad into the front room and told him what they had found. The old man's face crumpled, his features disappearing, and Nicholas saw tears sprouting from rhinoceros-like folds of skin. He placed an awkward hand on his grandad's shoulder.

'We need to call someone,' Nicholas said. 'I don't know who to call.' And as he said this he remembered the man they had seen leaving the house.

'We need to call the GP, Dr Shipman,' Grandad said.

'If you give me his number I'll call him.'

Within twenty minutes, a car could be heard pulling up outside the house. Nicholas looked out of the window. The same man was walking up the garden path as they had seen leaving the house on their arrival. Nicholas went to open the door. The man looked surprised to see him, but merely muttered something unintelligible and insinuated his bag into the space between Nicholas and the door jamb in order to gain entry. Nicholas watched the doctor's back as he walked upstairs, then went into the front room to wait with Grandad.

Eventually, they heard the doctor making his way downstairs. Nicholas went to open the door and the doctor entered the front room. Grandad tried to stand, but Nicholas went over to him and encouraged him to stay seated.

'She was all right when I left her earlier,' the doctor said, as if it were merely annoying that the timing was awry.

Grandad frowned.

'The doctor was here earlier,' Nicholas explained. 'He was just leaving when we arrived.'

'Her heart gave out,' the doctor said, scratching his chin through his scruff of white beard.

'Her heart gave out? She was fine. She was perfectly fit and well,' Grandad said.

'How can her heart just give out?' Nicholas asked.

'She was eighty-odd.'

'Eighty-six. Just,' Nicholas said, profoundly irritated by the doctor's manner.

'We all have to go sometime,' he said.

'What?' Nicholas shouted. 'Is that the best you can do? *We all have to go sometime?*'

The doctor's face twisted into a self-pitying grimace.

'I'll be in touch,' he muttered.

He turned to go but the doorway was blocked. Jonny was standing there.

Jonny said: 'When's Nana going to wake up? Daddy? *Daddy?* Why won't Nana wake up?'

There is silence when Grace finishes. She keeps her head down, so it isn't immediately clear that she has indeed finished. Also, because she read for so long, much longer than one would normally read during such an exercise, many of those around the table got so used to the sound of her deep, cracked voice, even became mesmerised by it, that they were no longer waiting for it to stop.

But then someone claps and another person follows and soon the whole room is applauding. Finally she looks up – at me. I look away and smile at those faces around the table that are turning towards mine. Slowly the clapping dies down.

'Quite a substantial piece,' I say. 'Hardly half an hour's work.'

'What was your object, Grace?' someone asks.

Resting one of her elbows on the tabletop and picking at her lip with her fingers, she looks at me again.

'My object was Paul,' she says. 'And you're right, Paul. I didn't write all of that this morning. But you are my inspiration. There's no question about that.'

There's a pause while people take this in, each interpreting it, presumably, in their own way.

'I don't know what to say,' I say, reaching for a smile and not quite getting there. 'Does anyone have a question?'

Lawrence Duncan – or Duncan Lawrence – signals that he wishes to speak. I give him a nod.

'I'm just kind of like playing devil's avocado here, dude,' he says to Grace, 'but what you've done there, mixing up the real and the fictional, you know, bringing a real person into your novel, is that OK? How does that play? I mean, in terms of, like, taste?'

'You mean, is it in bad taste?' With the fingers of one hand she is still picking at dry skin on her lower lip.

'I guess.'

'I don't think so, because it really happened.'

'Right.' He nods, and then his eyes grow wide. 'Really? Shit.'

'Yeah, really.'

'You mean it really happened to someone you know?'

Lawrence Duncan – or Duncan Lawrence – is like a man trying to keep hold of a bar of soap. Grace, meanwhile, appears to be carefully considering her answer.

'Yes,' she says. 'It happened to someone I know.'

There is an interesting discussion to be had here about morality and taste, but I'm not about to encourage it. Plus, there are a lot of people with pieces to read and only a limited amount of time. I suggest we move on. I notice that Grace finally removes her fingers from her mouth and as her hand returns to the tabletop it is shaking.

After lunch, I get through the first two tutorials on autopilot. I dish out my standard advice. *Carry a notebook. Read your work out loud. Go for long walks.*

The third slot – the last one of the day – is Helen's. She comes to find me – I'm sitting outside staring at the far side of the valley – and says, 'I've got to get out of here.'

'Good idea,' I say, getting to my feet. 'Where do you want to go?'

'Let's go for a drive,' she says.

'Er, OK,' I say, shooting her a glance, to which she responds with a breezy smile.

I unlock the car as we approach it and she jumps in. I reverse out of the cobbled area in front of the house and drive slowly up the steep lane in first gear.

'Where shall we go?' I ask when we reach the road.

'Which way are you familiar with?' she asks.

'That way,' I say, pointing to the right.

'Go left then.'

I go left.

'So shall I just drive?' I ask after a couple of minutes of listening to the rushing sound of the tyres on the road.

'Whatever you like,' she says, playing with her ponytail. 'You can do *whatever you like.*'

I turn to look at her. She gives me a lopsided smile.

When I see a turning, I take it, and when I see another I take that as well. Five minutes later we are parked in a field, tucked in behind a hedge. I switch off the engine and release my seat belt. I barely have time to register the sound of birdsong from the hedgerow before Helen climbs across and straddles my lap, hitching up her skirt. I put my hands up to the back of her head. I release her hair from the bobble that she uses for the ponytail and she shakes her head, laughing, so that her hair goes everywhere. I have never seen her with her hair down before. There suddenly seems so much of it. She places her mouth against mine. Our teeth clash. Her mouth tastes citrusy. I can hear the birds singing. I trace the outline of her breast through her cotton top. She leans into me with her hips and runs a hand under my T-shirt, over the small soft mound of my stomach. Her other hand goes to my belt. I lift her top at the back so I can undo her bra. With a shrugging motion, she removes this from her sleeve and I stroke her breasts through the top and then underneath the top and she undoes my jeans and I press back in my seat until I can push them down and she helps me and I remember the last time I parked my car in a field and she kisses me harder and her teeth catch my upper lip and I taste blood and I hear birdsong and she removes her top and her breasts rise and fall in front of my face and she presses them into my face and there's blood on her breast and the sound of birdsong is constant and I now know what sound it was I could hear that time above the low growl of the engine and the chug of the exhaust and the increasingly faint protests of the children. That sound that I couldn't put a name to at that time. A sound that should be beautiful both in itself and by association. It's not, though, it's not for me. But then nothing is. Nothing is beautiful. Nothing makes me feel anything. Everything either exists or it doesn't. Everything either has a physical presence or it doesn't. Everything – everyone – is either alive or dead. And that's about all I can say.

Helen climbs off me, still laughing or laughing again. I don't know what is funny.

'Look,' she says.

The car is surrounded by cows. At the windscreen, the driver's window, the back passenger window and the rear windscreen, cows stand with their great heavy heads pointed towards the interior of the car.

'How long have they been watching us?' Helen asks.

'I don't know,' I say, as I study their long eyelashes, their indifferent gaze.

'It's like yesterday morning,' says Helen, 'when I read my piece about me and you in your car and everyone around the table was staring.'

'Were they?' I say, looking at her and then back at the cows surrounding the car, their huge jaws sliding from side to side like machines made of flesh.

'You know Grace?' she says.

I look at Helen again.

'Is she for real?' she says. 'Is she authentic?'

'One might ask you the same question,' I say.

Thursday evening. Everyone is gathered in the snug. It's Grace's turn to read. Half the students are reading tonight, the other half tomorrow. Of those who are reading tonight, all but two have already read and their performances have been received with due warmth and enthusiasm, but there's an obvious tension in the air, a sense among the students that Grace is not done yet.

She has been sitting slightly apart, in a corner of the room. It's a small room and there are a lot of people; someone has to sit in the corner. But still.

She slides forward to the edge of her seat and looks up. Having secured the attention of everyone in the room, she looks down and starts to read.

◆

Most people never meet a murderer. Jonny met two.

At the time when Harold Frederick Shipman was committing his crimes, no one knew he was a killer. One or two had their suspicions; eyebrows were raised and checks were made, followed by more checks, but Shipman went on killing. And although Jonny's nana died almost certainly at the hands of her doctor, that's another story, one that would begin to be told three years later in court. Convicted in January 2000, of fifteen murders, Shipman was told he would spend the rest of his life in prison.

He did.

On 13 January 2004 he hanged himself in his cell using bed sheets tied to the bars of his window. He was fifty-seven, just a day shy of fifty-eight.

Jonny was fourteen.

The first report of the Shipman Inquiry, which followed the trial, had already concluded that the former doctor had killed 215 people. Jonny's nana was not named among them, but that figure would later be revised upwards. The thing was, no one would ever know for sure how many killings could be attributed to Shipman.

Jonny kept files. He had an ever-growing collection of box files filled with press cuttings on the Shipman case. His copy of Brian Whittle and Jean Ritchie's *Prescription For Murder: The True Story of Mass Murderer Dr Harold Frederick Shipman* fell apart through overuse.

Puberty hit Jonny like a train. Nicholas or Liz would often find themselves knocking timidly on the bathroom door to ask Jonny if he was all right, he'd been inside for so long. But shaving your legs and your chest and your armpits took a while and so did deliberately cutting your arms and then waiting for the bleeding to stop.

There were no girlfriends. There were no boyfriends. There was a crush on a rather butch English teacher called Miss Fletcher that was never really going to go anywhere, but Jonny took up all her recommendations for books to read. He was behind in some subjects (science, maths), but he excelled in English.

Nicholas and Liz were determined not to spoil Jonny, but what harm could it do to let him have a laptop and a broadband connection in his bedroom? Like any fourteen-year-old boy, Jonny used the Internet to look at porn, but his consumption of it was not straightforward. He didn't especially like looking at pictures – or videos – of naked women unless they were accompanied by men, and soon he started to wonder if it was the men he actually wanted to look at. So he tried gay sites, but that didn't make the issue any clearer. He didn't know what he liked and he felt he ought to like one or the other. But something inside him was stopping him from developing a preference. He wondered if it was grief or anger, but it didn't seem as direct as that. If he felt desire it was a desire for change, a need to put something right that felt wrong. His dissatisfaction and confusion were linked to what had happened to him, he was sure of that, not so much tied to Nana's death but to an earlier tragedy that was never spoken of in his adoptive family.

One of Jonny's box files contained press cuttings on Shipman just like all the others, but only on top. If he delved a little way down, he would find his secret collection of cuttings on the murder of Laura Taylor and the attempted murder of Jonathan Taylor, twins, aged three. There were blurry pictures of his natural father, whom he hadn't seen since the tragedy. Jonny had been in touch with the Probation Service and found out that his father had spent time in Strangeways and Parkhurst, but since 1999 he had been incarcerated in Wakefield Prison, coincidentally where Shipman ended his days.

When the news broke about Shipman's suicide, Jonny thought for the hundredth time about his father being within the same prison walls as the mass murderer. Had he and Shipman known each other? Had they ever eaten together or folded sheets in the laundry at the same time? But then Shipman was gone and Jonny found that his interest in his nana's killer waned. He kept the files only to conceal the one he maintained on his father.

There was love in Jonny's life; he knew that his adoptive parents were doing their best in difficult circumstances. They cared for him in every sense of the word. They offered affection, which he found impossible to accept. It was like being handed a piece of machinery he didn't know how to use. He felt nothing. Still there was no attraction to other girls – or boys. His flickerings of desire for Miss Fletcher guttered and died. He had an idea, which he'd had for some time and not expressed to anybody. It bubbled away in the back of his mind like a spring in a cavern. He frequented chatrooms, called helplines, saw the family GP, who refused Jonny's initial request point-blank and offered to refer him instead to a psychologist. Pragmatically, Jonny took up the referral. He told Nicholas and Liz that he had issues around grief, trauma and bereavement, which of course was true and would always be true, but when he got to see the psychologist he told her what was in his mind and he reminded her that she was bound by the Hippocratic oath. When she looked doubtful, he insisted that he was Gillick competent. In just over a year's time, he said, he would be sixteen. He had similar discussions with the GP, who said there would be no question of acting before Jonny's sixteenth birthday, with or without the written consent of his adoptive parents.

What had been an idea became a plan, a project, an obsession. It began to seem to Jonny to represent his only chance at any kind of a life. Not just for him, either. That was the point, really. For his sister.

Why should he have been the one to survive? Why not Laura? Maybe if she had survived and he had not, she would have felt the same as he did, that it wasn't right, that what had happened wasn't itself survivable, even for the survivor, without drastic action, fundamental change. Maybe, maybe not. Either or. Either him or her, or her or him. Either one or the other. This was how the cards had fallen – one face up, one face down. All he knew was he couldn't go on the way things were. There was just a chance that by acting now, he could achieve a kind of resurrection, the twins reunited in a single body, in a state of grace.

Jonny kept up the pressure on his GP and at sixteen, after submitting to endless assessments, he – or she – was accepted on to the gender-reassignment programme.

She – Grace – knew how it would go down. Three months of psychotherapy before even taking the first hormones, and then up to two years spent living in her desired gender role before surgery, a period known as the Real Life Experience (RLE). The NHS liked a two-year RLE, since the evidence showed that while many patients made it through the first year, the dropout rate increased during year two. It was the NHS' insistence on the two-year RLE, they believed, that resulted in such a high satisfaction rating among the post-op transgender population.

Even with the two-year RLE, Grace was hopeful she would be able to complete the process and embark on her new life before her father was released from prison, which he would be, she was confident, after a minimum of fifteen years. Life rarely meant life for parents who killed their own children. They were not thought to represent a danger to members of the public. Whatever impulse had driven them to murder their offspring had most likely been smothered, certainly when the prompt for the impulse was the banal, tedious one her father would presumably have cited – the threat of losing one's children through the break-up of one's marriage. Big yawn. Big, big yawn. Little more than an extreme form of midlife crisis, it was in danger of becoming a cliché. An item in brief on page four, relegated to the news 'where you are'. Had it really become boringly common or was it just that Grace – that I – was oversensitive to such stories?

◆

Whether Grace continues reading when I leave the room, I don't know. As I'm packing my bag I can hear a murmur of voices from down below. The layout of the rooms is such that I am able to walk downstairs and leave the house without being seen. The car starts first time and I reverse out. At the top of the lane, a sudden flash of white at the windscreen startles me. I brake and the engine stalls, almost causing me to crash into the drystone wall. Quick, shallow breaths steam up the windscreen, but the barn owl is gone.

Careering down the A646 towards Todmorden, I have to fight an impulse to drift over to the wrong side of the road on blind corners. When I reach the M62, I'm lucky the traffic is light, since my lane discipline is non-existent. I know that if I were to be stopped by the police I could end up back inside. A murderer is only freed on licence. At this moment I don't care if I go back to prison. I join the M60, come off at junction 1 and park the car just off the one-way system in front of a rollover door marked ENTRANCE IN USE 24 HOURS.

The glass sides of the Stockport Pyramid glow blue and green in the purply-orange night. I walk stiffly across the road and force my way through dense foliage, coming up against a blue fence only a little taller than me. I could climb it, but I decide not to. Instead I back away and lean on the parapet over the river. There's a drop of twenty or thirty feet and the water is as flat as a mirror, any turbulence hidden within. A little way downstream the river turns shallow over scattered rocks and debris brought down by flood waters, but where from? Where *do* the shopping trolleys and old tyres get tipped in? Whose old clothes *are* those?

I hear the approach of jet engines and turn around. In the sky to the north-east hangs a pair of white lights, close-set as a spider's eyes, quickly increasing in size and brightness. By the time the plane passes above my head, it is 1,500 feet from the ground.

I walk around to the path between the river and the road. It leads down to the river's edge. The bank is heavily overgrown, colonised by Himalayan balsam, its sickly sweet scent invading

263

my nostrils. Bats swoop low over my head. I follow the path down into a dip and then up the other side. A series of steps on the left leads down to a wooden platform over the river. I walk down and stand on the platform, swaying slightly. The river is not especially high, as there's been little rain, but at this point the waters swirl and eddy. You can drown in an inch. You'd probably die of exposure just wading out in this. All I can see in my mind's eye is Grace – her face from various angles, the scars on her arms, her forest-trail scalp. I try to see Jonathan's features in hers and I tell myself that I can, but I don't know if that's only because of what I now know (assuming she is telling the truth).

After an indeterminate length of time I climb back up the steps and continue down the riverside path away from the Pyramid. I know that on the flat land beyond the fence on my right, which I have heard referred to more than once as the Valley of the Kings, there have in the past been plans to build two more pyramids, but the money ran out. The path narrows and darkens as trees close over my head. The drop to the river is steep and long. I pass a tubular metal pedestrian bridge and keep going. There are gaps here and there in the wooden fence on my left. Brambles and rowan contest the available space; rosebay willow herb appears among the nettles and shrubs on the right-hand side of the path.

I pass beneath the motorway, the concrete bridge low above my head, graffiti adding sparkle to the supporting wall. Beyond the motorway the path curves and descends, following the course of the river. Bats are my only companions, guiding me. Another aircraft slips by away to the left. The path widens. Horses stand motionless in a field on my right. Erect on the remains of a railway bridge, a heron's profile is as still as the slender weeds that sprout from the brickwork. I come to a complicated gate with different access points for cyclists and horse riders. I walk a little way along a metalled road and then encounter another similar gate, after which the path rises and winds through high blackberry bushes and low rowan trees. Power lines approach on the right, strung between enormous bristling pylons. A large bird forms an interrogatory silhouette perched on top of one of these. My blind pursuance of this path cannot silence the questions in my head. How long has Grace known who I am – if indeed she does? (She must.) Was it a coincidence that she applied to the institution where I was teaching or was she several steps ahead of me? Why is she writing what she is writing in her novel? What did she hope to achieve by exposing me at Lumb Bank? *Did* she expose me? Would it have been clear to the other students whom she was talking about? Did my sudden exit confirm suspicions or remove any doubts? What is her motivation? *What does she want?*

I collapse on a humped rise on the left-hand side of the path overlooking the dark ribbon of the river. The bird on the pylon – its neck in the shape of a question mark identifies it as a cormorant – has not moved.

What does Grace want? What do *I* want? What are my choices? That they are fewer now is the only thing I feel certain of. Do I have any at all? Is it up to Grace what happens next? Do I stop or go on? Either or. Do we achieve reconciliation or do I let her destroy me (once again, assuming that is what she wants)? Everything is either or, and inside each either or is another either or, like Russian dolls.

I move off the mound and take a couple of steps down towards the river, unsure what I am doing but feeling impelled to do it. Not really thinking beyond the next few seconds. The river is a channel of black ink. With it I will write the rest of my story. I picture my head going under, unseen by anybody. There is a tree on my right, a thicket of brambles, nettles and Himalayan balsam between me and it. A bird sings. Not the cormorant; a songbird, hidden in the tree. The notes slip out on to the soft night air like some kind of benign alarm or unknown signal. My foot slides on a flattened frond of bracken. I put my arms out for balance, look down and see a corner of gabardine emerging from the vegetation. The tail of an overcoat.

I hear a different sound and look up. A beating of black wings. The cormorant has left its perch.

I bend down, lift the corner of gabardine and see more overcoat material underneath. I drop it and straighten up, prod with a toe, meeting resistance. I sit down again, my previous course of action interrupted. I look at the power lines, at the procession of pylons across the fields on the other side of the river. I watch a plane sideslip towards the airport. I listen to the bird singing from somewhere in the blackness of the tree, its song a repeated pattern of descending arpeggios.

I have never used this path before, but it can't be long before it reaches the playing fields at the back of Parrs Wood High School and then, beyond the playing fields, Wilmslow Road. The Parrs Wood end of the same dismantled railway line that I can access from the humpback bridge near my house can be no more than a third of a mile away. Either Overcoat Man walked here, lay down and fell asleep, never to wake up, or was carried here and his body dumped in the undergrowth.

I find a recently fallen branch still festooned with foliage and lay it over the exposed area of gabardine before returning to the path and walking on, more quickly now, downstream. I turn right up a path perpendicular to the river that runs between the golf course and the school playing fields, and when I reach the top I cut across the Green Pastures housing estate and reach the end of the dismantled railway line. From here it's a straight line; I can be home in ten minutes.

The dismantled railway line will soon be cleared so that the tram system can be extended along it. A line will run from Trafford Bar via Chorlton to East Didsbury. It will take years for the line to be constructed and for all that time, once they have been down here and cleared the way, the path will be fenced off to the public. I think about the crowd of young people I saw jostling Overcoat Man on the humpback bridge. I picture them carrying his body down this path in the same thick, knotted darkness through which I am currently advancing in the opposite direction. They could have done it the night after I discovered the body. I picture Overcoat Man making his own slow, painful way down here instead, either in daylight or at night. I had assumed he was dead when I found him lying in the nettle bed, but he may very well not have been. Maybe he was still alive even now, down by the river? Although I doubt it. I could have been wrong once, but not twice, and in this case I doubt that I was wrong at all.

When I get home, I stand at the window of my study, panting slightly from the exertion. I'm looking down at the humpback bridge over the dismantled railway line and the beginning of the path that leads down to the old trackbed from which I emerged only a couple of minutes ago. When my breath steams up the window and I can no longer see, I allow myself to fall forward until my forehead presses against the cool glass. The misty grey field in front of my eyes swims in and out of focus.

Only when I am too tired to remain upright do I go to bed.

In the morning I walk down the dismantled railway line as

far as the bottom of Burnage Lane, where I stop and listen to the sound of my own breathing. I face a choice. Either I go left up to Didsbury Road and catch a bus to Stockport in order to pick up the car, or I go straight on through the little tunnel and then down to the river and Overcoat Man.

Either or.

Either I'll walk up to Didsbury Road and sit and wait for a bus to Stockport and I'll pick up the car and call Helen and meet her somewhere and either we'll have sex again in the car or we won't but either way I'll never see her again after that. She won't quit the course, but she'll stop attending and it won't be long before someone talks to the university and an investigation is carried out and I will be relieved of my position. It may be impossible to get rid of staff who underperform or who complain about this or that injustice while taking sick leave at the first sign of sniffles, but failure to disclose a previous identity and by extrapolation a criminal record will be reason enough. I'll be out of a job. I'll email Grace, but she won't reply. I'll give it a few days, I'll give it a week, but she still won't reply. I won't know if I expect her to. I suppose I'm not surprised, I'll think to myself.

One afternoon I'll drive down Kenworthy Lane in Northenden. I'll knock on Erica's door, but she won't answer. I'll wait outside in the car. An hour will pass and finally she'll walk down the street, coming home from work. I'll open the car door. She won't want to get in, but I'll persuade her. I'll tell her we'll go for a drink, for a meal, whatever she wants. I'm depressed and confused, I'll tell her, I don't know who else to turn to. With obvious reluctance she'll get in. I'll start the engine and drive the car to the end of the road, where it turns into footpaths and cycle paths that go off into the woods and under the motorway. While I'm in the middle of executing a three-point turn I'll look at the line of four concrete bollards that I'll remember from the last time I saw Erica. I'll remember specifically thinking about driving into them at speed. I'll picture the moment of impact.

I'll still be thinking about the bollards as I'm driving back down Kenworthy Lane towards the main road with Erica in the passenger seat. We'll take a meandering route over to Stockport. There won't be much conversation in the car. I will try, but Erica will resist. We'll reach the roundabout over the river and I'll take the exit for the Pyramid. I'll pull in to the side of the road and Erica will stiffen in the seat alongside and I'll try to reassure her that I don't mean any harm. I'll tell her, I just want to know about the Pyramid. I'll ask her, How can I get inside? Can't you get me inside? What's that window there on the east wall, why is it different? See, one window on the east wall is different. It's not a different size or anything, the windows are all the same size, but it's a different colour. It's kind of blank or opaque, while the others are semi-reflective. What's special about it? I'll ask her.

It's the body door, she'll say. I'll say, What? What's the body door? But she won't say any more about it, just that it's the body door. Perhaps it's something she's heard someone say. It's not even an Egyptian pyramid, she'll remark. It's more Aztec or Babylonian. I'll wonder if she's right. I'll look up at the steps near the summit. Two steps. The clear glass of the apex. An interior ladder goes right to the very top, but you'd climb it on your own. A pyramid is a house for one. Only one person can occupy the highest point at any one time. It's narcissistic, solipsistic; it's about power and the individual. I guess that's why I'm drawn to it.

I'll ask Erica if she can get me inside the building. This will be the last time I will ask her. Either she'll say yes, in

269

which case I will go in there and climb to the second floor and throw myself out of the body door. Or she'll say no, and I'll turn the car around and return to the roundabout. I'll take Didsbury Road and drive in silence right through Heaton Mersey and East Didsbury and Didsbury Village with one hand on the wheel and the other resting on my leg, ready to change gear. When I look down, I'll notice Erica's leg. I'll notice its constant tremor.

I'm not dangerous, I'll tell her. She'll look at me briefly, then back at the road ahead; she'll be like a porcelain figure, fragile, brittle. I'll turn left into Victoria Avenue and I'll drive past the house where they filmed *Cold Feet* while I was in prison and then past the house of Elizabeth Baines and once I'm past the next junction the houses will get bigger and I'll turn right, driving past even bigger houses belonging to doctors and lawyers and drug company executives until I turn left into Holme Road and right at the bottom into Dene Road West and I'll skirt the speed bumps with the nearside wheels as I floor the accelerator. The stop sign will be obscured by the overgrown bush, the white line hidden by the last of the speed bumps. I'll drive straight across Palatine Road. A car travelling from north to south will pass behind me so close it will feel as if it's passed right through the back of the car. The woosh of air, the shriek of the engine. The scream of the horn, the explosion of brake lights – once we've missed each other and it's too late for a warning, but not for a rebuke. I'll turn to look at Erica as the car's suspension reacts to the change in camber by bouncing into Mersey Road. She'll be looking at me, eyes wide, mouth moving, but no sound coming out, or none that I'll be able to hear. She'll attack me, blows raining down on my arm as I continue to drive one-handed. I won't feel a thing, but then I haven't felt a thing for more than fifteen years. Under assault I'll be unable to change gear and when the road bends to the right I'll have to slow down and the engine will grumble. I won't be able to hear it but I'll feel the car begin to shiver and shake and I'll have to brake and come to a halt and Erica will open her door and get out and run back down Mersey Road towards Palatine Road, where she will turn right and continue running and walking back to Northenden. I'll take a deep breath and reach across to close her door, then I'll turn the car around and drive to and fro across Palatine Road between Mersey Road and Dene Road West without stopping or even looking. I'll do it five times each way, ten times. I'll do it until I hit someone or until I've had enough, whichever comes sooner.

There will be a period of time spent figuring out what to do, trying to see Grace and trying to get back in touch with Helen. Neither will return my messages. I'll walk the streets. I'll see Dog Man without his dog, looking lost, bewildered, but still leaning forward. I'll work on my novel, but it won't come. Everything I try will seem forced. I'll turn to my author's copies of *Rites*. I'll flick through each one, noticing that I no longer seem to have a copy with a folded corner. A picture will enter my mind of Helen at Lumb Bank handing me her copy for me to sign.

I'll spend hours looking at my other books – the white-spined Picadors, the orange and green Penguins – taking them off the shelf, blowing off the dust, smelling the pages, putting them back. I'll take the remnants of Veronica's collection and distribute them among the charity shops in the village as I become increasingly aware of a need to get away somewhere, somewhere different, a long way away. Eventually I'll book a flight to New York.

Landing at JFK in the early afternoon, I'll jump in a cab

to Brooklyn and I'll notice that most of the houses we pass have pumpkins outside them, often as many as two or three sitting on different steps, all elaborately carved. I'll be wearing a simple dark jacket and white T-shirt and I'll wonder if it will be enough to keep me warm. I'll either walk around Park Slope hoping to catch sight of either him or her and if I do I'll follow them home and inveigle my way into their house, or I'll hang around the Community Bookstore on 7th Avenue, their local bookshop, their favourite one apparently, which will have a Halloween-themed window display with plastic spiders and fake cobwebs, and maybe one or both of them will bob in and I'll introduce myself. I've come all this way, I'll say, and they'll have to invite me back. He'll be politely affable in a reserved kind of way and she'll be more outgoing, friendlier. She'll be wearing the black and white striped cardigan and the dangly earrings that I'll recognise from the magazine articles; he'll look relaxed in a grey zip-up cotton jacket over a soft brown shirt tucked into belted black jeans. His eyes will be hidden behind aviator-style sunglasses; hers will shine like opals from their deep settings. They'll walk with me back to their house, which will have a pumpkin with an evil-looking grin sitting on the stoop, and we'll go in and I'll find myself standing in the living room with the olive-green leather sofa and the shiny round coffee table stacked with books. The stacks will look slightly less neat than in the photographs. *Conjunctions 49: A Writers' Aviary* will still be there, although it will have migrated to the left-hand pile. Joe Brainard's *The Nancy Book* will be lying open, as if in the middle of being read. Paul will mutter something about having to make a call. He will shake my hand and withdraw to another room and Siri will smile and lead me to her study on the fourth floor.

Standing in front of Siri's desk, with its silver Apple laptop, assorted knick-knacks of sentimental value and a half-full bottle of San Pellegrino (but no glass – does she swig it from the bottle?), I'll find my eye drawn to the shelves above, to the top right, but there'll be no sign of the orange-spined book previously spotted in the Writers' Rooms picture. Perhaps she is reading it, I'll think to myself. Perhaps it's lying on her nightstand.

I have one of these, you know, I'll say to her, resting my hands on the back of her Herman Miller Aeron chair. Really? she'll say. Yes, did you know that Geoff Dyer, Alain de Botton and Francesca Simon all have one as well? She'll say, I didn't know that. I'll ask her what she's working on and she'll tell me a little about the memoir she's writing, *The Shaking Woman*. She'll tell me about her mother and her migraines. I'll say it sounds fascinating, that it explains a lot about *The Blindfold*. I'll tell her what I thought of *The Blindfold*. I'll tell her about the strange déjà vu experience I had while reading it. She will look at the floor and then up at me and say, I am delighted by your déjà vu experience because when I set out to write the novel, many years ago now, I was guided only by the thought that I wanted to write an uncanny book – *unheimlich*, as Freud said – and your reading falls squarely into that category.

And then either she'll ask me what I'm working on or she won't, and if she does, I'll tell her I'm working on a novel but that it's taken a funny turn and is threatening to fall apart. It's beginning to remind me, I'll tell her, of a first novel by David Pirie called *Mystery Story*, which held my attention all the way through and remained plausible, indeed strangely compelling, spellbinding in fact, and then right near the end the action shifted to America and it just seemed to go off-key somehow.

Pirie must have thought so himself, too, because twenty-one years later he published another novel and on the jacket it said, This is his first novel.

There will be a silence and I will say that I should go, they must be busy. She will escort me downstairs and as we pass what I imagine to be Paul's study I will hear the low murmur of a one-sided conversation. Siri will smile at me in the hallway and I will thank her for her kindness. She will hold out her hand and I will hold it briefly in mine.

Outside, the sky will have darkened a shade as afternoon edges towards evening. On the streets, a lot of people will be in Halloween costume. There will be zombies and vampires and Dead Barbies and people wearing red plastic horns and carrying tridents with flashing lights inside them. It will still be a little early for trick-or-treating, but people will be getting in the mood.

As I approach Bergen Street subway station, I will notice a man in a devil mask coming directly towards me. I'll think he might be drunk and that it would be wise to get out of his way. Being unable to see his eyes will mean I can't be sure of his intentions. His mask will be red with strong black markings and two small rubber horns. He'll open his arms and force me to enter into his embrace. Still I won't know if he's intoxicated or murderous. I'll sniff for alcohol fumes creeping out from behind the mask but all I'll be able to smell will be the man's sulphurous cologne. I'll feel something cold in my stomach and then hot – and then, as he releases me and steps back, cold once more. There will be blood pulsing out of a wound in my stomach rapidly turning my white T-shirt red.

I will collapse to my knees, remembering the last line of a short story by Daphne du Maurier. *Oh God*, I'll think, *what a bloody silly way to die.*

Or I'll keep on going and pass through the tunnel under Didsbury Road and I'll slip across the narrow waist of the Green Pastures housing estate and get back on to the path that runs downhill through a small patch of woodland until the school playing fields are revealed on one side and the golf course on the other. Down at the bottom will be the river, where I'll turn left. It won't be especially high, but the combed fringe of vegetation on both banks will reveal that it has been higher. On the far side, in a sandbank, I'll notice a number of holes like tiny caves: nests for sand martins, which will have flown south at the end of summer. I will approach the first pylon and pass under the power cables. Shortly after the path turns to the left, I will leave it, going to the right, towards the river itself, using a small tree as my landmark. The tree will have seemed bigger in the dark. Something – a dog, the wind – will have moved the fallen branch so that the corner of gabardine is once again visible. I'll check the path in both directions. Either there'll be a man walking an Alsatian or there won't be. When the coast is clear I'll move a few yards away from the body and take a tentative first step into the brambles. I'll take long strides towards the river, thorns catching in my jeans, until I'm beyond a line level with the body, then I'll turn right. I'll sting myself on a nettle and curse quietly.

Eventually, still keeping an eye out for runners or cyclists, I'll lower myself into a crouch between river and tree. I'll feel the muddy bank beginning to slope away beneath my feet. I'll wonder why I didn't bring gloves. As I extend them through the undergrowth, my hands and lower arms will be etched with red scratches, reminding me of the marks on Grace's arms, but finally I'll catch hold of a scrap of coat and I'll work out – from a hard, bony protuberance and the arrangement of the coat – that I'm touching a shoulder. Reaching for the other shoulder, my fingertips will alight on a surface as damp as the coat but colder. My hand will shrink back from the contact and the edge of my palm will snag on something sandpapery and I'll remember reading somewhere that it's a myth that hair and fingernails continue to grow, post-mortem, for up to seventy-two hours. Instead it's shrinkage in the skin and the flesh – hair follicles, nail housings – that's to blame.

As I get my hands under the arms and start pulling the body further down towards the river, into the concealment of thicker, taller undergrowth, I'll notice, for the first time, the smell. It will remind me of the time I emptied the salad drawer of contents that had been left in there far too long. I'll leave the body close to the lip of the bank, the legs anchored by tough brambles, and retreat, doing my best to leave the vegetation looking as undisturbed as possible.

Back on the path, I'll start walking upstream. When I reach the Pyramid, I'll look up at it and wonder, as I've wondered before, about the window in the middle of the east wall that's a different colour from all of its neighbours. I'll cross the roundabout at the lights and retrieve my car and drive to the university, where I'll look up an address. I'll get back in the car and drive to Fallowfield or Oldham or Blackley or Swinton, wherever her records show her as living. The house will be a little redbrick terraced two-up two-down with a landlord living in Didsbury or Prestwich or Altrincham or Ellesmere Park who'll have several places like it on his books, but either there'll be no answer to my knock on the door or it will be opened by a girl in denim shorts over black tights who'll say she hasn't seen Grace in over a week and I'll leave and drive around aimlessly for a while before heading back home and parking not outside my house but outside a house a couple of streets away with scaffolding climbing up the walls.

I'll bang on the door until he answers it and I'll walk into his house without being asked. What the fuck? I'll say to him. What the fuck? *Ksssh-huh-huh*, he'll go, in his lounge surrounded by his world movie DVDs and his Neil Roland photographs and his seven copies of *Straight to Video* published by Strangeways Books. What? What the fuck, I'll say again and then I'll smack him. And then I'll either leave him lying on the cheap, lumpy wooden floor, rubbing his stubbly jaw, or I'll pull him up to his feet and suggest that we go out to the car and we'll drive out to the Peaks and I'll drag him up the hill and dig and dig and dig and show him that nobody's coming through that fucking mountain. The remains of his family were cleared up years ago with the wreckage of the plane. Crashed aircraft do not move through solid earth. The dead do not come back to life. The Ancient Egyptian Book of the Dead is a work of fiction. Pyramids are nothing but monuments to obscene power and colossal vanity. And he'll go, What the fuck?

That night, after driving back and dropping Lewis outside his scaffolding-clad house, I'll stay up drinking until I succeed in numbing the pain or until I replace the pain with a new pain in a different place but that's acute enough to distract me from the original pain and then I'll go to bed and I'll fall into a fitful sleep and I'll be woken by the rain. I'm not normally woken by rain unless it's particularly heavy rain and then I hear it in my dreams as it's blown against the windows and as it pours out of the gutters and splashes on to the ground at the front of the house. I'll exit my dreams and lie there thinking about the body perched on the edge of the riverbank, albeit tethered by thorny stems. I'll try to get back to sleep, but I'll be unable to and I'll know from experience that it's hopeless, so I'll get up and dress in the dark and make a cup of tea that I'll sit and drink in the kitchen staring at the rain lashing against the windows.

Dawn will break without my being aware of its happening. One moment it will still be night, the next the sky will have turned a uniform misty grey. At the same time the rain will have eased off. I'll leave the house and walk down the dismantled railway line through a fine drizzle. I'll pass through the tunnel under Didsbury Road without hesitating and across the middle of Green Pastures and then I'll be down on the riverbank and the rain will have stopped, but the water will have risen by an appreciable amount. The sand martins' nests will not only have filled with water but the force of the flow will have swept away parts of the bank. The pylon will be emitting a strange buzzing noise as if affected in some way by the rain. A thin grey tablecloth of mist will have been laid over the field on the far side of the river.

There'll be no one on the path, no cyclists, no horse riders, no trans-Pennine ramblers. I'll step off the path into the brambles, which will resist my progress as staunchly as if I had never before penetrated them, but I'll finally reach the spot where I expect to find the body and I won't immediately see it and I'll have visions of it having been dislodged by the fiercest of the flood and dragged into the flow and carried downstream until arrested by some obstacle and left hanging in a grotesque tableau to be discovered, with awful, clichéd inevitability, by a dog walker, but then I'll smell it and I'll suddenly see it and I'll realise I'd hidden it better than I thought I had. I'll make sure the body is still secure and I'll check the height of the water and I'll observe that it's unlikely to rise much higher than it is at the moment and I'll slowly and carefully extricate myself from the brambles and nettles and return to the path. I'll stand there for a moment and sniff the air, but I won't be able to smell anything, and so I'll start walking back towards Parrs Wood.

When I get home I'll find the model aircraft that I salvaged from the garden beyond the back fence and I'll get the broken pieces of red plastic and I'll put them all on the kitchen table. From the drawer I'll take a tube of superglue and I'll fix all the pieces back together and then I'll sit and look at the aircraft. I'll turn it this way and that, examine every angle. I'll allow most of the morning to go by in this fashion and when I feel the first pangs of hunger, instead of getting some lunch, I'll go outside and get in the car and drive round to Carol and AJ's and I'll park outside on the opposite side of the road and sit and watch their house. I'll sit there for a long time and either I'll see Carol at one of the windows or I won't. And if I do, either I'll wave or I won't. And if she sees me she'll either wave back or she'll ignore me because she doesn't recognise me, and if she waves back I'll get out of the car and I'll walk up the drive to her front door and she'll come down and let me in, and I'll smile at her and either she'll invite me in or she'll ask me what's up and if she invites me in I'll go in and she'll close the door behind us and I'll walk into her kitchen and I'll ask if AJ is there and she'll say, No, he's at work. Some of us have jobs to go to. And I'll laugh and she'll look a little uneasy and either I'll say, Look, this was a mistake, and leave, or I'll tell her that it doesn't matter that AJ's not in because it's her I've come to see. I'll start to tell her how I feel about her, and it will occur to me that I don't know how I feel about her. It will occur to me that I don't actually feel anything about her apart from a basic, almost animalistic attraction that I might feel for anyone but that I just happen to feel for her, and she'll either slap me across the face or look away and start picking at the cuticle of her thumb. I'll tell her I'm sorry and that I had to see a friendly face and there was no one else I could think of. I'd have gone and seen Lewis, I'll say, except I saw him last night and I'm sick of seeing him, to be honest, and she'll say *Who?* and I'll repeat his name and she'll say, Who's Lewis? And I'll say, You remember, and she'll say, I think you should leave now.

I'll drive home past Elizabeth Baines' house, past the second-hand bookshop, through the centre of the village, where I'll see Umbrella Lady waiting at the lights for the green man to appear so she can cross over and begin the long, slow trek down School Lane. I'll park outside my house and sit in the car for a few minutes listening to the ticking of the cooling engine and looking at the front of the house. Staring, really; watching, gazing. Thinking, calculating. The front door will close behind me. I'll look in the kitchen and see the red model aircraft standing on the kitchen table. I'll walk upstairs and enter my bedroom. Expending considerable effort, I'll pull the bed away from the wall into the middle of the room. I'll do the same with the chest of drawers and the wardrobe, rucking up the carpet. I'll be sweating by the time I stand back and survey my work, trying to summon up ghostly diagonal lines coming up through the floor from the four corners of the house. In the bathroom the adjustable feet of the wooden cabinet will squeal in protest, leaving dirty marks on the tiles. I'll look at the fixed items ruefully – the bath, the toilet, the washbasin. Will I have to stop using them, make do with the toilet in the cellar? I'll run upstairs, to my study, where I'll find Cleo curled up on my Herman Miller Aeron chair. I'll kneel down on the bare floorboards next to the chair and stroke her sleek black fur and very soon she'll start purring. And then I'll stand up and grab hold of my desk and yank it away from the wall. Power cables will reach their full extent and drag various pieces of kit on to the floor. I'll gather them up and stuff them under the desk in the middle of the room. I'll start pulling the books off the shelves and stacking them on the floor next to the desk and then I'll take hold of the Herman Miller chair and lift it up on to the desk. I'll climb up on to the desk myself and then, taking care to keep the chair steady, I'll lever myself up on to the chair. Cleo will shift resentfully, so I'll gather her up into my arms as I balance on the chair and I'll ask her if she knows who else has one of these chairs and she'll say, Geoff Dyer, Alain de Botton, Francesca Simon and Siri Hustvedt, and I'll say, That's right, Cleo, that's right. Good girl. And then she'll wriggle out of my arms and like a streak of tar she'll leap down to the desk and then on to the floor and she'll run out of the door, leaving me, crouched on the chair, alone, lifting my head to the pyramid roof.

In the end, I walk on through the tunnel under Didsbury Road. I cross Green Pastures and join the path down to the river, where I turn left. Above the power lines, a medium-size jet is making its final approach to Manchester Airport, under-carriage down, ready to land. The branch is still in place. Without moving it, and making sure first that no one is coming from either direction, I find more fallen branches from the other side of the path, where, beyond the pylon, there is a nature reserve. I lay these down over the makeshift grave to create more of a barrier to inquisitive dogs and then I walk back along the river towards Parrs Wood. I turn right up the path between the playing fields and the golf course. I cross Green Pastures and head back down on to the trackbed of the dismantled railway line.

When I get home I write an email to Grace suggesting we meet. The cursor hovers over the send button. I reread it and click back in the body of the email instead and rewrite it, *asking* if we can meet, doubting that she will agree or even get back to me. I hit send.

I open the folder marked 'Novels' and reread the last few thousand words of my work-in-progress to see if I can get going again, but I can't. I check my emails to see that nothing has arrived. I take out my phone and call the university and get Grace's contact details. She lives in West Didsbury, less than a mile away. I key in the number, but there's no answer and apparently no voicemail service. I send her a text. I check my emails again.

I leave the house and walk for five minutes to a quiet street just around the corner from Lewis' house where there are always a couple of minicabs sitting waiting for jobs. I ask one of the drivers to take me to Stockport. He says he's not insured unless the job is booked through the office. I shake my head and walk to the other car and repeat my request and get the same response. So, I pull my phone out of my pocket and call the number of the cab firm. The controller asks where I want to go and I tell him and he asks me where I am and I tell him that too. He tells me his drivers can't pick up passengers on the street, so I ask if they can pick me up from the address of the house outside of which we're standing and he says, No, that's not where you live, that's just where you happen to be standing. So I say, Right, and give him Lewis' address and ask to be picked up from there. He asks when I want to be picked up and I say in two minutes. He says, Sure, no problem, and I hang up. I give the driver of the cab a humourless smile and walk to the end of the street and turn right. After a hundred yards I reach a house covered in scaffolding and walk up the drive. The windows are dirty and it's hard to see inside, but the place looks dead. By the time I've turned around to face the street, the cab has arrived and is pulling up at the side of the road. It's one of the two cars from around the corner. I walk back down the drive and open the rear door and the driver says, Hiya mate. Stockport, yeah? And I say, Yeah.

Throughout the journey I check my phone for texts and emails and I look out of the window. When I see the Pyramid sliding into view I ask the driver to let me out. He says, What, here? And I say, Yes, here. I pay him and get out. I cross Didsbury Road and make my way towards the system of footpaths and subways that negotiates the roundabout suspended over river and motorway. I pass close to the Pyramid and think about scaling the fence and seeing if I can get inside, but I'm not sure there's much point. Instead I walk on and eventually reach the spot where I left the car. It's still there and no one has clamped it or taken a half-brick to the windscreen. I get in, start the engine and drive back to the roundabout, giving the Pyramid another look as I get on to Didsbury Road and head for home.

I leave the car outside my house and walk over to West Didsbury. The address I've been given for Grace is on one of the roads that run from north to south between Lapwing Lane and Barlow Moor Road. These are narrow roads with cars parked on both sides; tall, narrow Victorian houses mostly divided into flats. I stand outside hers and look up at the windows, which give nothing away. Because of the age of the house, any windowsills on the inside will be too shallow for anything to stand on – plants, ornaments, a row of books – that might reveal something about the residents. In the front room of the raised ground-floor flat I can see men's shirts on hangers hooked over the picture rail.

There is a strange fluttering in my stomach, an odd lightness contrasting with a heaviness somewhere higher up. It's so long since I've felt anything like this, I don't recognise it. It feels alien to me. But it *feels*. It is a *feeling*.

I walk up to the door and ring the bell for flat C. I hear a faint, intermittent buzz somewhere in the house, presumably the top floor, but that is all I hear. I press it again, but there is no response. I step away from the door and return to the street. I look back up at the windows, but there is nothing to see.

The feeling inside me has not gone away.

I walk through the streets. Leaves are beginning to fall; they form wide circles on the road and the pavement below the lime trees that line Parkfield Road South. I don't know what time it is when I'm finally standing outside Lewis' house, but the light is different: there's a softness to it, an amber hue, a sense of liquidity. It feels as if the world could become trapped in this moment. My hand lifting the door knocker, striking the door, once, twice, three times. Lewis doesn't answer. I peer through the stained glass, but it's hard to see anything clearly. The windows of his front room are streaked with dirt. I knock again and a moment later find myself pulling open the garage door, which scrapes on the tarmac. I slip into the garage and move past some bits of old junk to reach the side door, which is unlocked.

I step into Lewis' kitchen, my shoes crunching on grit. If I didn't know this was Lewis' kitchen I wouldn't immediately guess it from what I see around me. The cupboards and cabinets have gone. The floor, too. I'm standing on bare cement. Everything has gone. It looks as if it has been stripped, or abandoned halfway through building. There's a business calendar hanging on the wall, some dates ringed with red pen, scribbled notes that are impossible to read. On the floor, something catches my eye. I bend down to pick it up. A creased photograph of a woman with flaming red hair and two little blonde girls. I go to put it down somewhere, but there's nowhere, so I drop it on the floor again and walk out of the kitchen into the hall, which looks similar. I enter the rear living room. More of the same. No furniture, no big plasma-screen TV, no Neil Roland framed picture on the wall. No carefully chosen DVD collection.

I'm about to go back into the hall to go and explore upstairs when I hear a sound coming from outside, possibly the garage. Then gritty footsteps in the kitchen. I look around for somewhere to hide. There's nowhere. A figure appears in the doorway.

'Grace!' I say.

She enters the room. Her squat body seems packed with unpredictable intent. Her hair has been tied back, emphasising her square jaw.

'What are you doing here?' I ask.

'I followed you,' she says, stopping a few feet away and thrusting her hands into her jeans pockets. 'I don't know what to call you. Paul? Dad? Neither feels right.'

'I keep wanting to call you Jonathan,' I say.

'Jonathan's dead,' she says.

She looks at me, as if challenging me, then lowers her head to the floor.

'What do you want me to say?' I ask her. 'I don't know what to say. Do you want me to say I'm sorry?'

'It would be a start.'

I pause, then say, 'I am. I'm sorry. If I don't say it easily or often enough, it's because it isn't adequate. I know it isn't adequate.'

'Do you think,' she asks with sudden bite, 'that saying that makes it all right? *Do* you?'

'No. Nothing will make it all right. I know that.'

Neither of us speaks for several seconds. Half a minute. I breathe out; she looks around.

'What are you doing here anyway?' she asks.

'I know the guy who lives here.'

'Doesn't look to me like anyone lives here.'

'I reckon he's done a bunk.'

'What are you talking about?' she says, twisting her face up as she looks at me. 'No one lives here – or *has* lived here for *years.*'

'What do you mean?'

'Look around you. Look at the dust. At the desolation. The abandonment. It's, I don't know, a refurbishment put on hold. They ran out of money. Absent owner. Whatever. But no one's lived here for a long time.'

'How do you explain the calendar in the kitchen, in that case?'

She rocks back on her heels. 'What calendar?'

'Calendar in the kitchen.'

Grace turns and walks into the hall and I follow her. She enters the kitchen and the calendar is still there hanging on a nail. As she approaches it, she brushes the photo of the redhead and two blonde girls to one side with her shoe, without noticing it. I bend down and pick it up while she's inspecting the calendar.

'See?' she says.

'What?' I say as I fold the photograph in half and slip it in my back pocket.

'Check the date, Daddy-o.'

She points and stands aside and I see that the calendar dates from 2006. I wonder how I had failed to notice that before. I turn and walk out of the room. In the hall I look at the pile of junk mail on the floor behind the front door. I crouch down. Pizza delivery leaflets, Indian takeaway menus, flyers for cleaning firms, drive-layers and gutter-clearers. Free newspapers, plastic bags for charity donations. A small handful of franked letters in window envelopes addressed to a variety of names, none of them Lewis'.

I stand up and turn to the door to the front room. It is as bare as the main living room at the back of the house. I step back into the hall and look at the stairs. I think about what I'm doing as I climb the stairs and I think that if there was any point at all in my checking every room downstairs, there's surely no point in my even *going* upstairs. I've never been upstairs in Lewis' house. How will I know whether what I see is the same as it was during the times I visited Lewis' home or is any different? And what difference would it make? A box room at the top of the stairs is empty. The next bedroom looks larger than it is only because there's nothing in it – no bed, no wardrobe, nothing. The main bedroom, at the front of the house, is the same. I enter it nevertheless and walk across to the window and look out at the street. I take my phone out of my pocket and find Lewis' number. I dial it and get a message saying the number has not been recognised. I put the phone away and stare out of the window, past the scaffolding poles, at the street. I don't know how long I've been standing there when I hear a light tread on the stairs and I'm aware of Grace entering the room behind me. For a while she doesn't say anything and I continue looking out of the window.

Finally, she says, 'Who's your imaginary friend, then?'

'Lewis Harris,' I say.

'So who is he? Or, should I say, who *was* he?'

'Just a guy, a guy with an annoying laugh. A writer. He lives round here. He lives *here*,' I say, gesturing at the house itself as I turn to face her.

'Yeah, right. Has anyone else ever met him?'

'What are you talking about?'

'You're a fantasist. Always have been.'

'Lots of people have met him. *I* met him at a mutual friend's barbecue.'

'That woman you had your affair with, she was never going to be with you. You destroyed your marriage for nothing. And the lives of your children. For nothing.'

'I slept with her twice and then *I* called it off. It was a mistake, but your mother made mistakes as well.'

'Yeah, marrying you.'

Grace is looking at me. I look at her briefly, but I can't hold her gaze.

'Why?' she says, in a low voice. 'Why did you do it?'

I look up. I can see she doesn't mean why did I marry her mother, nor why did I sleep with Susan Ashton.

'Do you think I haven't asked myself that question every day?'

'And?'

I stare at the floor.

'Your wife leaving you,' I say, 'is one thing. When she says she's going to take the children and you'll never see them again, that's another. Part of you dies.'

'Don't try to universalise it,' she says, her voice full of scorn and venom. '*You* did this, not some universal archetype.'

Neither of us speaks for a moment. I turn and look out of

the window. A breeze stirs the fallen leaves. On the other side of the street, a man walks past. When I was young I used to look at other people and think how *strange* it would be to *be* them.

'The part of you that died,' she says, 'what was that? Your conscience? Your humanity?'

I don't respond. The scaffolding poles moan in the wind. Between us in the empty bedroom the silence spreads like water. I do have something to say, but I have never said it. I have thought it to myself, but there has never been anybody to say it to. It has never been spoken out loud. I don't know how weak it will sound. Or how wrong.

'It's like it's already happened,' I say. 'It's like something inside you *goes* – cracks, snaps, dies, whatever – and then it's like it's already happened. Like you've already done it. There's an inevitability about it, a feeling that you don't have a choice. It's going to happen, because in a way it already has. You become an instrument, nothing more.'

'Bollocks,' she says. 'Pretentious, self-serving bollocks.'

'I thought it might be,' I say. 'It's the best I can do. Why would I want to kill my children? Why would anybody want to kill their children? The answer is you don't. You don't want to kill your children. You're consumed by a compulsion to hit out, to punish. What punishment could be worse? It's not the suicide – that's nothing. If someone does that to you, leaves you thinking you're responsible for their death, they're beneath contempt, not worth bothering about. But taking the children, that's unforgivable, the ultimate punishment. That *is* contemptible. There can be nothing *more* contemptible. You're leaving me? Threatening to take the kids? Well, how about this, I'm leaving you and everything else and taking the kids with *me*.'

'Don't you dare make this my mother's fault.'

'I'm not. I did it. I'm the one who's to blame. All I'm saying is, it happens without you deciding it should happen. Those thought processes, you don't go through them. You work them out afterwards, trying to make sense of what you've done. Not make sense of it, but trying to understand how you could have done it.' I pause. 'Where is she, though?' I ask her. 'Your mother. You didn't write about that, did you? She just seemed to disappear.'

'She wasn't perfect. She couldn't handle it. But there's no comparison.'

'No. I know that.'

I realise I'm tired of standing and I sit down on the dusty floor. Grace does the same. Between us the pool of silence expands and becomes deeper. We don't say anything for several minutes. I think about Lewis, about meeting him at AJ's barbecue. Had others interacted with him or had he only ever spoken to me? *Ksssh-huh-huh*. I picture him at the pub. Did he speak to the other guys? Did he get a round in? I reach into my back pocket and bring out the folded photograph. I unfold it and look at the woman and the two blonde girls.

'What's that?' Grace asks.

I look up and see her sitting on the other side of the black pool that lies between us. I reach across it, offering her the photograph. She stretches out an arm, then holds up the photograph to her eyes in the darkening room.

'Who's this?' she asks.

'Lewis' wife and daughters?' I say, my intonation rising at the end of the sentence. Grace, being a young person, won't necessarily hear it as a question.

She gets to her feet and walks around the black shadow

in the middle of the floor until she reaches the window, where there's more light. She holds the photograph up for a closer look. I get up also and stand a foot or so away from her. While she's studying the photograph, I take another step towards her, holding my breath. The dying light falls across her face and a tiny pool of shadow collects in the little round scar at the corner of her eye. She looks up and I raise my hand to take the photograph back and as I do so our fingers touch and I feel a sudden stab of emotion like an electric shock. I grab hold of her hand and the photograph falls to the floor. She looks at me, mistrust and confusion in her eyes. I pull her towards me and wrap my arms around her. She struggles and she's strong, but I'm stronger and I use all the strength in my arms and upper body to hold her close and not let her go. Her struggles become less frequent and when she's not trying to make me release her she stands rigid as a statue. Her face is pressed into my chest. I wonder if she can breathe. Her hair smells of grapefruit. We stand like that for half a minute, forty-five seconds, a minute, maybe longer, until I become aware that one of us is shaking. Either it's her, or it's me. Maybe it's both of us. I think, after a short while, it is both of us. Eventually, I feel her relax her muscles and a moment later I release my hold and let her go. She remains where she is for a few seconds, then steps back.

I offer her a tissue, but she pulls out one of her own. She turns away to blow her nose.

'There's something I have to ask you,' I tell her, my voice slightly unsteady. 'That piece about the tramp that was read out in class, was it yours? Did you write it?'

She blows her nose again before answering. 'That was an anonymous exercise.'

I wait, in case she might add something, but she doesn't.

'Right,' I say.

I watch her back. She stands tense and hunched over her tissue. After a short while she puts the tissue away and walks towards the door.

'Grace?' I say, but she doesn't answer, just keeps walking. I hear her feet on the stairs and then noises from downstairs. I turn to the window and watch her walk down the drive and turn left. I wonder if I will ever see her again.

I walk over to Grace's road and push an envelope through her door. I hear it land on the hard floor, the keys inside it clinking together. Briefly I look up at the top-floor window, but there's nothing to see. I turn and walk away. I start walking back to my house, but then stop and change direction. This time – the last time – I won't take the path along the trackbed of the dismantled railway line. I join the river at West Didsbury instead, via a stile at the bottom of Stanton Avenue.

It's early, an hour after dawn. A thin layer of mist lies above the river, which sits low in its channel, greenish-grey in colour. I walk upstream, due south, for a quarter of a mile. The river starts to meander and soon the only clue to orientation is a steady stream of planes coming in to land at Manchester Airport. I stop and watch a heron picking its way along the opposite bank, using its spindly, anglepoise legs to find the best footholds in the mud. When it draws level with me, it stops and looks back upstream. It stands very still. I also stand very still watching it. It doesn't twitch or move even a fraction. When it does move again, I will carry on walking upstream. I will watch the planes coming in to land as I walk, my shoes damp from the dew. It will take me at least half an hour to get there, maybe longer, and when I get there I will call the police and I will wait there until they arrive and then I will go with them.

ACKNOWLEDGEMENTS

Thank you to Paul Auster, Julian Baker, Christopher Burns, Jonathan Coe, James Dingemans, Gareth Evans, Tom Fletcher, Dan Franklin, Myriam Frey, Steve Hollyman, Siri Hustvedt, Juliet Jacques, Stan Jawando, Christopher Kenworthy, Ladies of Lumb, Joel Lane, Stephen McGeagh, Jeannie Mackie, Frances MacMillan, Steven Messer, David Milner, More Maniacs, Mark Morris, Victoria Murray-Browne, John Oakey, Ra Page, Geeta Roopnarine, David Rose, Nicholas Royle, Kate Ryan, John Saddler, Ros Sales, Michael Marshall Smith, Joe Stretch, Colin Thompson, Will Vandyck, Conrad Williams.

Thank you to my family for their encouragement and support and to all my students and colleagues, past and present, at the Manchester Writing School at MMU.

I would like to mention Stars of the Lid, whose album *And Their Refinement of the Decline* I listened to constantly while writing the book, particularly the tracks 'Tippy's Demise' and 'December Hunting for Vegetarian Fuckface'.

Some short sections of the novel first appeared in earlier versions in *Ambit*, *Black Static*, *Exotic Gothic 2* (Ash Tree Press), *Rainy City Stories* and *Vertigo*. Thank you to my editors, Martin Bax, Andy Cox, Danel Olson, Kate Feld and Gareth Evans, respectively.

www.vintage-books.co.uk